Spoiled FOR Choice

Kings of League BOOK 1

E.J. MASDEN

Copyright © 2020 by E.J. Masden

Cover design: Nicole Highland -

www.nicolehighlandwrites.com

Cover image: Sachin Bharti / Pexels, Pixabay / Pexels

Editor: Lauriel Masson-Oakden

ISBN: 978-0-473-51315-3 (Kindle)
ISBN: 978-0-473-51394-8 (Paperback)

Also by E.J. Masden

Novels

Undoing the Damage (2019)

This book is dedicated to all of those who don't fit into society's neatly labelled boxes

CHAPTER ONE

Carrie stepped backward on dangerously high, red six-inch heels, and looked critically in the full-length mirror hanging in her bedroom. The flowing black dress made her look like she was off the cover of a seventies era Mills and Boon, just waiting for a buff, blond, long-haired hero to throw her over the back of his horse and whisk her away, rescuing her from the drudgery of life as she knew it.

'All that tulle, you look like a princess!' Jess had told her at the dress shop a week earlier. 'It's pretty, but sexy, and classy, but hot... and god damn! Have you seen how amazing your tits look?'

Swept up in the moment, Carrie had purchased the far-too-expensive black tulle and silk dress, before moving on to the shoe shop next door and treating herself to a pair of shiny red Louboutins.

'*Sex on legs*' was how Jess had described her as they'd stood together under the harsh lights of the changing room, but now, looking at her reflection in the mirror, all

Carrie could see was a chunky imposter. Cinderella dressing up for the ball she didn't belong at.

The squeak and slam of the front door was quickly followed by Jess's sing-song voice. "Hello, lovely lady, I'm *heeeeeeere* and I have *wiiiiiiiiiine*!"

Like she'd expect anything less from her best friend. The woman drank wine the way most people drank water.

No one had been more surprised than Carrie when she and Jessica had become best friends years earlier. They'd been thrown together in their Year Eleven biology class and had been inseparable ever since.

Jess was loud, while Carrie was quiet. Jess lived in the moment; Carrie was a planner. University had been one long, drunken orgy for Jess; Carrie, on the other hand, had been in a relationship with one guy for the entire three years, and only let her hair down between semesters.

Feeling defeated, she called out, "I look like shit, Masters! Dunno where you got princess from, or any of those other things you told me I was at the shop."

"You better not be getting out of your dress! I'll come in there and kick your ass!" Jess called back, the tell-tale clink of crystal ringing out telling Carrie there was a glass of wine in the kitchen with her name on it.

As she walked down the hallway, toward the kitchen, Carrie sighed. "Please, be honest. If I look awful, you need to tell me."

Jess, looking glamorous as ever in a tight-fitting, low-cut black dress that no doubt cost more than a month worth of mortgage payments, rolled her eyes. "Carrie, you look great. I mean it. You look hot, and if I was a lezzy, I'd totally be hitting on you right now."

"You're so full of shit," Carrie laughed. "But I guess it's good enough for me."

Jess shot her an impatient look and handed her a crystal flute. "Drink! The taxi will be here soon."

Carrie tipped her head back and drank the wine down in one long gulp, the acidity at the back of her throat making her screw her face up.

"That's my girl!" Jess cheered, topping up Carrie's glass.

"You have it. I'm worried enough about tonight without the possibility of making a dick of myself because I'm drunk."

"You've got nothing to worry about," Jess promised, making quick work of Carrie's wine.

Sure, nothing to worry about. She was only going to Sydney's—if not Australia's—*biggest* fundraising gala of the year, raising funds for the Children's Hospital.

Recently single, Jess had begged her to go as her plus one and Carrie had reluctantly agreed. She didn't do big groups, especially not big groups of people she'd never met before... but, for Jess, she was willing to put herself out of her comfort zone.

The blast of a horn sounded from the driveway and Carrie picked up her red bolero. "Better go," she said, finding Jess had moved on from drinking out of a wine glass, to going directly to the source and drinking out of the bottle.

Jess burped and giggled. "Okay."

"If you end up a drunken mess in the middle of the gala, don't expect me to rescue you, Jessica Marie

Masters!" Carrie warned, even if they both knew she didn't mean it.

Jess winked at her. "Yes, Mum."

The horn sounded again, and this time Jess left the wine bottle on the bench and picked up her emerald-green clutch. Turning on her heels, she walked to the front door and Carrie followed closely behind, relieved to see her best friend was walking in a straight line. The last thing she needed that night was a drunk Jess to deal with.

***

Twenty-minutes later they were getting out of the car outside the swankiest hotel in Sydney, surrounded by a slew of people primped and preened to within an inch of their life, all looking fabulous. Carrie contemplated getting back into the taxi, but it was too late, the taxi was long gone.

In front of a large backdrop adorned with the logos of the hospital and the major sponsors, a photographer was taking photos of important people. Individuals. Couples. Groups. Beautiful dresses, well-cut tuxedos, elaborate hairstyles for the women, a large majority of the men looking like they'd been to the barber that afternoon.

And again, she was reminded how out of place she was; an insignificant nobody in amongst a crowd of somebodies.

"Isn't this the best?" Jess gushed, pointing out famous people as they walked toward the entrance.

"Uh, sure."

"Come on, Carrie, let yourself have fun for once!"

Carrie glared at her. "I have fun!"

Jess appeared to give up, though it may have had something to do with the fact that she was rooted to the spot, staring in the direction of the photographer.

"Carrie! Those guys getting their photos taken? They're from the Kings! You know, the league team?"

"Ooooh, right!" Carrie had *no* idea.

"You're useless. They're one of the best teams in the comp at the moment, and more importantly, for like, the last six years, they've been voted the hottest team in Aus!"

"Because that's what matters, right?" Carrie sniggered.

The men, tall and broad, made for an imposing sight and she had no doubt they were cocky as hell. She didn't really see why girls went so crazy over guys who played sports, though the cynic in her said it was to do with the big fat dollar signs.

Chris Hemsworth on the other hand... phwoar! She could look at him all day, in fact, late at night when she needed a little orgasmic relief, it was him that usually came to mind and got her over the finish line.

"I wouldn't kick any of them out of my bed," Jess said, eyes glued to the group of rugby league players.

Carrie nudged her best friend playfully. "If you need me to, I can get a taxi home by myself later."

"Hopefully, I can take you up on that offer," Jess said, the twinkle in her eyes telling Carrie there was a high likelihood she'd indeed be riding solo.

She envied her best friend's confidence. When it came to men, Carrie was shy and unsure, never really knowing how to act for fear of coming across like a complete idiot. Now, more than ever, she was convinced she was going to grow old and lonely—your run-of-the-mill crazy cat lady.

If it wasn't for her role as a senior editor at Heartbeat Publishing, there would be zero romance in her life; at least her job meant she got to read about romance... not that words on a page was the same as having a warm body to cuddle up to in bed. Nor was it the same as feeling the weight of your lover on top of you, or his sturdy frame below you, his hands tightly gripping your hips as you—

"Earth to Carrie!" Jess was snapping her fingers.

"Oh, sorry I was—"

"Jed Atkins totally just looked at me! Like *really* looked at me! You know, like a man looks at a woman, kind of melting her clothes off with his eyes and—"

"I get it!" Carrie cut her friend off. "And I'll just pretend to know who that guy is that you're talking about."

Jess shook her head, exasperated. "One of the Kings, Carrie!"

Carrie nodded and smiled apologetically. "Gotcha. Well, that's very exciting."

"Let's get inside, I want a drink and maybe then I'll accidentally bump into Mr Atkins and his friends."

Carrie knew better than to argue. "Lead the way."

The grand ballroom was right out of a fairy tale, decorated in floaty whites and pale pinks with dashes of the lightest possible green. Ribbons, streamers and balloons were suspended from the high ceiling, while the chairs were covered with delicate white fabric tied at the back in an over-the-top bow, each table punctuated by a centrepiece of pink and purple orchids mixed with fern fronds.

Wait staff were dressed in customary black and white, carrying trays of champagne, or tiny delectable bites of food she imagined would be good enough for a banquet at Buckingham Palace.

Jess swooped on a waiter and took a flute of champagne for each of them, and they walked around the expansive room looking for the table Jess's boss had purchased on behalf of his employees. Working for the most reputable HR company in the city certainly had its perks, and as they sat down at the table, Carrie felt an impending sense of not being good enough creeping up again.

The four women already seated at the table were wearing gowns, likely sporting the names of Chanel, Gucci, Alexander McQueen and Vera Wang, and she didn't need to look beneath the table to know their shoes sported similarly fancy names.

Her Louboutins mightn't look out of place, but the rest of her outfit did. The four-hundred-dollar Karen Walker dress she'd purchased from David Jones was her idea of fancy, but in amongst all the finery straight off the catwalks of Europe, she might as well have been wearing a grubby Hessian sack.

Why had she let Jess talk her into any of this?

Carrie spent the next hour wishing she was home, curled up in her bed with a good book, or at least a Chris Hemsworth movie. She attempted to join in on the conversation around the table, but it was almost impossible, and she was sure that, after a few minutes, no one at the table registered she was there.

Occasionally her eyes drifted a couple of tables away to one group of the rugby league players Jess had pointed out earlier. Some were accompanied by glamorous looking women, wives or girlfriends she guessed, while others were clearly on 'bro-dates', no doubt on the look-out for a gorgeous specimen of femininity to take home after the gala.

It was hard to imagine they were thinking any other way, not with the constant stream of stories in the media about rugby league players and the sticky extra-curricular situations they regularly found themselves in. Only the previous week, a huge scandal had erupted when two players from the same team had a punch up after a game, as it had come to light one's wife had been cheating on him with the other player.

Jess was right though, the men at the table were all spectacularly good looking, clearly there was something in the water at Kings HQ. It should be illegal, Carrie thought to herself, to have so many attractive men in one place. Two men in particular had caught her eye more than she'd care to admit.

The first one was tall, around six foot four, and almost as wide. She'd never seen such a broad frame on a man and couldn't get over how well he filled out his black tuxedo. It was no wonder she'd zoned in on him, he was a classic red head, something she'd always found so sexy in a man. His jaw showed the merest hint of ginger stubble adding a little extra roughness to his look. Not that he needed it.

He exuded raw, masculine strength and it was hard not to imagine the ease with which he would be able to lift a woman up and pin her against the nearest wall before doing unspeakably wicked things to her. Watching him raise a glass of water to his lips, she noticed how big his hands were and a hefty jolt of something impure shot through her as she imagined exactly what type of magic he could work with those long, thick fingers of his.

The other man looked to be a bit younger and certainly wasn't as physically massive as the other one but was just as enticing to look at. He was a few inches shorter than the first man and was lean, as opposed to stocky, but there was still an aura of power, and that same masculine strength about him. His coppery brown hair, untamed and wild, was the perfect length to fist in one's hands while holding on for dear life as he went to town with his mouth and tongue, licking said woman into a frenzy and—

And she *really* needed to stop that train of thought.

"Quite taken, are we?" Jess said, nudging her playfully.

"What do you mean?"

"You were drooling over Bodhi Hook and Dalton Kendry, don't even bother denying it!"

Carrie felt her cheeks flaming. "I wasn't drooling, I was looking."

"Sure, looking at them like you wanted to tear their clothes off."

"Oh, stop it. Not everyone is as obsessed with men as you!"

Jess winked at her. "Perhaps they should be, especially if they've been in a dry spell for over a year."

"My sex life is just fine, thank you."

"A vibrator and occasional orgasm do not a sex life maketh," Jess said, an unsurprising champagne slur to her voice. "You need to let loose, Caz, grab yourself a man and fuck him good and proper."

Naturally as she spoke those words there was a lull in the noise and more than a few people sniggered in response to Jess's impassioned rant.

"I'm going to the ladies' room," Carrie said, before she fled from the table in embarrassment.

She should just leave. Jess wouldn't miss her and no one else would wonder where she'd gone. Agreeing to go to the gala had been a stupid idea, one she'd known she'd regret and just over an hour in, she'd proven herself right. Where was the bloody exit? There were so many people milling around, she began to feel claustrophobic. Damn Jess and her so-called good ideas.

One minute she was zigging and zagging around groups of people, on a mission to escape, the next she slammed heavily into a concrete slab dressed in a white shirt and black tux. The breath shot out of her lungs and for a second, she wondered if this was it for her.

"Shit, I'm sorry. Are you okay?" A large hand caught her elbow and when she looked up, she became breathless for a second time.

It was one of the league players—what was it Jess had called him? Dayton? Brodie?

"Uh-I'm-yes, I'm fine." Carrie tried not to make eye contact but failed because looking down at her were the richest chocolatey eyes she'd ever seen.

"I'm Dalton," the man said. "And you are?"

"Carrie. Carrie Lucas."

Dalton reached out and shook her hand. "Lovely to meet you, Carrie."

"You too," Carrie said and tried to move away but her feet appeared to be glued to the floor.

"Escaping your friend, huh?" Dalton surprised her by saying.

"Oh crap, you heard too?"

Jess and her big fucking mouth.

"Gotta love friends like that, right?" he chuckled, and smiled in a manner that could be mistaken for shy. "Did you want to get a drink?"

No, she wanted to go home and forget all about that night, but before she could politely turn him down, her voice betrayed her. "Sure, that would be lovely."

Carrie followed him to the bar, her heart was racing so fast she was worried she might go into cardiac arrest. Why had she agreed to a drink with someone like him, who was so many levels above her in the social pecking order? She was getting in over her head and couldn't see a way out.

'*Calm the fuck down*', she chastised herself. It was just a drink, and an apology one at that. If he got her a drink, he would no longer feel bad for almost killing her when they'd bumped into each other. Maybe if he wasn't so big and hard and—

Oh crap. She could just imagine how big and hard he would be.

An ache developed between her legs and she clenched her thighs tightly in an attempt to fight it off. Not that it helped. All the clenching did was make her wonder how it would feel to be tightening *around* him as he filled her.

"What can I get you?"

Dalton looked amused and she wondered how long he'd been trying to get her attention.

"Champagne, thanks."

"Be a love and get me a beer," said a male voice from behind her.

Instinctively, Carrie turned in the direction of the voice and found herself face-to-face with the other man she'd been ogling. Oh shit. His smile... it melted her fucking panties and, once again, that previously dormant ache resonated deep between her thighs and she had to bite down on her lip to halt the moan that threatened to escape.

"Carrie, this is Bodhi. Bodhi, this is Carrie," Dalton said, getting the introductions out of the way.

"Nice to meet you." Bodhi smiled.

"Um, you too," she stumbled over her words, overwhelmed by the close proximity of both men.

"Escaping your friend, I see," Bodhi teased.

Carrie frowned. "I'm going to kill her."

Dalton waved in the direction of some empty tables around the outer perimeter of the room. "Did you want to sit down?

"Thanks, but I should probably go back to Jess."

Bodhi pointed across the room. "I'm not too sure she'll notice if you go back."

Carrie looked towards their table and, considering the way her best friend was currently sticking her tongue down some guy's throat, she didn't think Jess had even noticed her absence. Rolling her eyes and resigning herself to the fact she'd be finding her own way home that night, Carrie shrugged then smiled at Dalton and Bodhi.

Butterflies were duelling in the pit of her stomach and she giggled nervously. "I guess one drink can't do too much damage!"

'*You need to let loose, Caz.*' The words Jess had spoken rang sharply in her head as she took a seat, with Dalton and Bodhi sitting on either side of her, and she couldn't fight the feeling she was about to get in *waaaay* over her head.

The prospect excited her more than she dared to acknowledge.

CHAPTER TWO

Carrie blinked to try and rid her eyes of the grit of sleep. The sun was too bright, and her eyelids instinctively snapped shut; it was Saturday morning and she had no need to be awake so damn early.

A light rhythmic sound to her left roused her curiosity and, turning her head slightly, she expected to find her cat, Tiger, curled up beside her.

Oh, shit.

Carrie clasped her hand over her mouth, her eyes so wide it was a miracle her eyeballs didn't pop out. The sweet sounds of sleep coming from beside her were not from a cat, but an especially large red-headed beast of a man. Awareness dawned on her; she was naked and judging by the bare skin her sleeping companion had on display, so was he. She'd had her first ever one-night stand, but she hadn't gone home with any old guy, she'd gone home with a bloody rugby league player.

A movement behind her made her freeze. She was looking at the ginger hottie—Dalton she remembered his name was, so why did it feel like there was someone else in the bed with them—

Oh.

Fuck.

An arm wrapped around her waist and she was pulled backward against a solid wall of heat, and breath mingled against the crook of her neck, followed by the slightest sensation of lips pressing against the sensitive skin below her ear.

She hadn't gone home with a rugby league player. She'd gone home with *two*!

Her brain started flooding with memories; being in an elevator and kissing Dalton, then Bodhi; wandering hands during the ride home in a taxi; buttons popping off shirts, her dress dropping to the floor, hands on her hips and breasts, zippers undone, lingerie flying... Louboutin heels staying on. There had been kissing. So much kissing. Two different mouths on her nipples at the same time. Her hand wrapped around two very hard c—

Oh, dear God.

Carrie waited for the horror to set in and tried to devise an escape plan; she didn't even know where in Sydney she was, let alone how she would get home or if her dress was in wearable condition.

Yet, instead of shame or embarrassment, all she felt, lying in between those two men she hardly knew, was deliciously sexed-out and sated.

And just a weeny bit turned on.

The arm around her waist tightened and another lazy kiss was dropped on her neck.

"Morning," Bodhi whispered.

"Morning," she whispered back, hoping her voice didn't convey how nervous she suddenly felt.

"Sleep okay?"

'*How about like someone who'd been fucked into a coma?*' Carrie thought, but instead opted for a safer, "Yes, I did."

Bodhi kissed the back of her neck again and whispered, "You have anywhere to be?"

"No-not really," Carrie said. Her breath hitched when Bodhi's lips made contact again and he kissed a slow path up to her earlobe.

There was no mistaking the hard ridge developing against her ass, and she was relieved Bodhi couldn't feel the hunger returning to her veins, or so she thought, until he began lightly rolling one of her nipples between his fingers. Her body gave away just what his touch was doing to her and as a result her hips started rocking; she could feel his cock growing harder against her, his breath coming faster, much like her own.

For a moment, Carrie forgot there was another person in the bed with them but when Dalton rolled over in his sleep, she found herself almost face to face with him, and wondered if she and Bodhi should stop before they got too carried away.

They should stop, but she didn't want to.

Bodhi's fingers were pulling the tension of pleasure tighter inside her with each tweak and tug of her nipple. Her bottom lip was trapped between her teeth in an attempt to stifle a moan of delight that was fighting to escape, and her back was arching in response to his fingers, willing them to squeeze tighter.

Any chance she had of remaining silent was blown apart when Bodhi moved his hand from her breasts, ghosting down over her ribcage and belly, lower and lower until he reached the part of her anatomy silently screaming for him.

"Oh fuck," she half-whispered, half-moaned as her swollen folds were gently parted by eager fingers.

"Uh huh." Bodhi's own reply was more of a grunt which turned into a growl as he worked his fingers down the length of her slit, coming to rest with one finger against her hole.

Carrie held her breath, waiting for his long fingers to settle inside her. Her pussy throbbed with impatience, but still, no fingers. Usually she wasn't one to speak up in bed and say what it was she wanted, but the intensity of her sudden craving outweighed any potential embarrassment, and she put her hand on top of his and pushed gently downward.

"I n-need you."

Relief washed over her as two fingers pressed slowly inside her, the swollen state of her pussy meaning every little spot he hit was more sensitive than usual, heightening her response.

"Oh fuck."

She moved her top arm behind her and gripped onto his upper thigh, aware her nails were digging into him, but she didn't have it in her to care in that moment.

"You feel so good," Bodhi whispered. "Soooo fucking good."

"I need-I need..." What did she need? Him to use another finger? To move harder? Deeper? She was flustered, she just needed... "You. I need you. Inside me,"

Carrie gasped, shocking herself with her apparent lack of shame.

"Hold on a sec," Bodhi's fingers slipped from her body and he rolled away from her.

She could hear him fumbling with the box of condoms and wished she was one of those irresponsible girls who said 'fuck it' to condoms and tell him to just get inside her. Nothing compared to the feeling of a bare cock moving against wet, swollen flesh, but now was neither the time nor place.

Dalton's eyelids flickered, and she held her breath as he opened his eyes and sleepily took in what was going on right in front of him. For a second, she worried he might get pissed off and leave the room—who wanted to wake up to their friend having sex with some woman in the same bed?—but a grin clutched on the corners of his mouth and, without any warning, he moved closer to her and licked his lips as his eyes zeroed in on her hard nipples.

Behind her, Bodhi repositioned himself and moved her top leg back over his waist, leaving her spread for him. The thick head of his cock grazed against her hole and even as he tilted his hips and the first inch pressed inside her, she started crying out. His hands found her hips and, achingly slowly, he pulled her back against him, his cock filling her all the way, shocks of pleasure sending shudders through her body.

What really made her cry out though? The feeling of one of her nipples being sucked deep inside Dalton's mouth, his tongue massaging the sensitive bead as it was pressed against the roof of his mouth.

Bodhi inched out of her until he'd almost left her body then pushed back inside, his fingers digging in as he moved his hips back, almost leaving her body again. This time when he thrust forward, Carrie pushed back against him and moaned loudly as the tip of his cock made heavy contact with the back of her pussy.

On and on it went—it felt like ten minutes but was more likely two at the most—until her cries were drowned out by Bodhi's loud grunts with each thrust. Dalton's mouth was punishing her nipple, and she'd never experienced anything more erotic. To be taken from behind while having her nipples sucked created a pleasure that she'd never imagined possible.

Forcing herself to let go and stop resisting the orgasm she knew was ready to explode, Carrie felt her pussy contract; every muscle in her body felt as if it was on fire. Bodhi's cock was continuously striking sensitive spots, Dalton's mouth was overpowering her nipple with the most intense balance of pleasure and pain... she couldn't hold back any longer.

She screamed as her orgasm hit, pushing into Bodhi allowing him to hit harder. He gasped and groaned and with one final, powerful thrust, his own orgasm took hold, his arm tight around her waist, his dick so deep and thick, she couldn't tell where he finished, and she began.

Dalton closed the gap between them, the evidence of his arousal pressing against her belly. She wished she had the energy to take him in her hand and work him until he came too; the way he was twitching against her belly told her it wouldn't take long, but she was a lost cause. Even as Bodhi was carefully slipping out of her, Carrie could feel her brain becoming foggy with exhaustion as her body gave in to another great need. Sleep.

**

When she eventually woke, it was with the stark realisation that she needed to use the toilet, badly, and had no idea where it was. Neither of the men were in bed and for a minute she wondered if they'd ditched her, but no, she could hear sounds coming from the other end of the house, the smell of bacon suggesting they were in the kitchen.

Spying her dress on the floor beside the door, Carrie crept out of the bed and darted across the room, picking up her dress and climbing into it as quickly as she could to save herself any embarrassment should Dalton or Bodhi come back into the room. Who was she kidding? After what she'd done with both of them in the past twelve hours, the embarrassment train had long left the station.

After finding the bathroom next door, Carrie went about her business and used the opportunity to take some deep breaths in an attempt to calm herself down.

How was one meant to go about such a morning after? Should she walk into the kitchen long enough to say goodbye and escape, or should she act like it was no big deal, sit down and see if a coffee was on offer, or even if there was a piece of bacon to spare?

She wasn't clued up about normal post one-night-stand etiquette, let alone what to do after a bloody threesome.

Carrie splashed cold water on her face, then looked at her reflection in the mirror and giggled. Her hair had that freshly-fucked look about it, while her eye makeup was smudged and, instead of a smokey eye, she looked like she'd rubbed soot straight from the fire around her eyes.

But that grin. When was the last time she'd smiled like that? Her whole face was lit up and even her eyes seemed to be smiling. *Ah*, the magical powers of breaking a sexual dry spell. She'd forgotten how spectacular the post-orgasm high felt and only hoped it would last the rest of the day.

Knowing it was time to face up to what—who—she'd done, Carrie walked out of the bathroom, and down the hallway, toward the noise and the breakfast smells. She paused. What was she going to do? Just walk on in and say, '*hey boys, what's up?*?

'*What's up?*' reminded her of what *had* been up, and a flush crept up her cheeks. How was she going to be able to look either man in the eye?

Taking another deep breath to compose herself, Carrie stepped into the kitchen and found Bodhi sitting at the table, while Dalton, only wearing boxers, stood at the stove, tending to the bacon.

"You want a coffee?" Dalton asked, not even turning to look at her.

"Yes please, milk and no sugar."

"Big cup, small cup?"

"Bigger the better," Carrie said, not missing the way Bodhi snorted. She turned to him and rolled her eyes. "Shut up."

"Not sorry," Bodhi laughed and pulled a chair out for her. "Come, sit down if you want."

"Don't mind if I do." Though she hadn't gotten drunk, she felt hungover and wobbly on her feet.

"You want some food?" Dalton asked. "We've got bacon and mushrooms and there are some English muffins too."

"As long as I haven't outstayed my welcome," Carrie said, unsure whether they were just being polite in inviting her to have breakfast with them, or if they really didn't mind her presence.

Dalton walked over with her coffee and said, "We've got a game tonight, but until then, not a hell of a lot on. Be rude of us to kick you out without at least feeding you."

Before she had a chance to take his '*kick you out*' comment seriously, Bodhi clarified, "What Dalton means is, we're not the type of inconsiderate bastards who'd tell you to bugger off."

"It's okay if you want me to go," Carrie said. "I've never done this before so I have no idea what the rules are for the morning after."

"Never had a one-night-stand, or..."

"Uh, either. Never had a one-nighter, never had... well, what the three of us did last night."

"And this morning," Dalton added with a mischievous wink, as he put a plate piled with greasy food in front of her.

"And that," Carrie said, busying herself with her food so she didn't have to make eye contact.

"FYI, it isn't something we've done before either," Bodhi said.

"Well, individually we've done it," Dalton added. "But not together."

If she didn't know any better, she'd have thought Bodhi was blushing as he spoke, "And it's not something either of us does a lot."

"But when the mood takes you..." Dalton finished, a sparkle flashing in those chocolatey eyes of his.

Carrie giggled. "Fair to say it took all of us last night."

"See!" Bodhi laughed. "Who said morning after conversation has to be awkward."

They ate in silence, but as she sneaked looks at Dalton and Bodhi, Carrie could tell they, much like her, were thinking about what had happened between them. It was a pity it had to come to an end, really, because both men seemed lovely—not that she knew them very well. Okay, she hardly knew them at all, but she'd always been a good reader of people and could tell the two men she'd spent the night with didn't belong in the scumbag category.

After breakfast, Bodhi excused himself to have a shower, leaving Carrie alone in the kitchen with Dalton. It surprised her to realise she felt more nervous being alone with one of the men, than she had been with both.

"Want another coffee?" Dalton asked, standing and taking their plates.

"If you're having one."

"I am. Go into the lounge if you want to, it's nicer in there."

What Carrie really wanted to do was stay where she was, so she could watch a topless Dalton moving around the kitchen. Every movement the man made rippled one muscle or another and gave her the overwhelming urge to bite him all over.

Biting... and more. She *really* needed to get out of there.

In the lounge, Carrie was pleasantly surprised by the view, looking out over Coogee Beach. That meant she wasn't too far away from her own house, around three kilometres away in Clovelly; if she really wanted to, she could escape out the front door and walk home, never to see Bodhi or Dalton again.

Why did an idea that should appeal so much not appeal at all?

"You guys have got a lovely view here," Carrie said when Dalton came in carrying their coffees.

Dalton put the coffees on the dark wooden coffee table in front of the couch and sat down. "One of the perks of playing for the Kings!"

"A major perk if you ask me," Carrie said. "I live in Clovelly, would have loved a beach view but that was way out of my price range."

"We're as good as neighbours!" He smiled at her as she sat next to him and picked up her coffee.

"Might as well be." She took a large gulp of her coffee, not caring it burnt her throat on the way down. "I don't think any amount of coffee will be enough today."

He took such a big mouthful Carrie was surprised he didn't finish the drink in one go. "I know that feeling."

"Were you and Bodhi friends before you joined the team?"

"I'd heard of him, but never met him. We both signed the same year and the club put us in this place together, since then, we've been pretty close."

So close they'd fucked the same girl, in the same bed, at the same time...

Dalton's face went bright red. "Not usually as close as last night though."

"Just so you know, I had a lot of fun." Why did words insist on coming out? Surely, she should be going to any length to avoid the subject.

He put a hand on her knee. "I did as well."

God, she must look hysterical sitting there in her fancy dress with mussed up hair and smudged eyes. If anyone was to walk in, there'd be no way to explain her current look.

"It wasn't at all how I expected the night to turn out."

"Neither did I. I'm glad it did though," Dalton said, his voice taking on an unusual husk that woke up something heated inside her.

"Sorry about this morning... you know, what you woke up to."

"In case you didn't notice, I very much enjoyed what I woke up to."

"It was a bit rude of us though, of me and Bodhi, I mean. We should have—"

"It wasn't rude, or inappropriate, or any of the negative stuff you're obviously thinking. It was fucking hot. I only wish I'd been the first one to wake up..."

"You should have woken me if—"

The rest of her sentence was cut off by his lips moving against her own. Strong hands gripped her hips and, without breaking the kiss, Dalton moved her, so she was straddling his lap. The kiss was long and lingering, and with each passing second, she could feel him growing harder between her thighs, her hips soon rocking in time with his.

"I'd ask if there was room for me, but I don't think three on that couch would be too comfortable," Bodhi's voice was a chuckle behind them, causing her and Dalton to freeze.

"I-I'm-I should be going," Carrie said, caught off guard by Bodhi's appearance in the lounge and worried he was going to be pissed off she and Dalton had started fooling around without him.

"No, it's fine. You two have fun, Mum just rang and invited me out for lunch. Like I can say no to a free feed!"

She could feel him moving closer behind her and gasped when she felt his breath on the back of her neck.

"I had a great time last night, you made a very boring gala anything but." Bodhi's words made her insides flutter and when he bit down lightly on the crook of her neck, she shuddered into Dalton.

"Uh huh," Carrie said, though her words were more of a groan.

"If you don't have plans tonight, you should come to the game."

"Maybe I will." Carrie had no intention to but she could hardly say '*no thanks*' to his face.

"Be back about three," Bodhi said for Dalton's benefit.

"See you then."

Bodhi left, and the house was silent, except for her heart beating out of her chest. Carrie peered down at Dalton, taking in his beautifully long eyelashes, and the smattering of freckles on his nose, she felt compelled to do something very un-Carrie-like.

Standing up, she made quick work of unzipping her dress and stepping out of it, before settling back on Dalton's lap.

"You've just woken up," Carrie set the scene for him. "I'm straddling you, kissing a path up your chest, my nipples keep brushing against you and you can feel the heat of my pussy against your cock..."

In one easy movement Dalton stood up, his hands on her ass holding her close. He forged a determined path out of the lounge and down the hallway, kicking open the door to a bedroom she'd not been inside of yet. Turning them around, he then sat on the bed and fell backward, putting Carrie in the exact position she'd just described to him.

Dalton reached across to the bedside table and opened the top drawer; Carrie took out the box of condoms before he had a chance and removed one. Wiggling backward she carefully tore open the foil wrapper and carefully extracted what was an impressively sized erection out of his boxers; just the sight was enough to make her pussy clench and squeeze. She'd never been so hungry for a cock and, as she sheathed him then positioned herself over him, she couldn't decide if that hunger was a good thing, or a bad thing.

She sat down on him and, feeling that agonisingly good stretch as he filled her, she had her answer. It was too much of a good thing.

She was screwed.

CHAPTER THREE

"What made you suddenly want to come to a league game?" Jess shouted to be heard over the rowdy crowd of rugby league fans.

"No reason," Carrie yelled back.

"It's because of last night, isn't it?" Jess winked knowingly.

"What do you mean?"

She couldn't know, could she?

"I saw you perving on the Kings table at the gala, and look, I don't blame you, they're a pack of hotties and it's my honour to attend your first game with you."

"Oh gee, am I that transparent?"

"Well, you are a hot-blooded woman, there'd be something wrong with you if you didn't want to watch twenty-six men running around in tight shorts and even tighter tops for eighty minutes!"

Oh Jess, if only you knew.

Carrie felt naughty for keeping such a huge secret from her best friend, but what had happened between her, Dalton, and Bodhi was something she wanted to enjoy by herself for a while. She liked knowing both men had been inside her and that she'd driven them both to the point of desperation with her body. *She* had done that. Boring, old, responsible Carrie. A few times already, Jess had caught her smiling and asked why she was so happy. It would have been so easy to say, '*I had a threesome last night*', but it was far more enjoyable to make her wonder.

She'd acted suitably shocked when Jess told her that, before leaving the gala, she and the guy she'd left with— Dave, who was occasionally contracted by the firm she worked for —had had sex in a public toilet in the foyer of the hotel. When Jess had gone on to tell her about having sex on Dave's balcony and being sure a bunch of people in nearby apartment buildings had seen them, Carrie had managed an oh-my-god-you-must-be-joking gasp, while, at the same time. screaming in her head, '*Well I had a threesome. Beat that.*'

She knew she shouldn't be so cocky, it had been a one-off and would be the only wild sex story she'd ever have to tell. Jess had had her fair share of threesomes, though none had been with professional rugby league players!

The crowd erupted around them and Carrie cheered along, everyone looking in the direction of the tunnel in anticipation of the players running out. She'd seen it on TV before when stuck watching league with her dad but being part of that atmosphere in person was something she hadn't been prepared for. When the players ran out, she was screaming and jumping with everyone else.

As she watched Dalton and Bodhi run onto the field, Carrie felt dizzy. They looked so massive, and strong... physical perfection if ever she'd seen it.

What the hell had they seen in her? They hadn't been drunk so couldn't use beer-goggles as an excuse. Had it been a bet of some sort? A huge joke between them and their teammates? She didn't think that was it, but who knew what went on in the heads of men.

Carrie felt clueless about what was happening on the field *and* what had happened off the field, in Bodhi's bedroom. At least when it came to the game, she only needed to follow the cues of the people around her to get the general gist of what was happening. Loud screaming and clapping meant the Kings had scored a try, swearing and booing meant the other team had scored. Chanting '*off off off*' meant the other team had done something bad to one of the Kings players, while '*come on ref!*' meant one of the Kings had done something to a player on the opposing team.

It was easy to get swept away in the excitement of it all, and Carrie wondered why she hadn't been to a game earlier. Even if she didn't know anything about the game, she could enjoy being part of a loud, raucous crowd.

If she'd had the impression Dalton and Bodhi were big, hard men before the game, by the time the final whistle blew, she was utterly stunned by how the human body could put up with so much physical punishment. With a lot of the tackles, especially the ones Dalton had been part yet, you could hear the bone-rattling *thud* as body made impact with body. On more than one occasion, a player had been aided off after a head knock, trying to persuade the medic he was perfectly fine while zigzagging to the sideline.

How did parents watch their kids playing this sport? And the wives? How did they handle it week in, week out, seeing their men getting bruised and bloodied, knowing there was a chance a season—or career—ending injury was just one play away? Everyone knew a player needed to be physically and mentally tough, but surely the same went for their families and friends too.

"I want to go down and see if I can get close enough to smell the sweat on the players," Jess said, making Carrie laugh. "Maybe I can catch Jed Atkins's eye again."

Carrie shrugged. "You're my driver tonight so I guess whatever you say goes."

Jess rolled her eyes. "Wow, way to sound excited, Caz."

"Fine, I am happy to go with you! Lead the way."

Jess caught Carrie's hand and pulled her along the row of seats they were in and down the numerous steps until they reached the bottom. They followed the rest of the crowd waiting to get down to the area of the field cordoned off for players meet and greets, and slowly moved along until their shoes touched solid ground. Considering it had been raining most of the week, the grass was surprisingly firm underfoot.

That didn't stop Carrie stumbling over her own feet when she noticed Dalton standing four metres away. Any hopes of him not seeing her were dashed when Jess pulled her in his direction. Maybe she did know and she was about to make a scene in front of the thousands of fans at the stadium.

Dalton hadn't noticed her yet, he was far too busy signing autographs and taking photos, mostly with kids, and something about that made her heart turn into a pile of mush. He was taking his time to talk to each kid and made sure to get down to their level while photos were taken. He might have been a huge hulk of a man, but he looked to have a wonderful way with his younger fans.

How tiny would a newborn baby look in his arms?

No, Carrie. Dangerous territory. Avert thoughts, avert th—

"Carrie! Fancy seeing you here."

Dalton. Oh crap, he was talking to her. Jess looked at her questioningly.

Carrie raised her hand with a little wave. "Uh, hey, Dalton."

"Enjoy the game?"

"I did!"

"You guys played sooooo well, as usual!" Jess piped up.

"Thanks."

"We should let you get onto the rest of your fans," Carrie said, knees weakening when he smiled at her. It was a smile that said, '*remember this morning when I was buried inside you and you rode me like a cowgirl?*'

"Bodhi will be around somewhere, you should stop and stay hi to him."

"*Bodhi*—you know Bodhi Hook?" Jess screeched, making everyone in earshot look at them.

Dalton laughed and opened his arms to her. "It was nice to see you."

"You too," Carrie said, not at all repulsed by the sweaty hug, and very conscious of Jess's eyes burning a hole in the back of her head.

She watched Dalton move a metre to the left where he was accosted by a little boy who could not have been more than four years old.

Jess turned her around roughly. "How the hell do you know Dalton Kendry and Bodhi Hook?"

"I met them at the ball last night," Carrie said. "You know, when you hooked up with that guy and completely ignored me?"

"Stop being dramatic," Jess laughed.

"Not being dramatic, Jess. Just telling you how I met Dalton and Bodhi."

"First name basis, huh."

"It's what happens when you meet people, they tell you their name, you tell them yours."

Jess opened her mouth to say something, but was interrupted by Bodhi, who chose that second to call out to her.

Carrie turned and smiled at the man whom she'd been naked with less than twelve hours earlier. "Hello."

"I'm glad you came!"

Carrie snorted and winked at him. "Glad I came as well," then added in a whisper, "every single time."

Bodhi laughed loudly and looked her up and down appreciatively. "Mmm, so am I."

"Seriously though, I'm glad I came to the game. It was a pretty cool experience."

"It's a nice surprise to see you... funny how that happens, you're just thinking about someone and they magically appear."

"You were thinking about me, eh?" Carrie teased.

"You have no idea."

"Oh," Carrie said. "I do."

Bodhi looked around as if searching for someone. "Where'd your friend go?"

Carrie turned around on the spot slowly, looking for the familiar bottle-blond ponytail, but came up empty. Jess had been standing beside her a minute earlier, and now she was nowhere to be seen.

"She's probably scouting her next conquest," Carrie said, still looking for that ponytail.

"Not hard to get lost with all these people, probably easier to ring her."

Deciding Bodhi was right, Carrie took her cell phone out of her handbag, not surprised to see she had a message from Jess. She expected it was probably along the lines of '*I followed a player into the locker room and now I'm lost! Help!*'

She couldn't have been more wrong. The message read, '*I know when I'm not needed. I'm sure if you ask Bodhi or Dalton, they'll happily give you a ride home.*'

"What the actual fuck?" Carrie said loudly, earning her a few unimpressed looks from people standing nearby.

"You okay?" Bodhi asked, and Carrie handed him her phone, so he could see for himself. "Oh wow, that's harsh, but if you do need a ride, I'm more than happy to oblige. Dalton said you live out our way anyway?"

"No, I don't want to put you guys out, I know it's probably not just as easy as getting changed and leaving the stadium."

"Not quite, but you can hang out inside with the rest of the friends and family, it's not a problem at all."

"I can just get a tax—"

"Look, we're going through your suburb, it'd be stupid to make you fork out for a taxi. I insist."

"If you're sure?"

"Wait while I finish up here and you can come inside with me."

Carrie had to stifle a laugh at the combination of the words '*inside*' and '*me*', finding herself more amused than she should be. Bodhi smirked knowingly, and she felt not only her face burning, but another part of her body too, one that seemed to be dramatically affected *whenever* he flashed that suggestive smile at her.

***

The car came to a stop outside Carrie's house and she was still in the midst of a silent battle with herself. To ask them in, or not to ask them in... that was the question.

Asking them in could be considered an invitation for sex and that was something she wasn't sure if she wanted. It was one thing to have sex once (... or twice), but to do it again, at a different location, was to tread into very dangerous water. But if she didn't invite them in, it could be seen as rude because they had given her a ride home, and her mum had taught her the polite thing to do in that situation was to invite the person in for a drink.

Her mum's lesson in manners hadn't been intended as words to live by after a one-night stand... but asking them in was still the right thing to do.

They'd likely politely refuse the offer, anyway.

"Did you guys want to come in for a drink?"

Bodhi replied first. "Sure!"

"Why not!" Dalton said, pushing open the driver's door and hunching over to get his huge frame out of the vehicle.

The men followed her up to the front door and she'd never felt more self-conscious about what someone would think of her house. It wasn't big or fancy, she didn't have sea views and her furniture was mostly second-hand; but it was *her* house. She owned it and had worked damn hard to be able to achieve that particular dream.

It was only when she opened the fridge to tell Dalton and Bodhi what was on offer that she remembered she hadn't done the groceries yet.

"I don't have any beer, sorry. I can do orange juice or lemonade, or coffee or tea, or water. If you want beer, I can go to the shop."

"Orange juice is fine," Bodhi called.

"Can I be really outrageous and ask for an orange *and* lemonade?" Dalton asked.

Orange and lemonade? Who'd have thought such a sexy beast of a man would want such a tame drink? It was quite adorable.

For old times' sake she poured herself an orange and lemonade as well; it reminded her of holidays at her nana's house when she was a kid... '*kid fizzy*' the old woman had called it, and it was quite the delicacy.

Carrie walked carefully into the lounge; she knew she'd taken a risk by carrying all three glasses at once. If she spilled the drinks she'd look like a right twat, wouldn't she? By some miracle, the three drinks made it to the coffee table without a single drop being lost to the floor.

It was only when she had safely delivered the drinks that she paid attention to where the men were sitting, on opposite ends of the cushy black couch.

Great, another decision to make. Did she sit between Dalton and Bodhi, or did she sit across the room from them on one of the recliners? So many fucking decisions to make. She hadn't signed on for this!

Buying herself a little time she walked over to the entertainment unit and fiddled with the iPod until she found a radio station that played a little bit of everything. That was why the single life was so much easier. She didn't need to worry about what someone else liked, or have to take their opinions into consideration when deciding on any of the mundane daily tasks, such as choosing what to have for dinner, or what movie to watch. The loneliness that came with singledom almost seemed worth it when looked at from that perspective.

Almost.

Fuck it. Why shouldn't she sit between the two men? It made more sense than having to shout half-way across the room at each other, and it wasn't as if sitting by them meant anything sexual had to happen. After they left that night, she doubted their paths would cross again, and in the meantime, there was nothing wrong with enjoying their company.

With no idea how to start the conversation, she introduced a topic she knew was safe. "You guys must be happy you won the game?"

"I could have played better," Dalton said and shrugged his shoulders, a movement that felt as if it shook the whole couch.

"Sure, forty-four tackles, such an awful effort!" Bodhi said.

"What? We all know you're going to say that two-hundred and thirty metres is a shit amount of metres run!"

"Not awful, but I could have done more!"

"Can I just say, as someone who knows sweet fuck all about league, I thought you both had awesome games?" Carrie interjected.

"Thanks," the men said sheepishly, at the same time.

"But I get that you are always trying to do better. I'm the same in my job—not that I have to run or smash into people, but I always want to perform better."

"High up in the editing team, you must be impressing someone with your work." Bodhi smiled, and Carrie lost her train of thought for a moment.

"Guess so," she said. "Doubt I look half as good as you guys do when I'm working, though."

Dalton screwed his face up. "Because smelly and sweaty and covered in mud is *soooooo* hot."

Winking, she confessed, "I'm more thinking of those short shorts and tight tops."

"You look just as good in a tight top," Bodhi teased.

Dalton added, "You're the type of chick that would look good in anything."

She frowned and shook her head. "I beg to differ."

"See, that's what makes you so hot!" Dalton turned to face her. "You don't realise you're sexy as hell. You're one of those girls that sees all these flaws that no one else does."

"I don't th—"

"Dalton is right. Last night at the gala every guy who walked past turned to look at you, most of them were undressing you with their eyes, but you were sitting there talking to us idiots, completely oblivious to all the attention you were drawing."

"Pretty sure anyone who looked at me was thinking, 'What the hell is she doing here?'"

Dalton scoffed and looked so intensely at her, she had to turn away.

"More like *'Jesus Christ, what is that smoking hot piece of ass doing with those two losers?'*"

Carrie laughed at the absurdity of the description matching her. "Hot piece of ass... sure."

"You need to stop being so down on yourself," Bodhi said softly, stroked her upper arm with his fingertips.

"I don't agree with this muppet often." Dalton chuckled. "But Bodhi is right. You need to give yourself more credit."

Carrie opened her mouth to tell them they were idiots, but Dalton put his hand on the back of her neck and her capacity to talk ceased to function.

Bodhi and Dalton moved closer and desire surged through her veins. There was no cell in her body that didn't want this, didn't want them, and as two pairs of lips pressed against opposite sides of her neck, Carrie moaned with delight.

Lips were all the same, but it was incredible to notice the differences in the way they kissed her. Bodhi's tongue grazed softly against the skin below her ear, his lips soft, creating contact so light it tickled; Dalton, on the other hand, was lightly sucking and occasionally biting down on the tender crook of her neck, his kisses hungrier, more insistent.

Bodhi kissed a trail along her jaw until he reached her mouth, and those gentle kisses of his resumed against her lips. It was she who initiated the first contact of tongue against tongue and, when he groaned into her mouth, something charged inside her. Something powerful and determined. She was brought back to earth by Dalton's teeth, digging into her neck, causing her to cry out with a mix of surprise and pleasure.

Carrie hadn't expected the change in intensity and felt like she was free falling. Toward what, she didn't know.

"If you want us to stop..." Bodhi mumbled against her mouth.

"Don't!" Carrie gasped. "Please."

Dalton pulled away. "Did you hear something?"

Carrie tore her lips from Bodhi's and paused for a moment. "I don't hear anything."

"I was sure I h—"

She didn't give Dalton a chance to finish, putting her hand on the back of his neck and pulling him toward her, leaving no question she wanted him to continue where he'd left off.

Before he could mark her neck any further, there was a loud knock at the door.

Carrie groaned. "Fucking hell, who comes to someone's house this late at night?"

She stood up and went to answer the door.

"Oh shit, Caz. I'm so glad you're home! I'm sorry! It was such an asshole move, leaving you at the stadium like that, pleeeeeeease forgive me." She held her hands together as if praying, and fluttered her eyelashes, giving Carrie puppy dog eyes.

Now things were awkward.

"Uh, no, it's okay I—"

Jess pushed past her. "I'm so thirsty! You got a beer?"

"No, no beer," Carrie said. "Why don't you come over tomorrow morning, we could go for lunch or something, spend the afternoon together."

"I just feel so bad!"

"I'll get over it, Jess." Carrie said, trying to get between the lounge door and Jess, but she wasn't fast enough.

Jess walked into the lounge and stood still, rooted to the spot.

"Clearly, you really missed me!" Jess snarled. "Stupid fucking slut!"

"Hey, that's enough of—" Bodhi started but Jess interrupted him.

"No, I know what I just walked in on, and it's fucking disgusting. I guess it's true what they say, league players really will sleep with any woman who throws herself at them! It's fucking pathetic!"

"Jess, that isn't what happened," Carrie said, hands on her hips. "The guys brought me home after *you* left me stranded. I invited them for a drink, end of!"

Yeah, she'd left out a few details, but that wasn't the point.

"I thought you had class, Carrie. Obviously not. And you didn't even go for two of the big names on the team... I suppose these two were the only ones who'd stoop so low." Jess's laugh was cold. Nasty.

Dalton came to stand behind Carrie and placed his hands on her shoulders. He looked at Jess. "I think you need to leave now."

"I think *you* need to leave," Jess spat back.

"No! You can leave, Jess, before you say something you'll really regret." Carrie said firmly.

Jess rolled her eyes. "Whatever, whore. Have fun getting whatever disease from these two dirty cocks. See ya."

The lounge door slammed. The front door slammed. Outside a car started and sped away.

What the hell had just happened?

"You okay?" Dalton asked, cautiously.

She shrugged. "No. Not really. But I will be." Though it went against everything her body was telling her, she looked apologetically at the two men. "I'm sorry guys, but it's probably best if you go as well. I don't think I'm going to be much company to anyone. I'm going to have a shower and go to bed, try and forget what just happened." She attempted a smile. "The stuff with Jess I mean, not what happened before that... I was really enjoying *that.*"

Carrie wasn't sure if she was disappointed or relieved when the men picked up their cell phones from the coffee table and slipped their shoes back on.

"Thanks for coming to the game," Dalton said as they followed her to the front door. He leaned down and kissed her on the cheek. "And for inviting us in."

"I hope your friend calms down and gives you the biggest apology known to mankind," Bodhi said, also kissing her. "She usually that psycho?"

Carrie frowned. "Never seen her like that."

Bodhi hugged her and opened the door. "Well, maybe we'll see you at another game."

She smiled and nodded, meaning it this time when she said, "I will make sure of it."

***

Carrie hadn't been in bed long when her cell phone vibrated on the bedside table. Picking it up, she saw she had new message notifications on Facebook Messenger. Probably Jess with another attack, or an apology. Always a stickler for punishment, she opened the messages, but it wasn't Jess she found.

Bodhi H wants to connect with you on Messenger.

DJ Kendry wants to connect with you on Messenger.

Nothing could ever happen between them romantically, she knew that—two guys, one girl might work in pornos, but not in real life—but it didn't mean they couldn't be friends though. What did she have to lose?

Accept.

Accept.

CHAPTER FOUR

Lying in bed on Saturday night after the drama with Jess, Carrie decided nothing more would happen with Dalton and Bodhi. The last thing she wanted was to earn herself a reputation, even if the three of them were single, consenting adults who had every right to do whatever they wanted – and *whoever* they wanted.

Two days later, the aftershock of Jess's words was still with her. She'd never been called a slut before, or a whore, and hearing the words coming out of the mouth of her best friend had been more alarming than the words themselves.

The easy part was knowing she shouldn't have sex with Bodhi or Dalton again, the hard part was making her body remember that the next time she saw them in person, if she did. It would be easiest to cut all ties, to never lay eyes on them again, but the idea of never seeing them again made her inexplicably sad. They hadn't known each other long, there was no reason she should care if she saw them again, or not.

It didn't help that, after accepting their message requests on Facebook Messenger, the three had been chatting regularly, and the more they spoke, the more she wanted to see them again, even if it was just as friends.

Just friends. It was the only solution in their situation; one woman and two men, it didn't exactly have relationship potential. Casual sex wasn't a realistic option either; what were they going to do? Make a schedule of the nights Carrie would spend with each of them? No, it was far too complicated for anything as simple as friends with benefits.

Pity, she'd enjoyed all the time she'd spent with them over the past few days—in and out of bed.

She'd just finished her chicken noodle salad for lunch on Tuesday, when the Messenger icon showed up on her notifications. As she opened the message, Carrie convinced herself she was smiling because she'd had a shitty day at work and looked forward to the distraction. It was most certainly *not* because she missed Bodhi and Dalton.

Bodhi: Carrie, you need to settle this debate we're having.

Carrie: What debate is that?

Dalton: Bodhi thinks his pizza is better than mine, but I know mine is far more superior.

Bodhi: Whatever, you don't even make your own sauce! You just use store-bought shit.

Dalton: Well your crust tastes like crap.

Carrie: Okay, okay, settle petal! How can I help settle said debate?

Bodhi: Come to our place for tea tonight? We'll both cook a pizza, you can decide which you like best!

Dalton: Break it to Bodhi softly though, he might cry... doesn't handle criticism well.

Bodhi: Ha! I've got nothing to worry about because I'll totally win.

Carrie: Such a mature argument. What if I don't like either?

Bodhi: Not a chance! You're gonna love mine so much, it'll ruin all other pizza for you.

Dalton: Much like I've ruined all other men for you...

Bodhi: Dream on.

Carrie: You're both idiots. Fine, I accept the challenge. Want me to bring anything?

Dalton: Some sort of runner-up prize for Bodes...

Carrie: *laughs* Is anything not a competition between you two?

Bodhi: Well, you're not...

Carrie: Good, because there is plenty of me to go around. I mean... plenty of my friendship to go around. My platonic friendship. Nothing else. Just... two guys and a girl... friends.

Dalton: You blushing, Miss Carrie?

Carrie: Shuddup. Get back to training! (see you around 6?)

Bodhi: Until 6pm...

Dalton: Peace out, friend.

Going to dinner at their house didn't have to be awkward. It was what friends did all the time. There was nothing wrong with socialising, spending time together and enjoying one another's company; she'd done it with other friends numerous times, and it wouldn't be any different that night, with Bodhi and Dalton.

Focusing on work for the rest of the afternoon was harder than she'd expected, and she was disappointed in herself. Carrie prided herself on her commitment to her job and giving one hundred percent of her attention to whichever manuscript was in front of her. That afternoon was a total write-off.

What was it about those two men that had her so distracted? Sure, they made her laugh and whenever they asked her a question seemed genuinely interested to hear the answer, and of course there was the sex... but why was she so taken with them?

A lot of the manuscripts that came via her desk contained sex, some extremely graphic, and she'd always enjoyed reading those scenes. Some of them made her horny as hell and made her wish she had a man to go home to. But that week? Even the steamiest of the scenes she'd read had paled in comparison to the vivid memory of what she'd done with Dalton and Bodhi.

It wasn't just at work. All she could think about was the sex, reliving that night over, and over again. She couldn't forget how it had felt when Dalton had taken her from behind while she sucked Bodhi's cock, or riding Bodhi's cock while sucking Dalton's. Then there had been the way Dalton had sucked her nipples on Saturday morning when she'd been filled with Bodhi. The way Dalton had looked beneath her as she rode him when they'd gone to his bedroom after breakfast had been arousing enough on its own, without the addition of his massive dick which had stretched her to the point she'd thought her vagina would be forever changed.

She'd been so wet afterward she'd had to change her panties.

Carrie guessed Jess's interruption on Saturday night had been a good thing because the way they were headed, they'd surely have ended up back in bed. Spending one night with them had turned her memories into a non-stop porno, two nights would have rendered her completely useless.

Deliciously, blissfully useless.

***

Knocking on Dalton and Bodhi's front door, Carrie willed the butterflies in her stomach to calm the fuck down. Why was she so nervous about a simple meal? In that moment, she hated herself. *Three* times she'd changed her outfit before finally deciding on what to wear that night, a red embroidered off-the-shoulder top, paired with light blue jeans. She'd even gone to the extreme of wearing a strapless bra, so she could properly show off her shoulders, one of the parts of her body she actually liked.

The heavy wooden door opened, and Bodhi greeted her with a hug that severely damaged her resolve to keep things platonic. He smelled so damn good and all Carrie could imagine was the scent on his bare skin as he hovered above her teasingly before plunging inside her.

Shit. This was going to be harder than expected.

"How was your day?" Bodhi asked, leading her through to the kitchen, where Dalton was busy putting toppings on his pizza.

"It was good." What else could she say? '*Terrible, all day the only thing I could think about was you fucking me, which in turn made me incredibly horny*'?

"Hope you're ready to be blown away by my pizza," Dalton said, walking around the kitchen island to give her a hug.

Oh, God. He smelled even better than Bodhi... This was not good.

"Drink?" Bodhi asked, before opening the fridge and taking out two bottles of beer.

"I'll have a beer too."

Because alcohol was definitely the best way to deal with the rapidly increasing urge she was experiencing to drag both of the men to the nearest stable surface so she could ride one or both of them.

The pizzas were ceremoniously put in the oven and for twenty-five minutes they sat outside on the balcony, enjoying the last of the early spring daylight with a view of Coogee Beach.

"I can't wait for the weather to warm up," Carrie said. "Love spending the day at the beach!"

"Best thing about living here," Bodhi said, smiling as he looked out to the horizon.

Without thinking, Carrie said, "We should all go sometime!"

Immediately, she regretted it.

Like she could deal with being around those two wearing nothing but their swim shorts. All that bare skin, all those muscles, the enticing trails of hair heading south from their belly buttons, reminding her of what lay just beneath.

"Great idea," Dalton said with a nod.

Bodhi gave his approval of the idea, "Let's do it!"

Hopefully they'd forget before the weather warmed sufficiently to make beach visits a possibility.

Grasping for a change of subject, and ideally a change of her train of thought, she broached the most dangerous of topics. "So, tell me more about these pizzas."

Luckily, her ploy worked and for the next few minutes the men talked up their own pizzas while bagging on the other's. The conversation soon turned to what their favourite meals had been growing up, and the best places to eat in Sydney. Bodhi and Dalton told her about an awesome Argentinian steakhouse they'd eaten at when playing in Brisbane, and she told them about the delicious seafood she'd eaten on a holiday in New Zealand the previous summer.

Even though the conversation revolved around food, Carrie's thoughts were still firmly planted in the bedroom and it was only getting worse.

She found herself wondering how sturdy the guardrail on the balcony was and how much of the area was visible to their neighbours. The wooden table they were sitting around felt solid and, though she tried her hardest not to, she couldn't help imagine laying on it, the breeze turning her nipples into hard buds as either Bodhi or Dalton feasted between her legs. Maybe they'd take turns. Later, she could repay the favour, getting on her knees and s—

A loud beep rang out from inside and Carrie had never been so relieved.

"Time for my pizza to shine!" Bodhi said, getting off the canvas chair and walking in the direction of the kitchen.

"Dream on," Dalton called, running after him. "You're gonna lose!"

Carrie giggled, amused to see two big men being so competitive about something as trivial as pizza.

The smile on her face as she joined the men in the kitchen was genuine and she was glad she'd been invited to dinner; sure, she was attracted to both of them, but the more time spent with them, the more she found herself enjoying their company.

As an adult, it could be hard to make friends, but Carrie had a feeling that, on Friday night, when she'd found herself talking to Dalton and Bodhi, she'd unexpectedly made friends for life. It was hard not to imagine how differently things might have played out if she'd only met one of them, and knew there was every chance a friendship could have evolved quickly into a relationship, but watching the two men pushing each other around in the kitchen, Carrie knew better than to dwell on the what-ifs, and to be grateful for what she did have.

Bodhi and Dalton were being better friends to her than her own best friend was at that present point in time, that was for sure.

It wasn't until they were sitting at the dining room table with the pizzas waiting to be eaten, that Carrie realised she would actually need to 'judge' the pizzas, and do so in a way that no feelings would be hurt.

Looking back and forth at the pizzas, she raised her eyes to the men. "Which is which?"

"We're not telling," Dalton said. "That way you can be impartial."

"That seems fair." She tried not to laugh at how seriously they were taking the stupid pizza tasting.

Taking a piece from the first plate, she took a bite. The sauce was lovely, tomato-based but with a hit of chilli, the base was pretty standard and the toppings well apportioned, the barbecue sauce swirl on top was smoky and tangy. Overall it was pretty good, a lot tastier than she'd expected.

She repeated the same process with the second pizza and looked up to find the men staring at her, impatiently awaiting her verdict. The sauce wasn't as nice, but the base was the best she'd ever had, and it was loaded with mushrooms, a plus in her book, and it was finished off with a creamy swirl of mayo.

Carrie knew she had her work cut out for her.

"I like both of them," she eventually said. "I don't know if I can pick a winner."

"So, pizza was the winner on the day?" Dalton joked.

"The first one, that sauce was lovely. The second one, the base was amazing... and I really can't pick one over the other."

"The sauce is mine," Bodhi said proudly, flashing her that grin she'd quickly come to love.

"Well, it's really tasty," Carrie replied. "And Dalton, I have to get the base recipe off you! It is sincerely the nicest I have ever had... and I eat a lot of pizza!"

"I don't give it to just anyone," Dalton said, winking at her in a way that made her want to tear her clothes off and tell him to get inside her. "But I guess I can give it to you."

"If you guys teamed up, you could make a pretty sublime pizza," Carrie said, only realising what she'd said about 'teaming up' because of the smirks on the men's faces.

"Like us teaming up, do you?" Bodhi said innocently, shifting uncomfortably in his seat and Carrie didn't need to ask why.

"Don't know what you're talking about," she said, looking down at the pizza to avoid making eye contact with either man.

"You're telling us you haven't been thinking about it non-stop, like we have?" Dalton teased.

"Well, yeah, I have been... but it can't happen again, right? I mean, what good can come from a threesome? Someone will end up getting hurt if it happens again, and I don't want to come between the two of you—"

Bodhi and Dalton burst out laughing and Carrie clasped her hand over her mouth.

"You didn't have a problem with that on Friday night," Bodhi said with a sexy smirk.

"Or Saturday morning," Dalton added.

Like she'd forgotten!

"But with regard to it happening again, as long as we're all on the same page, I don't see the problem," Bodhi said. "It's not an expectation. We're all single and if we willingly fall into bed together, then that's what happens, and no doubt a lot of fun will be had. If it doesn't, well, it doesn't."

Dalton nodded, signalling his agreement. "What he said."

"I enjoyed it. A lot," Carrie said. "And I've been telling myself it can't happen again, but I can't stop remembering Friday night. I've never done anything like that before and it felt good to let go and enjoy myself."

"Let's just take it as it comes," Dalton suggested. "We can chill out and watch a movie or something, see where the night does or doesn't take us."

"I'd like that." Carrie smiled.

Standing up from the table, Bodhi pointed toward the lounge. "USB is plugged into the TV and loaded with movies, why don't you go in and choose something for us to watch and we'll get the dishes sorted then join you."

"You don't want a hand?" Carrie asked, giggling when she caught herself. "Actually, don't answer that because I'm sure I know the answer."

Bodhi bit his lip while looking her up and down. "Lady, you've got no idea just what I'd like you to do to me…"

… and he had no idea just how badly she wanted to do all of those things to him.

CHAPTER FIVE

If her plan was not to think about sex for the rest of the night, Carrie's choice of viewing material for the evening had been a bad choice.

She'd heard of the TV show *Banshee* and had wanted to watch it but had never gotten around to it. When she saw the series was on the USB, and with Bodhi and Dalton's blessing, she'd put the first episode on, not really knowing what to expect.

Sex. That was what she should have expected. The first sex scene involved the main character taking a woman up against the wall in the basement of a bar; every thrust, every grip of the hips, every groan that came from the TV, she could feel. Another episode started in the bedroom of a husband and wife, the wife spread-eagled while her husband went down on her. Naturally, her mind wondered how it would feel to have Dalton or Bodhi working her the same way.

The way she was sitting, her back resting against Bodhi's chest, and her feet on Dalton's thighs, didn't help.

Bodhi's arm was slung over her shoulder and the more she relaxed into him, the closer his hand and magical fingers came to her already-hardened nipples. Dalton was absentmindedly stroking her lower leg and Carrie knew how easily that hand could glide up her leg, higher and higher until...

If only they weren't being such gentlemen! As close as Bodhi's fingers were to her nipples, he didn't once 'accidentally' touch one of them, and Dalton's hand stayed below the knee, no matter how much she willed it to move to where she most wanted it.

The men weren't unaffected either. She could hear Bodhi's breathing change with each sex scene, or flashback of sex, and beneath her foot she could feel Dalton's penis was in a semi-hard state. She could sense, by the tension in Bodhi's body, that he was fighting an internal battle to control his need to give in to certain biological impulses.

Carrie was torn between appreciating the control he was exhibiting, and wishing he'd give in to them, because her own body was screaming for him.

Sex was a bad idea, she knew that... but sitting on the couch between those two men, it also seemed more essential to her survival than breathing. Bodhi said there was no expectation on it to happen again, but did that mean he didn't want it to happen? It wasn't what she'd taken away from their earlier discussion, but there was a chance he was just being polite and didn't want to hurt her feelings.

One way to find out.

She moved her hand from where it was sitting in her lap and put it behind her, unsurprised, but still relieved when her fingers brushed against what was an incredibly hard erection. Bodhi shifted in his seat and nipped at her neck which Carrie took as a sign he wasn't exactly hating the new location of her hand.

For good measure she rubbed up and down the ridge of his hard-on a couple of times and was met by a sharp hiss of breath, and the feeling of him throbbing beneath her palm. Any thought of his reaction being a reflex rather than an indicator of his arousal was quashed when he arched his hips in an attempt to increase the level of hand-cock contact.

"You're very naughty," Bodhi whispered into her ear, the sensation of his breath making her shiver with delight.

This time she gave him a gentle squeeze and his breath hitched, his chest vibrating lightly as he emitted a silent growl. A harder squeeze and she could feel him swelling in her hand; she had to bite back a moan as she remembered the way he'd felt inside her.

Movement on the other end of the couch forced Carrie to pull her hand away from Bodhi's groin; she looked up, knowing guilt was written all over her face when Dalton locked eyes with her. She'd been worried about causing a rift between the two men and now it looked like that fear was coming true.

If he was pissed off, Dalton didn't show it, his smile warm and inviting. "I'm going to go to bed," he said and stretched his arms above his head as he yawned, putting a sliver of his belly on display, making her mouth water. "You two have fun though."

"Are you s—"

Carrie's question was cut off by Dalton pressing his lips against hers in a surprisingly soft manner.

"I'm very sure. Maybe I'll see you in the morning."

If not for the genuine smile on his face, Carrie would have doubted whether or not he was as relaxed about everything as he was making out, but she had no option but to believe him.

"See you in the morning," Bodhi said. "Just holler if you want us to turn it down."

"Will do, don't stay up too late you two!"

Bodhi sighed. "Okay, Dad."

"Good boy," Dalton chuckled and, after giving Carrie another brief yet toe-curling kiss, he left the lounge.

Carrie turned to face Bodhi when she heard Dalton's bedroom door close. "Do you think he's okay?"

"Yeah, fine. Why's that?"

"I'm just worried that me... doing what I was doing... made him uncomfortable, or angry, or something like that, and that's why he went to bed."

"If he had a problem with it, he would have said something. Believe me."

"You're sure?"

"I'm sure," Bodhi said, cupping her face in his hands. "But if you aren't comfortable, we don't have to take things any further."

"Are you crazy?" Carrie laughed and moved so she could straddle him. She linked her hands behind his neck, marvelling at the heat of his skin, and pulled him toward her, stopping when he was millimetres away from her. "I know what I want... and I think you want the same thing."

Bodhi placed a hand on the back of her neck and one on the small of her back, pulling her against him as he seduced her mouth with an impatient kiss. He didn't hold back, and Carrie instinctively met his greed with her own.

The way his tongue was stroking hers translated directly between her legs and she moaned lustily against his mouth, imagining it was her pussy his tongue was exploring, that it was her clitoris he was lightly sucking on. Her hips moved as if she was riding him and he was buried to the hilt inside her. A kiss had never, ever, caused such an overwhelming response in her body, and she couldn't control the urgency building inside her.

She gripped his hair in her fists, holding his mouth firmly against hers, refusing to let the kiss end. The way his tongue danced against her own was hypnotic and when she felt her pussy starting to grip tightly, realised just how turned on she was.

Oxygen was a necessity however, and when she felt as if she was going to pass out, she reluctantly pulled back. His breath was coming fast and shallow. She could feel his penis pressing against the seam of her jeans, and the cotton of her panties was noticeably wet. Carrie couldn't resist rocking against him, her eyes rolling back in her head when he pulled her down at the hips; the friction of the layers of clothing between them sent pure heat surging through her clit.

Bodhi put a hand behind her neck and pulled her in to kiss her again, breaking it off after a few seconds to mumble, "We should go to the bedroom." He pulled her down again and looked deep in her eyes. "I need to be inside you."

Carrie whimpered, his words having almost as much impact as if he'd just slammed inside her. "Yes. Please. Now." She ground her hips against him as hard as she could, taking great confidence in the strangled groan he tried to stifle. "I want you to fuck me, Bodhi. Hard."

"Remember the way to my bedroom?" he asked with a devilish grin, telling her he knew it was a stupid question.

She moved off his lap holding stood up, holding a hand out to him. He took it and stood up, surprising the hell out of her by swooping her into his arms and kissing her.

"Think I've forgotten the way, you should probably take me, so I don't get lost," she said with a wink.

To start with, she felt self-conscious about Bodhi carrying her. She was by no means a tiny size six, but he seemed to be more than capable of carrying her; in fact, he made it seem easy, or at least he did until she knocked her head against the door frame in his bedroom.

"Shit, I'm so sorry!" Bodhi exclaimed, putting her down so he could check her head for signs of blood.

She giggled. "It's okay, let's face it, it's one of those things that is always way sexier in the movies than in real life."

"Just so you know, there is no blood, but I think you'll have a bit of a bump in the morning."

"A battle scar," Carrie offered, but she could see he felt bad. The best way to counteract that? Snaking her hand beneath the front of his t-shirt and dipping her fingers into his boxers, closing her palm over the tip of his swollen cock. "I don't care about *my* head... this is the only head I care about right now."

It was a corny joke, but it made him laugh, and judging by the jolt against the palm of her hand, it took his mind off her most minor of injuries.

"I should probably inspect the rest of your body for injuries," he said, giving her a serious look, but for that twinkle of desire in his eyes.

Carrie liked the direction his thoughts were taking. "Yes, you should."

He grabbed the hem of her shirt and lifted it up and over her head, casting it aside, his eyes settling on the lacy red bra she was wearing.

"Everything looks okay here, but I should probably remove your bra, so I can double check."

She giggled when he moved an arm behind her and tried to undo the bra using one hand, but eventually giving up after some struggle.

"Another thing the movies make look way easier!" he commented as he moved both of his arms around her, meaning she was pressed nice and snug against him, as he undid the clasps on the bra. "There..."

He stepped back and watched as gravity did the job for him, leaving her bare and at the mercy of his gaze.

"Bloody hell," he uttered, placing his hands on her hips and walking backward until he was perched on the edge of the bed. "You're perfect," he said, running his hands slowly from her hips to her ribs, inching closer and taking one hard nipple between his lips.

Carrie gasped and threw her head back, her focus entirely on the sensation of his tongue against her nipple as Bodhi licked it to an even stiffer peak, before he caught her off guard and sucking it firmly, drawing it between his lips.

He moved his mouth to the other nipple and gave it the same treatment, licking it before sucking harder, and harder. The pleasure was so intense Carrie thought she was going to come from that alone.

"Breasts and nipples seem bloody amazingly perfect," Bodhi said, tracing a path from her sternum down to the waistband of her jeans. "One final check to go."

"Whatever you think is necessary," Carrie said, her breath coming in short, sharp gasps.

He stayed sitting on the bed and opened the button of her jeans then pulled the tab of the zipper down. Very slowly, he pushed her jeans over her hips, down her thighs and knees, until she could step out of them. Carrie had expected to feel vulnerable standing before him completely naked, bar her panties, but all she felt was powerful. The way his eyes were bulging out of his head, the loud rasp as he tried to swallow, made her feel very in control and for the first time in her life she felt like a *real* woman.

"Um, j-just one more," he stumbled over the words, which only served to make Carrie feel more powerful.

Nodding her permission, she wove her fingers in his silky hair, which was longer on top than she was used to. She liked the idea that there was more to hold on to. There'd be no grasping at the sheets to anchor herself when he was going down on her... not that she was getting ahead of herself or anything.

His hands moved up her legs, fingers coming to rest at the flimsy band of her panties. It felt as if it took him half-an-hour to complete that particular job, and as she was kicking the scrap of lace aside, she knew it was only half the job.

"It's only fair, Mr Hook," she said with what she hoped was a tone of authority to her voice, "that I now get you into a similar state of undress."

Bodhi stood up and kissed her with plenty of heat. "That's fine, but my tits are nowhere near as impressive as yours," he said and laughed. "I'm sorry, that joke sounded way better in my head."

"You're an idiot." Carrie laughed, hooking her fingers in the waistband of his track pants and without any ceremony, pulled them down.

"Impatient?"

"Very."

She took a few seconds to rub him through his boxers, but as Bodhi had pointed out, she was very impatient, and soon they joined the rest of the discarded clothing on the floor.

Seeing his cock bobbing and twitching, standing at attention, Carrie almost decided to forgo the removal of his t-shirt, but there was no way she was going to miss out on the opportunity to feel his body pressed against her and enjoy the contrast of soft skin and hard muscle.

Speaking of hard... she was sure his erection had doubled in size since she'd freed him from his boxers. Dalton may have had more girth, but Bodhi definitely won out in the length stakes and, for the first time, she found herself feeling more than curious about the concept of double penetration. With one of them inside her, she had felt so full already, she worried she might just explode if she had one in her pussy and one in her ass.

Now she was *really* getting ahead of herself.

Skin against skin was what finally tore her from her fantasy, and she realised Bodhi had dealt with his top himself, while she was busy imagining having two cocks inside her.

"That's better," Carrie said, her mouth dry... unlike another part of her anatomy.

For the second time that evening, Bodhi lifted her into his arms, but this time her legs were around his waist as his cock was sandwiched between them. His body already felt so good pressing against her, she had no idea how she was going to last long enough for him to get inside her.

Bodhi sat back on the bed, Carrie in his lap, and fell backward, the change in position meaning his cock was perilously close to her aching wetness. Every instinct in her body told her to take him in her hand and direct him into her; she could just imagine how silky his cock would feel against the tender walls of her pussy, and how intoxicating the friction created between their bodies would be.

She wasn't that much of an idiot though.

Carrie leaned across and was just able to reach the bedside table and the drawer the condoms were in. She took one out and dropped the box back in the drawer, before turning her attention back to Bodhi, straddling him at the hips before she removed the condom, and rolled it down his cock; she was relieved the condom didn't break, because it would have added an extra thirty seconds before he was inside her. That would never do.

Finally, she took him in her palm, and guided him to her entrance, slowly sinking down on top of him; she shuddered with delight as her pussy stretched to accommodate him.

"You okay?" Bodhi asked.

Carrie nodded and began rocking her hips, slowly at first to get used to the feeling of him, but she was soon moving harder and faster as her body adjusted to him, spurred on by the pleasurable sensations as they moved together.

She needed more resistance, so she leaned forward and put a hand either side of his shoulders, which provided her with the added bonus of being able to kiss the man currently turning the blood coursing through her veins into lava.

He let her lead the pace with her hips, giving his focus to the kissing, alternating between soft and sweet kisses, and hungry, furious kisses. He kissed paths along her jaw, and up and down her neck, stopping every now and then to bite down and suck in a manner that would surely leave bruises, but she didn't care. She wanted them.

The pleasure pulsing through her body became laced with frustration; she needed more than she could manage herself. Usually she'd have just made do, but for whatever reason, with Dalton and Bodhi, she felt confident enough to speak up. More than that, she felt as if it was her right to.

"Can you pull me down?" Carrie panted, crying out louder than intended when Bodhi did as she asked, and the pleasure stepped up a level. "Oh fuck!" she cried into his neck, gasping and trying to catch her breath.

It didn't take long before the frustration began seeping through again and she looked at Bodhi with pleading eyes. "More, please. I need m—" Her words were cut off, instead coming out as a loud groan when Bodhi pulled her down harder.

"Spread your legs."

"Oh my fucking god!" she growled into his neck—the act of spreading her legs had intensified the friction against her clit, while allowing Bodhi to hit deeper. He felt larger inside her, and suddenly she could feel the friction everywhere.

"So. Fucking." Bodhi groaned. "Tight."

Pleasure flooded her entire body; she could feel it in her toes, her fingers, at the base of her spine. Everywhere. Fizzing and flaming, burning her from the inside.

She didn't have to say a word to Bodhi this time; it seemed he could read her cues because, right when she needed it, he began thrusting his hips up to meet hers, doubling the impact *and* the pleasure. Just when she thought it couldn't get any better, he pulled her down as he thrust upward, and she made a growling sound.

Fitting, because she felt like an animal. She'd never felt pleasure so fully. It made her completely unaware of her surroundings, all that existed in the world was the firestorm brewing inside her. Bodhi locked eyes with her and panic flashed through them, seconds before his eyes snapped shut and he threw his head back. His loud grunts flooded the room, and she could tell he was getting very close to the point of no return.

Carrie poured all her energy into rocking her hips and when that firestorm finally exploded, she screamed, her orgasm so intense her body went rigid and the sounds coming from her mouth left her throat feeling raw. The waves of bliss kept hitting her, and she was still riding the tidal wave that was her orgasm when Bodhi joined her, his orgasm causing him to bite down on her neck to stifle a groan so guttural it would be a miracle if it hadn't been heard a suburb over.

Fuck.

She collapsed on top of him, no energy left to move off him, so she simply lay there, their bodies a hot sweaty mess. Aftershocks from her orgasm continued to shoot through her body and, because he was still inside her, she had no doubt he could feel them too.

The aftershocks finally petered off and she could feel Bodhi starting to slip from her body; she wasn't ready for it to be over yet. She wished she could bottle up the way he'd made her feel, so she could experience it all day, every day.

"Let's add condom removal to the list of unsexy real-life things," Bodhi joked as she carefully lifted herself off him while he held the condom in place to keep it from sliding off.

Carrie laughed, watching him getting some tissues from the same drawer the condoms had been in. "Should be a slogan for an advertising campaign, 'Responsibility, it's just not sexy'."

"You sure you're not in marketing?" Bodhi joked, before standing up and disposing of the condom in the wastebasket beside the bed.

Bodhi joined her back in bed and Carrie found her way into his arms, resting her head on his chest. She had no idea if it was appropriate to do something intimate like cuddling after having no-strings attached sex, but it wouldn't have felt right to just roll over and go to sleep. She wanted that closeness, the feeling of connection she hadn't experienced in a long time.

CHAPTER SIX

Carrie couldn't remember the last time she'd woken feeling so refreshed. She told herself it was because she'd simply had a good sleep and it had nothing to do with being in Bodhi's arms all night, but who was she trying to kid? The couple of times she'd woken up during the night, she'd been enveloped in the security of his arms, her body pressing against the length of his. It usually took her a while to get back to sleep when she woke up in the middle of the night, but Bodhi's presence was so soothing she'd drifted straight back to sleep.

It was something a girl could get used to, and that was a big, fat problem.

Spending the night with Bodhi was the start of a very slippery slope, Carrie could tell. She didn't have it in her to cut all emotions and have sex *just* be sex—for her the two were intrinsically linked, and with two men involved, emotions were only going to leave her even more vulnerable than if there was only one. It would have been okay if she didn't really like either of them, but the more time she spent with them out of the bedroom, the more she liked them as people, and the harder it was to see them merely as sex objects.

She figured she just needed to get them out of her system. Before Friday night, she hadn't had sex for over a year, obviously her body was making the most of having two hot, willing, and able men at her disposal.

There was no way someone like her—so straight-laced and boring, as Jess had often referred to her—would get into a situation where she would get emotionally involved with two men at the same time. That was the type of thing that happened to women who didn't think before they acted, women who loved sex so much one man couldn't satisfy them.

Though still asleep, Bodhi tightened his arms around her and Carrie inhaled slowly in an attempt to remind herself she wasn't allowed to enjoy this part. She should get out of bed, get dressed and leave, her way of saying '*thanks for the sex, it's all I needed from you*'.

The soapy scent of his skin held a hint of citrus that made her think of summer, and made her want to spend the day breathing him in.

Carrie had a feeling that, even after playing a game of league, he would smell good enough to eat and found herself imagining what it would be like to get her hands on him before he'd showered post-game, all salty and citrusy. She'd climb in the shower with him and soap every inch of him, helping wash away all traces of the game. Having played eighty very physical minutes, he would be exhausted so afterward she'd lead him to the bed and...

She was doing *really* well at the not getting attached thing.

Feeling eyes on her, she looked up and was met with sparkling green eyes and a smile that caused butterflies to swarm in her belly. God, he was beautiful.

He kissed her on the forehead, still smiling that brilliant smile. "Morning."

Why did she feel so nervous all of a sudden? "Morning."

"Sleep okay?"

"Very well."

"Me too, funny that," he chuckled quietly and wiggled down in the bed, so they were face to face. "I enjoyed last night."

"I did too," she said.

No matter how hard she tried to ignore how kissable his lips looked, nothing was going to prevent her pressing hers against his. She wasn't quite ready for the heat that washed over her at the contact.

Lying as they were, all close and steamy, Carrie couldn't help notice the hard ridge developing against her belly just as quickly as the moisture pooling between her legs. His tongue caressed hers and, without Carrie intending to, her leg hooked over his hip, bringing him in dangerously close contact with her wet heat.

Breathless, Bodhi broke off the kiss and rested his forehead against hers. "I want you so badly right now, but I really need to get up... I don't want to, but we need to be in the gym by nine."

"I need to go to work anyway."

"You're okay, right?"

His question surprised her. "Yeah, I'm fine, why?"

"I just don't want you to think I'm making up an excuse to kick you out of my bed, because I'm not..."

"I don't think that," Carrie reassured him with a soft smile. "Besides... just sex, right? I've probably outstayed my welcome."

Bodhi looked surprised. "You haven't outstayed your welcome!" he promised. "I'd quite happily spend the rest of the day with you." He moved a strand of hair out of her face. "I'm glad you spent the night... even if it's just sex, it's still nice to have the whole night."

Before she gave in to the hunger building inside her, she sat up. "Should probably get out of bed and head home to get ready for work, I guess."

"Back to reality, huh," Bodhi said, rolling his eyes.

They got out of bed and Carrie trawled the room for her discarded clothes. Every article of clothing she picked up brought with it flashbacks of Bodhi removing that particular item from her body.

"I'm going to jump in the shower," Bodhi said, and she looked up to find him standing before her with a towel tied very low around his hips.

Beneath the towel, she could see his cock was twitching and she forced herself to turn away, for fear she would follow him into the bathroom. "Okay. Uh, is it okay if I grab a coffee before I leave?"

"Help yourself," he said and took her hand, pulling her gently toward him for a final kiss. "If I don't see you when I get out, have a good day."

"You too," Carrie said, watching him walk to the door.

When the door closed behind him, she wasn't sure if she was relieved he was gone, or disappointed. She secretly suspected it was the latter but told herself it was relief she felt.

Fake it 'til you make it, right?

Once dressed, Carrie walked through to the kitchen and was again torn between feeling relieved and disappointed when she saw Dalton wasn't in there.

Just how fucked in the head was she? She'd spent the night with Bodhi and now she was hanging out to see Dalton.

Would Dalton even want to see her after what she'd done with Bodhi? Exactly how much had he heard coming from the bedroom? It was only then it dawned on her that he probably wouldn't want anything to do with her; what she'd done with Bodhi was pretty disrespectful toward Dalton, and she was amazed he hadn't marched into the room the night before and told them to fuck off, so he could get some sleep.

Hanging around to have a coffee was not an option, she needed to leave... and never come back.

Before she could step away from the counter, two strong arms wrapped around her torso and the lightest of kisses dropped just below her ear. "Good morning, gorgeous."

"Hi, D-Dalton."

"Sleep well?"

Carrie turned around in his arms and looked up at him. "I did, thanks."

"Coffee?"

"Look, I'm sorry about last night, about me and Bodhi..."

Dalton looked confused. "Why are you apologising?"

"You must have heard it all and—"

"I did," he grinned. "The noises you were making got me so bloody hard."

She frowned, caught off guard by his reply. "It didn't bother you?"

Dropping his head down, he gave her the sweetest, softest of kisses. "Why should it?"

"Because Saturday morning I was having sex with you and then last night—"

"Last night I gave you and Bodhi time alone to do whatever it was you wanted to do together," he finished for her. "This little situation we've got going on might be a bit unorthodox, but all that matters is that it works for the three of us and that we're all honest about it. Me and Bodes talked about it before you came over yesterday, neither of us have any problem with you sleeping with both of us. It's not like we're doing it behind each other's backs."

"Kind of feels like I'm cheating on both of you," Carrie admitted, and again Dalton kissed her in that soft, gentle way that seemed completely out of character for such a big, imposing man.

"If it's too much for you, you just need to say so," Dalton whispered. "Like we said last night, no expectations."

"I think it's confusing for me because I know it should feel wrong, but it doesn't... and in the past I've always thought negatively of women who have more than one man on the go at the time."

"Society has a lot to answer for. Even as toddlers, we're told we'll have a husband or wife, that we'll have kids, that we'll be with this one person for life. It doesn't really take into consideration other types of relationships, which are just as valid as hetero monogamy."

"Never really thought of it that way!" she said, surprised by the insight he provided.

Professional sport players had the reputation of being idiots who rarely had serious thoughts, but what Dalton had just said resonated with her. He'd pinpointed exactly why she was feeling so confused, and had explained it in a way that made so much sense.

"While we're speaking of all things monogamous, I kind of have a favour to ask you."

Oh, this could not be good. Even though he'd just preached about the validity of alternative relationships, he was going to ask her to choose, wasn't he?

"And what would that be?" She was almost too scared to ask.

"It's my cousin's wedding on Saturday and my mum and her sister have this stupid competitive thing going, about who's going to have their five kids married off first. They're tied on four all at the moment, both with one to go. Anyway, Bodes was going to go with me, but Mum put her foot down and she is refusing to let me take a dude... I was just going to go alone, to really piss her off, but I was wondering if you'd want to come with me instead?"

His request wasn't at all what she'd been expecting, and though she considered saying no, she couldn't resist the opportunity to see Dalton in a suit. "Count me in!"

"Excellent. I promise it won't be too painful... my brothers and their wives will be forever grateful, because they won't have to sit through hours of 'where did I go so wrong with Dalton? why is he so unmarriageable?' at this wedding."

"Just how many brothers and wives are we talking?"

"I'm the baby of five. Harlan is the oldest, then Killian and Kellan—they're twins, obviously. Closest in age to me is Lachlan. They're all married and reproducing like it's going out of fashion. Harlan has three girls, Killian two boys, and a girl on the way, Kellan has three boys, and Lachie has one boy, with another on the way."

"That is a whole lot of reproducing!" Carrie giggled, just imagining what a crazy household his parents' house must be on the occasions when the whole family was home.

By the time she finally sat down for a coffee, Bodhi was out of the shower and joined her and Dalton at the table. Carrie was pleasantly surprised by how easily conversation flowed between the three of them and concluded that Dalton had been right, they were all adults and if they were open about what was happening, who cared what they did and who they did it with?

***

Though Carrie was only going to Dalton's cousins wedding with him as a favour, with each passing day she grew more nervous. It was one thing to be meeting the family when you were dating a guy, but when the extent of your relationship was a threesome and one morning of sex, it was a whole other story. She could just imagine the questions they'd get.

'*How do you two know each other?*'
'*Where did you meet?*'
'*How long have you known each other?*'
'*Are you dating?*'

What was Dalton going to say to his family? He couldn't very well blurt out that they'd met at a gala and taken her home for a threesome.

They'd had a few conversations about it online and Dalton didn't seem to be anywhere near as nervous as she was, explaining he would tell his family he was taking a friend he'd met a while ago. He'd told her to relax, which of course had the opposite effect. Even if he did tell everyone that story, would she be able to keep a straight face while he did? They would be able to see right through her, and she and Dalton would be thrown out in disgust.

It was also possible she was reading far too much into it and was letting her imagination run wild, but no amount of telling herself to calm down worked.

On Friday after work, she opened her closet to try on the dress she'd decided she was going to wear: her trusty black wrap-around she knew she looked half-decent in.

After rifling through her wardrobe for twenty minutes and still not finding her dress, it finally dawned on her: she'd lent the dress to Jess a few weeks earlier. Crap. She now had two options, get in touch with Jess and ask for it back, or avoid the inevitable confrontation and instead head to the mall to buy something new.

Ever the avoider, Carrie opted to grab her handbag and left for the mall.

Being a Friday night, the traffic was crazy, and the mall was as crowded as she'd imagined it would be. By the time she'd walked the length of the building and into City Chic, she was beginning to wish she'd grown some lady balls and asked for the dress back from Jess.

"Hi love, can I help with anything?" the girl standing at the counter asked as Carrie walked deeper into the shop.

"Just looking at the moment, I've got a wedding tomorrow and need an emergency dress!"

"You're not the first one tonight to come in looking for an emergency dress!" the girl commented. "If you need anything, just yell out."

She hated clothes shopping, but City Chic was the store she felt most comfortable in because she knew she'd find something that looked good on her. As a size sixteen, she often found that clothes in regular shops—where she was at the maximum end of the size range—didn't fit her body type properly, but at City Chic, a shop catering to plus size women, she was spoilt for choice.

Looking through the racks of dresses she found a few that caught her eye and draped them over her arm in preparation for the changing room. There was one in particular that she hoped looked good because it was the perfect mixture of sexy and sweet, formal and casual, appropriate for a wedding but also okay for a hot summer's day spent at the beach, or for the type of restaurant jeans and a t-shirt weren't considered proper dining attire.

Concluding six dresses were more than enough to try on, Carrie found a free changing room and, closing the curtain behind her, hung the dresses on the two hooks provided. She took her clothes off and placed them on the little stool in the corner then got the first dress from the hanger.

"I look awful! Like a big fat whale!" came a frustrated voice from the changing room beside her.

"You look gorgeous, honey," a man's voice followed immediately.

"No, Calum, you're just saying that because you're sick and tired of waiting for me!"

"I love watching you try on all these dresses, actually. You might think you look big and fat, but I think you look beautiful."

Carrie tried not to listen, but it was impossible when the conversation was going on very loudly right beside her.

"Well, enjoy it while you can, because when this baby arrives, my body is going to be ruined!"

"You could have fifty kids and I would still think you looked incredible."

"Fifty kids? Are you fucking crazy? One is turning me into a psycho, fifty would make me a permanent resident on a psych ward!"

Calum made the stupid mistake of laughing.

"Glad you think it's so funny! I hate you, Calum Reiner, you know that?!"

Carrie winced, wondering if she should leave the changing room to let the two next to her have it out in semi-private.

"Yes, sweetheart, I know you hate me, and I am okay with that, because even at nine months pregnant you look like a goddess, and I'm the luckiest man on earth."

'*Oh my god, how cute!*' Carrie mouthed silently. How could any woman be upset with a man who said something like that to her?

The woman in the changing room sighed and gave a quiet laugh. "I guess you aren't really that bad."

Unlike this dress, Carrie thought looking at her reflection in the mirror. The first dress was a definite no-go. The cut was all wrong for her and clung to her belly a little more than she liked. She was already going to stick out at the wedding, she didn't need a fashion disaster to go with it.

"Wait! I think I've found it!" the woman next to her cheered, sounding legitimately excited.

"It's a miracle!"

Hoping the other woman's miraculous dress-finding discovery would rub off on her, Carrie pulled on the dress she liked the most and crossed her fingers it would look okay.

It fit perfectly. She loved the way it accentuated her waist, and the sexy little detail provided by the corset-like eyelets and lace up the front of the bodice.

Hallelujah. With the dress private-changing-room-mirror approved, it was time to take things to the next level, stepping out of the confines of the cubicle to look in the large mirror on the wall at the end of the curtained off changing area.

"Do you think it looks okay?" the woman from the cubicle next to her was standing before the mirror frowning at herself, her hand absentmindedly rubbing her bump.

The man who was with her—her husband, Carrie guessed from the gold band on his ring finger—stood up, smiling. "I'm not lying when I say you look beautiful, Nova. You look gorgeous, you and the bump."

"You really do look lovely," Carrie piped up, unable to stop herself.

Nova smiled. "Thank you. Um, I'm sorry you had to hear all of that. Bub is due any day now and I'm feeling more than a little sensitive."

"Understandable," Carrie replied. "I feel like that and I'm not even pregnant."

The woman laughed. "We're going to a wedding tomorrow and I had this beautiful dress all sorted, tried it on tonight to decide which of my boring ballet flats to wear with it, because my feet are so fat I can't wear any of my heels, and the bloody thing didn't fit. I only bought it last week!"

"I have a wedding tomorrow as well, and the dress I was going to wear is hiding in the wardrobe of my best friend, whom I've had a falling out with."

"The price we pay to look presentable, huh!"

"Exactly," Carrie said with a frown and shake of the head. "Anyway, good luck with the baby, I hope he or she arrives soon!"

Nova laughed and rolled her eyes. "Knowing my luck, I will go into labour tonight and won't even get to wear the damn dress after all this hassle."

Stepping back into her changing room, Carrie giggled quietly to herself and wondered if Nova would get to wear her dress, or if her baby would have other ideas on how they could spend the day.

Before she took the dress off, Carrie took a mirror selfie and, because she was so used to doing so, almost sent it to Jess on Messenger. Sadness speared her gut; as much as Jess had hurt her, Carrie still missed the woman who'd been her best friend for what felt like ever.

Rather than sending the photo to Jess, she sent it to Dalton.

'*Finally found a stupid dress. You think this will be okay to wear?*'

His reply came before she could even put her phone down.

'*No, it won't be okay because it is going to cause a rather large, hard problem in my dress pants...*'

CHAPTER SEVEN

"You look..." Dalton seemed unable to find the relevant adjective to finish his sentence but, given the look on his face, she had a feeling it would be a very complimentary one.

Even with drool almost dribbling down the sides of his mouth, she still felt obliged to ask for reassurance. "You sure?"

"That photo last night? I thought you looked hot, but seeing you... seriously woman, I don't know how I'm going to be able to keep my hands off you today."

Carrie eyed him pleasingly. "You don't look half bad yourself."

That was putting it mildly. Wearing a well-tailored charcoal grey suit, he looked every inch the billionaire businessman, a favourite trope amongst romance authors and readers alike. One of the books she was currently editing featured such a man and she knew when she was back at work on Monday, all she'd see when working on that manuscript was Dalton.

"I'm sorry, but I have to do this," Dalton announced before he stepped in to kiss her.

Carrie became lost in the kiss and didn't care who might be watching as things became heated on the doorstep. As promised, she could feel that hard 'problem' arising in his pants, the knowledge of which made her want to say 'fuck it' to being on time to the wedding and drag him through to her bedroom.

"I want you so badly," Dalton's voice was gravelly, full of the tones of a man about to lose control.

The heat of his breath against her skin sent a shiver of excitement down her spine, and she longed to feel that heat on other parts of her body. She'd had him in her mouth but was yet to feel his tongue on the part of her body currently screaming for him, the thought alone enough to make her moan against his mouth as she gripped the lapels of his suit jacket in her fists.

"L-later?" Carrie had to force the word from her mouth, in place of something more immediate, like '*right now on this doorstep*'.

Dalton cupped her ass in his hands and squeezed gently, forcing their bodies closer together. "I plan on it. All." A kiss on her neck. "Night." A kiss on her jaw. "Long." A ghostly soft kiss on the lips.

Feeling drunk, Carrie gently pushed him away and pulled the door closed behind her—the only way to prevent turning his promise of '*all night long*' into '*all day and night long*'.

***

A sucker for weddings, Carrie cried during the beautiful ceremony. A bit weird considering she didn't know either of the people getting married, but there was something about that atmosphere that got to her every time.

The bride looked spectacular, but what bride didn't on her wedding day? The groom had openly cried watching his bride walking down the aisle, and Carrie only hoped to have that effect on some poor, unassuming man one day.

At thirty-two, she felt like her chance at marriage and babies was slipping away, even if she was still young in the grand scheme of things. As a little girl, she'd dreamt of her wedding day and had had her life all planned out; from when she'd meet her future husband, to their wedding and the children they'd have.

During one of their conversations, her mum had told her '*It will happen when it's meant to*,' and Carrie hoped the woman she looked up to was right.

"Time for the fun part now," Dalton whispered, leading her toward a woman who was approaching them with the type of smile on her face a mum reserved for her child.

"Your mum?"

"It's okay, she won't bite."

The mention of the word 'bite' took her back to Bodhi's bedroom and the way Dalton had bitten her neck on that first night. She forced the memories from her brain, now was not the right time to be consumed by a sexy flashback.

Dalton hugged his mum and stepped back beside Carrie. "Mum, this is Carrie, this is my mum."

His mum hugged her tightly. "Hello, darling! It's so lovely to meet you!"

"You too, Mrs Kendry!"

"Oh god, please call me Viv. Mrs Kendry makes me sound so old."

Carrie laughed and felt more at ease than she thought would. "Okay, Viv."

"Come! I'll introduce you to the rest of the family since Dalton seems to have forgotten his manners" Viv took Carrie's hand, and lead her toward the other side of the room.

"Give me a bloody minute!" Dalton protested behind them. "We only just walked in, can't expect me to get all the introductions out of the way before we've seen anyone!"

Carrie turned and gave Dalton a 'save me' look. She was relieved when he caught her hand, just as they came to a stop at a table surrounded by men so big they could only be Dalton's brothers. Four couples turned to look at her, along with nine kids of various ages, and she gave a nervous smile.

"Carrie, this is everyone," he began and pointed to the couple closest to them, "Harlan and Lisa," the next couple, "Killian and Zara, Kellan and Nat, Lachlan and Emily. Everyone, this is Carrie."

"Hello" they all waved in unison and Carrie felt as if all the eyes in the room were on her.

"And the biggest loves of my lives are," he pointed along the row of his nieces and nephews, "Clara, Lucia, James, Hunter, Cooper, Amalia, Blake, Wyatt and Kingston."

One of the little boys came over and looked up at him, tugging on his sleeve. "Uncle Dolldoll! You forgotted Matilda!" He turned to Carrie. "That's the baby that is in my mummy's tummy that is going to be borned soon!"

"Wow! That's exciting!" Carrie said to the little boy, who smiled proudly.

"Sorry, Hunter, you're right," Dalton winked at her. "Matilda is chilling out in Zara's belly."

"And Gwayson in my mama tummy!" another of the little boys said excitedly.

"Annnnd like Kingston just pointed out, Grayson is joining the clan in a few months."

"Make us all sound like sex fiends, why don't you!" one of the brother's groaned.

Carrie laughed, already liking what seemed to be a very close-knit family. "Well it's lovely to meet all of you!"

"Terrifying, you mean," one of the wives joked and Carrie felt her face going red. "Don't worry, we've been in your shoes."

"If you don't mind, I'm going to take Carrie to get a drink," Dalton said.

"Hurry back!" Viv said. "We want to hear all about how you two met!"

As if things couldn't get worse, one of Dalton's nieces walked up to him and said, quite matter-of-factly, "Nanny said maybe you will marry her," pointing at Carrie, "and then you can have girl babies because she wants more girl babies to knit for!"

Dalton knelt down to the little girl's level. "You tell Nanny she needs to lay off Uncle Dalton or he might just marry Bodhi!"

The little girl laughed hysterically, which in turn made everyone else laugh and provided the perfect excuse for Carrie and Dalton to escape.

At the bar, he gave her an apologetic smile. "Sorry about my family, they're a bit eager."

"It's okay, you guys seem close, it's nice to see."

"Not close to your family?"

"We're close, but I'm an only child so it's pretty lowkey when we're together."

"Feel free to steal a couple of my brothers if you want," he joked. "Killian and Kellan are the most annoying, I think it's a twin thing, so feel free to take them off my hands."

"They all live in Sydney?"

"We all live within an hour of each other so we are able to get together quite a lot. Every Sunday we have dinner at Mum and Dad's house, it can get pretty crazy."

"My parents are in Brisbane, but I have an aunty who lives here, and I see her once or twice a month."

Just as their drinks were placed in front of them, Carrie felt something brush against the skirt of her dress and looked down, getting the fright of her life to see a little girl staring up at her.

"Lady, Nanny said you and Uncle Dolldoll need to go back and stop 'voiding her."

"Did she just, Clara-bear?!" Dalton exclaimed, before leaning down and picking the little girl up.

With her arms clasped around his neck, holding on for dear life, Clara looked tiny, and Dalton looked even bigger than usual. Bigger and way hotter. What was it about a good-looking man holding a child that made women go weak at the knees? He looked so comfortable holding his niece, and Carrie could tell he'd meant it when he'd referred to the kids as the biggest loves of his life.

"Poppa is there now, he had a beer with some man, because ladies are annoying when there is a wedding!"

"Better get over and introduce Carrie then, hadn't we?" he said to Clara, who gave her nod of approval.

"Poppa told Nanny off when she told me to come over here," she giggled and kissed Dalton on the cheek.

He clasped Carrie's hand in his and they walked back to the table his family were seated. An older man was sitting beside Viv and there was no doubt it was Dalton's dad—minus the obvious age difference, the two looked identical.

"Hi, stranger!" his dad said standing up and shaking Dalton's hand.

"Dad, this is Carrie. Carrie, this is Dad, Charlie."

"Lovely to meet you, Carrie," he said with a kind smile.

"You too," Carrie replied, once again feeling all eyes on her.

Over the next hour, the formalities got under way, speeches and toasts were made and then the buffet was brought out. There was little chance for probing questions, or even light-hearted banter, as the Kendry men loaded their plates and sat down to eat. All Carrie could do was watch in awe as they took in huge amounts of food and then sat impatiently waiting for the dessert bar to be opened. She didn't even want to think about how much money Dalton's parents had had to spend on food throughout the years; feeding five growing boys must have been a big job.

None of them had any difficulty squeezing dessert in when it was brought out, and she had a feeling they were all being polite not going back for seconds. Each of them had a ravenous look in their eye as they looked longingly at the decadent treats, Dalton in particular.

Although, Dalton's ravenous look was more aimed at *her* than the food on offer.

"How'd you two meet?" Viv asked, and Carrie wished for the floor to open up and swallow her.

"At a party, a while back," Dalton explained.

"It's funny, I've never heard you mention Carrie before," Viv replied.

"I don't talk about half of my friends to you guys! Why should I?"

His mum giggled, seeming to love that she was getting under her son's skin. "Because Carrie is a girl."

"We're just friends, don't get too ahead of yourself, Mum," Dalton said defensively.

"Someone's a bit sensitive, aren't they?" his brother Harlan commented.

"Fuck up."

Viv shot him a disapproving look. "Dalton! Language around the kids!"

"Leave them alone, you two," Charlie said, coming to Dalton's rescue.

Dalton nodded at Charlie. "Thank you, Dad."

Even though he'd shown his support, Dalton's dad couldn't help but give his two cents on the matter. "You do make a cute couple though."

Dalton did the very mature thing and poked his tongue out at his parents, then he stood up, looked at Carrie and held his hand out. "Want to dance?"

Carrie took his hand and stood up, too embarrassed about what his parents had said to even consider saying no. The interrogation by his mum hadn't been as painful as it could have been, but it was still awkward sitting there, having to listen to Dalton lying to his family on her behalf.

They made their way onto the dance floor and it was only then Carrie realised what they were going to do. Dancing seemed like such a couple thing to do; it was something you did with your significant other, not the guy you had had sex with a couple of times, and whose friend you were also screwing.

She wanted so badly to not get carried away by the dancing, but it was close to impossible. Dalton's hands were on her hips and he was holding her close, the way they were moving in time with the music reminded her, in a silly way, of how their bodies moved together while having sex. It wasn't a particularly slow song, nor was there a sexy beat, but being that close to him, feeling him against her... it was easy to imagine it was just the two of them in the room, and that no clothing was involved.

The next song that played was something slow and sensual, by Norah Jones, which made not getting carried away even harder. Their movements slowed, and Dalton held her closer, one hand on her hip, one on the small of her back, while her hands rested on his shoulders. She could feel his strength in every subtle move he made, and when he pulled her even closer, his cock was like steel against her belly.

His hand slipped down her ass and she imagined it slipping lower still, rounding her butt, his fingers grazing between her legs, teasing her through the lace of her panties.

A whimper tore from her throat, not escaping Dalton's attention. He looked at her and she could see he was biting his lip, caught up in a fantasy of his own.

Sandwiched between them, his cock was lurching, and Carrie could feel each pulsation in the swollen walls of her pussy.

Desperation bloomed in his eyes, and Carrie knew the same need was mirrored in her own, her mouth dry, the pulse in her neck beating wildly as they tried to communicate using eyesight alone. When Dalton dipped his head down and brushed his lips against hers, Carrie knew they were getting dangerously close to doing something they shouldn't, but needed.

"I want you so bad," Dalton said, his voice a tortured whisper.

"Here?"

"We shouldn't..."

"But..."

"I want to be inside you, Carrie. I want to feel you coming around me..."

"Dalton... please... *I can't wait...*" She was panting as she spoke, overcome by a hunger so intense it scared her.

He took her hand and led her quickly from the dancefloor, she wasn't sure if his haste was related to his need to be inside her, or his desire to get his very noticeable erection out of such a public place. Whatever it was, they walked so quickly through the room they were almost running by the time they reached the first available semi-private room.

The disabled toilet.

It was a trashy cliché if ever there was one, but the door locked, and when they were done, they could clean up. Trashy, but perfect.

Even as he was locking the door behind them, Dalton was kissing her and hoisting her skirt up with his spare hand. There was no time or need to set the mood, no chance of taking things at a leisurely pace. Undressing wasn't an option, though Dalton did drop to his knees to tear the side seams of her barely-there panties, pausing to put the ruined lace in his jacket pocket before standing back up.

Carrie moved her hands to his belt and undid the buckle, giving herself access to the button of his pants, and it was a miracle she didn't tear it off on her mission to free his throbbing cock from the snug confines. His zipper and boxers came down simultaneously and she gripped him tightly in her hand, loving the loud groan he couldn't hold back, not really giving a damn if anyone heard. As she swiped her thumb back and forth over the head of his cock, Dalton took his wallet from a pocket inside his jacket and, after extracting a condom, threw the wallet to the floor.

Batting her hand away, Dalton took the condom from the packet and shakily rolled it down his length.

Without a word or a look, he picked her up and pinned her against the wall; with one hand he guided himself to her opening then entered her with one swift thrust of the hips.

Carrie bit down on his shoulder to muffle her cries of pleasure at finally having him inside her, digging her nails into the back of his neck. Gentle was not going to be in their vocabulary in that cliché sex locale, nor did she want it to be; they were there for one purpose.

His thrusts started hard and fast, and stayed that way; she was at the mercy of his cock and she wouldn't have had it any other way. Each time his cock came in contact with the back of her pussy, she could feel her clit swelling, charging with energy, and every time she thought he was moving as hard as he could against her, he'd take her harder, her pussy bombarded with pleasure so divine it should have been illegal.

Dalton's face was buried in her neck in an attempt to smother the sounds of pleasure he had no control over. The feeling of his breath against her skin, and his teeth digging into the sensitive crook only increased what she was feeling, until she was silently screaming, her orgasm galloping ever closer.

He was pounding her into the wall, and she couldn't get enough of it as he began slamming into her, his grunting becoming louder, deeper, the sounds of a man dangerously close to orgasm.

Feeling inexplicably wicked, Carrie decided to take him over the edge, demanding in a rough voice, "Fuck me harder."

A loud roar filled the room as Dalton pushed inside her one last time and stilled, the pressure on her clit pushing her over the edge seconds later, her scream silent as her pussy contracted painfully around his cock.

Everything had been sapped from her and all she could do was cling to Dalton as they dropped to the floor in as a controlled manner as possible, given neither of them had use of their legs.

Minutes passed with them slumped together on the floor, their breathing jagged and shallow as they attempted to muster the energy to stand up, so they could go return to the reception, pretending nothing had happened. Maybe they could just leave the venue altogether, go back to her house and fall into bed to recover from what had been some ridiculously insane sex.

Dalton spoke first. "That was... I'm going to need a year to recover from..."

At least he'd managed words, all Carrie could get out was, "uh huh!"

"At the end when you said... bloody hell, I'm surprised you didn't kill me."

She giggled. "I had to."

"We really should get tidied up and get out of here."

Sadly, he was right. It was time. "Help me up?"

Dalton stood up on wobbly legs and held his hands out to her, pulling her to her feet. She walked slowly over to the toilet and tore off some toilet paper and passed it to Dalton, who carefully removed the condom and threw it in the bin. Not caring if he was watching, Carrie took some toilet paper and wiped between her legs, not that it was much use. She was so fucking wet she doubted she'd be able to walk anywhere without leaving a trail.

Dalton put his hand to the lock on the door. "Ready?"

She nodded and took a deep breath, hoping no one would be able to tell just from looking at her what had happened during their absence.

He unlocked the door and pushed it open, then glancing around quickly turned back to her. "Coast is clear."

They walked from the toilet hand in hand and, when they reached the door to the room the reception was being held in, they stepped aside for a couple walking out. Something about the man looked familiar, and the woman...

"Nova! What the hell are you doing here?" Dalton said, giving the woman a quick hug.

Carrie gasped as the dots connected; it was the couple from the changing room.

"Calum works with Luke. How do you—" Nova paused, eyes flashing to Carrie. "Hey! Wait, you're the lady from City Chic last night."

"I am... and yay, you got to wear your dress!"

Nova gave a little squeal of excitement. "Not for much longer! Started having contractions just before we arrived and they're getting a bit much now, so Calum decided it was time we headed to the hospital."

Carrie was about to congratulate the couple, when Dalton cut in. "Have you told Bodhi? He's going to be so excited!"

"No, don't want to bother him until we know it's the real thing," Calum answered for his wife.

Carrie stared at the three of them, confused. "How do you...?"

"Nova is Bodhi's big sister," Dalton informed her.

"I had no idea," Carrie laughed. "What a small world!"

Nova winced and clutched her belly; loving concern was written all over Calum's face as he smiled at them. "We better head off, don't want this little one being born in the car!"

"No, definitely not. Go! I won't mention anything to Bodhi," Dalton promised.

"Nice seeing you both," Nova said through the pain of her contraction.

"Go! Now! I don't know how to deliver a baby!" Dalton joked, but Carrie could see he was also a smidge serious.

They watched as Nova and Calum walked slowly, but determinedly through the foyer of the function centre and, when they were out of sight, Dalton turned to her and planted a kiss on her lips.

"My family are going to be coming to the worst possible conclusion right now."

Carrie snorted in a very unladylike fashion. "The right conclusion you mean.

CHAPTER EIGHT

When they'd arrived back at Dalton and Bodhi's house after the wedding, they'd been greeted by a very excited Bodhi, who had informed them that his sister was in labour. Instead of telling him they already knew and risk the chance of taking some of the shine off the moment for him, they had acted like it was news to them and let Bodhi tell them all about how Nova had gone into labour at a wedding.

The poor man had checked his cell phone non-stop all night, convinced that any second he was going to get the text message or phone call telling him he was an uncle. Little did he know his sister's labour was going to be a long one and the call hadn't come until late on Sunday night when Bodhi was in bed after the Kings' loss against the Chargers that day.

Carrie had gone to the game and, though she'd made her own way to and from the stadium, had ended up at Bodhi and Dalton's once they were home, for a late-night movie.

The three of them were in Dalton's bed when Bodhi got the call and Carrie loved how animated he became when he told them all about the baby.

"She was literally just born, like four minutes ago! How cool is that!"

"Congratulations, Uncle Bodhi," Carrie said and kissed him on the cheek.

Dalton leaned around Carrie, so he could slap him on the back in that way only men can. "Yep, welcome to the club!"

"They haven't named her yet, but she is eight pound and has a head of hair! Calum reckons she looks just like Nova."

"Well, no one wants their little girl looking like a dude in his mid-thirties," Dalton joked, earning him an eye roll from Carrie.

"I'm going to go in and see them first thing," Bodhi said, and she could already sense the impatience in his voice. "You guys should come with me!"

"Of course, we will," Dalton replied for both of them.

"You sure you want me to come?" Carrie asked. "I mean... I'm not exactly family or anything."

"Just want to spread the baby love, that's all," Bodhi said. "You don't have to come if you don't want to though."

"I don't want to crash what is going to be a special moment for you."

Without any warning, tears stung her eyes and she bit her lip in an attempt to stop more from coming. It didn't work though, and moments later she had the arms of two men around her while she cried like an idiot. She hadn't expected her stomach to drop the way it had, or for it to dawn on her that she couldn't keep it up anymore... Dalton and Bodhi, she had to end it.

"Are you okay?" Dalton asked, caution in his eyes.

"I'm… I just realised..." She took a deep breath. "This, the three of us... I don't think I can do it anymore." The men didn't say anything, and she knew they were waiting for her to continue. "Going to see a new baby isn't something you do with the guy you're banging, it's something you should do with a boyfriend or a husband... I just... Suddenly, it feels like—" Another deep breath. "I have had so much fun with you both, and I'm not just talking about the sex... but I'm the type of person who—" Tears began streaming down her cheeks and she wished she could click her fingers and disappear. Dalton and Bodhi didn't need to see her like this. "I don't do one-night stands. Nothing against them, it's just not for me... I need commitment, I need to know where I stand, and know that there are rules and parameters. I don't do spontaneous well... and what we have is about as spontaneous as it gets and—"

"Remember what we said about no expectations?" Bodhi said softly, moving her hair from her face and wiping away the tears gliding down her cheeks with his thumbs. "If you want this to end, it ends."

His words should have made her feel better, but they didn't, they made her feel oddly panicked.

"I-I don't want it to end though," she said and clasped her hands over her face, hoping it would mean she became invisible. "That's the problem."

"What you're really saying is you want some control over the situation, right?" It was Dalton who spoke this time.

"I guess so."

"If you don't want it to end, it doesn't have to," Dalton's words gave her a scratch of hope, though she didn't see where he was going with it. "We could always agree to make this a casual thing, but make it... I don't know, exclusive or whatever. Like, we're an officially casual thing, but we don't sleep with anyone else..."

Carrie turned and finally looked at him. "Makes sense..."

Bodhi picked up where Dalton left off, adding, "And when the time comes and we've all had enough, we end it... or if one of us meets someone we want to get to know better, I guess instead of a three-person agreement, it becomes a two-person thing."

Carrie looked from Bodhi to Dalton and asked, "Are you sure about this?"

"I think it's a good idea... have some transparency. We all know where we stand," Dalton said.

Bodhi nodded. "We just need to be honest with each other if we don't think it's working."

"It's not going to be a forever type of thing, obviously, but there is no reason we can't enjoy ourselves in the meantime," she said, hating the undercurrent of sorrow she felt thinking that one day there would be life without Bodhi and Dalton.

***

Waking up on Monday morning and still experiencing the after-effects of her conversation with Dalton and Bodhi, Carrie felt as if she was recovering from an emotional hurricane. There was no way she was going to go into the office that day and, not for the first time, she was grateful she had a job she could do from home if necessary.

Wedged as she was between two warm bodies, Carrie wondered what the chances were that Dalton and Bodhi would sleep the entire day, so she could stay right where she was. It was a cosy setup, tucked in between the two men, Dalton pressed up behind her, while Bodhi slept facing her, his mouth so close to hers she could have easily woken him with a kiss.

She had no idea what the time was but knew the men needed to be at their training facility for a 10 a.m. recovery session which would last a couple of hours, after which they were going to the hospital so Bodhi could meet his niece. Neither alarm had gone off, so it was before 8:30 a.m., which was all she needed to know.

Before they'd gone to sleep, Nova had sent Bodhi a few photos of the baby and he'd wasted no time in setting one as the wallpaper on his phone. It was touching to see him so in awe of the little girl he hadn't even met yet, and Carrie knew he was going to make the most amazing uncle, and one day, an even more amazing father. Dalton too, she could see the love he had for his nieces and nephews and, when his time finally came, he'd be a pro because of all the experience he'd had with his brothers' kids.

Secretly, she was looking forward to seeing Bodhi holding the teeny-tiny baby and only hoped her ovaries wouldn't explode from the cuteness overload.

Given the cosy confines of the bed, Carrie fell back into a peaceful sleep, only waking when two different alarms went off at the same time, creating a disturbing cacophony which took her from peacefully asleep to wired and sitting upright in a matter of seconds.

"I'll give you a ride back to your house," Dalton yawned, grazing his nails back and forth over her lower back.

"No rush," Carrie said. "Will ring my boss soon and let her know I'm working from home. Just drop me off on your way to training."

"Come here then," Dalton said, playfully grabbing her and pulling her down between him and Bodhi.

Moving her hands beneath the covers, Carrie took a man in each hand and gave them both a coaxing squeeze, the speed with which the penises in her hands became rock hard as a result leaving her feeling particularly proud of herself.

Dalton arched into her hand while Bodhi gave her a flustered look, his nostrils flared, eyes burning.

"Before you make me decide that I too can work from home today, I'm going to go and have a shower," Dalton said, the frown and pursed lips telling her he didn't really want to leave the bed.

"I'm not going anywhere," Bodhi said, his words dripping with suggestion.

Dalton smirked and winked at her. "Maybe you should tell him about what happened at the wedding yesterday..."

"What happened at the wedding yesterday?" Bodhi played along, the memory enough to send ripples of desire through Carrie's body.

"Have fun, you two," Dalton said with a smug look of satisfaction as he picked up a towel and left the room.

As it turned out, Bodhi quite enjoyed the graphic retelling of her sneaky, highly inappropriate tryst with Dalton at the wedding, and in return, she took great pleasure—of the literal sort—out of his explicit description of what he would have done to her in the same scenario.

***

"Are you sure it's okay that I'm here?" Carrie asked Bodhi as she rode with him and Dalton in the lift to the maternity ward.

"For the fiftieth time, yes! I even cleared it with Nova."

The lift dinged as it arrived on the fourth floor, leaving her no time to suggest she could just wait downstairs while he double checked.

"Room 407," Bodhi muttered to himself looking at the numbers along the corridor, eventually pointing toward the end room. "There it is."

Carrie hung back with Dalton, both of them laughing quietly, watching Bodhi as he jogged toward his sister's room. Pushing the door open, he walked into the room, then turned back and motioned at them to hurry up.

"I hope he won't be pissed when he finds out we saw them at the wedding!" Dalton whispered, his words mimicking her thoughts.

"Come on!" Bodhi said impatiently from the door and Carrie fought not to laugh.

Walking into the room behind Bodhi, Carrie smiled guiltily at Nova who was resting on the bed, a tiny nose poking out from a swaddle of blankets cradled in her arms.

Bodhi walked to his sister's bedside and hugged Nova who looked exhausted but elated. Slowly, he leaned down and dropped a kiss on the newborn in her arms; even though his back was to her and Dalton, Carrie could tell he was crying... which in turn made tears well in her eyes.

Weddings and tiny babies, two things certain to turn her into a gooey mess of tears and emotion.

Dalton put an arm around her shoulder, and she smiled shyly up at him, surprised to see his eyes had a bit of a glistening sheen to them.

"Congratulations Nova," Dalton said. "She is beautiful."

"She is, isn't she?" Nova gushed and then smiled at Carrie. "It's nice to see you again!"

"You've met?" Bodhi asked, and Carrie could feel her face flaming.

She was relieved when Nova was the one to fill in the dots. "Twice actually, at City Chic the other night when I was trying to find a dress to fit my whale-like figure, and then yesterday at the wedding! Cal works with Luke, the guy who, it turns out, married Dalton's cousin."

"Guess I don't need to do the introductions then," Bodhi shrugged.

"You should probably introduce yourself to this little one though," Nova said as she leaned slowly toward her brother, raising the baby to him, indicating it was time for Uncle Bodhi to have his first hold.

More tears for Carrie. It was such a sweet moment though, watching Bodhi taking his niece in his arms for the first time, cradling her and swaying gently from side to side as he whispered a private greeting to the baby girl.

Never one to be able to resist the pull of a baby, Carrie walked to his side and he ducked down slightly so she could take a closer peek. Complete perfection, that was the only way to describe the baby nestled in his arms.

Without thinking, Carrie put an arm around his waist and rested her head against his arm, earning herself a curious look from Nova. She stepped away from Bodhi and considered making up an excuse to leave, but the other woman smiled sweetly at her and pointed to a seat.

"Sit down if you want to, Carrie. Get the chair before either of these buffoons do."

"That's Uncle Buffoon to you," Bodhi said, and Nova laughed quietly, wincing as she did so.

"Don't make me laugh you idiot, I've got stitches in places you don't ever want stitches."

When Dalton screwed up his face in response, Nova frowned at him. "I'm sure you've heard all about that stuff from your brothers' wives."

"You have no idea. Can't have a family dinner without mention of someone's perineum."

Given what she'd seen of his family at the wedding, Carrie wasn't surprised.

The door opened, and a blond woman entered the room, the ease with which she said hello to, and hugged Bodhi, made Carrie wonder if she was another sister. Bodhi hadn't mentioned one, but then she hadn't asked either.

All thoughts of her being another sibling disappeared when the woman walked directly to Nova and gave her an emotion-fuelled kiss on the lips.

What the...?

"Carrie, this is Katrina," Nova said, completely flooring her by adding, "my girlfriend."

"It's nice to meet you," Carrie said smiling at the blond woman, wondering whether Nova meant girlfriend as in girl-who-is-a-friend, or girlfriend as in *girlfriend-girlfriend*.

"You too," Katrina said, giving her a friendly smile.

"Carrie is friends with Bodhi and Dalton."

"Oh, I see." Katrina gave her a look like Carrie had given her just seconds earlier—no doubt wondering what the situation was between the three of them.

Nova had mentioned she was having a bit of difficulty with breastfeeding, so when the baby began wailing, they took it as their cue to leave. When they told her they were going to leave, she said they didn't have to, but they insisted, and Bodhi promised he'd be back up later in the afternoon.

Feeling as if she'd been taking up all of their time lately, Carrie declined Dalton's offer of going for a coffee, knowing if she went with them, she'd end up back at their house and the following morning would be waking in one of their beds again.

"When are you playing this weekend?" Carrie asked as she got out of the car when they stopped outside her house.

"Friday night this week, but we're playing out west," Bodhi said. "Let us know if you want to come, we'll organise some tickets for you."

"I'll get back to you," Carrie said, though inside her immediate response had been to say, '*I'll definitely be there*'.

A break would be a good thing. She was starting to get used to being around them, and considering the casual nature of their relationship, that wasn't exactly healthy. It was one thing to get clingy in a relationship, but when it was more of a friendship based around sex? Not so much...

***

Carrie spent the rest of the day so absorbed in her work that the first time she stepped away was just after eight when there was a knock at the door. She knew Bodhi had been going to visit his sister and presumed the knock was him, stopping in on his way home, and she pretended for a second the thought didn't excite her as much as it did.

She opened the door, already smiling, ready to ask how the baby was and if the little princess had a name yet, but it wasn't Bodhi standing on the other side. Or Dalton.

It was Jess.

Her heart dropped, and she braced herself for whatever verbal lashing was about to be unleashed, but rather than yelling, Jess smiled sadly at her.

"Caz, I feel awful for what I said... Is there any chance you'll ever forgive me?"

Carrie felt completely blindsided and didn't know what to say, but the sad look in Jess's eyes melted the ice slightly and she stepped aside. "Come in."

Once in the lounge, Carrie didn't consider offering a hot drink like she'd usually have done, she just walked into the room and sat down in the middle of the couch, a silent way of saying 'do not sit near me'.

"How have you been?" Jess asked.

For the first time in her life, Carrie didn't follow her friends lead and enter into polite conversation, instead choosing to speak her mind. "What you did and said last weekend was nasty, Jess. Nasty and completely uncalled for."

Jess frowned and picked at an invisible thread on the recliner before finally looking her in the eyes. "I know it was, Carrie, and I'm so sorry. I was just... jealous, that's all."

"That's no reason to leave me stuck at the stadium the way you did, or to call me any of the shitty things you did afterwards."

"I just... well, I imagined it would be me with a hot tale to tell after the gala, and then they spoke to you after the game and didn't even acknowledge I was there, it felt..."

"Oh, I know just how it felt, Jess. It's the way I used to feel with you whenever we went out, like I was just there to give you someone to talk to until a better offer came along. I got over it though, because you're my best friend and I knew that the next day I would get all the juicy goss!"

Jess surprised Carrie by bowing her head in shame. "I'm sorry I made you feel that way, Caz."

"You are the one that always goes on about how predictable I am, and how I need to be more spontaneous. Well that's what I did when I went home with Bodhi and Dalton, and I thought you'd be proud of me. I didn't think for a second that you'd lash out the way you did."

"The part of me that isn't jealous is proud of you," Jess said. "I guess I need to stop being such a selfish bitch."

"Don't change too much though," Carrie joked.

Jess gave her a serious look. "So, are you still seeing them?"

What was the point in lying? She had nothing to be ashamed of. "Yes, I am. It's nothing serious, just sex," she shrugged. "We're all adults, we're all single... no one is getting hurt."

"Well, that's fair."

"Look, Jess, I'm willing to forget what happened, as long as you don't freak out on me again. It isn't like you haven't had fuck buddies before, or had threesomes— hell, I remember you telling me about the two couples you joined one night!"

"You've got me there." Jess laughed and didn't bother pretending to look embarrassed.

"That's the thing, you embrace it! You take it for what it is and enjoy it, so it really shook me when you reacted so negatively when I told you." It felt good to be saying what was on her mind and not hold back for fear of upsetting Jess. "I thought you'd be begging me for details, not calling me a whore!"

For the first time in memory, Jess looked truly ashamed. "I'm so sorry. I can leave if you want me to."

"No, you don't have to leave. I don't want you to." Carrie couldn't contain herself and giggled. "I need to tell my best friend *aaaaaall* about the naughtiness I've been getting up to."

"Yes, you do!" Jess laughed and stood up. "How about I go and get the bottle of wine from my car, that I put in just in case you gave me the time of day, and then you can tell me all about it."

"Don't bother going out to the car," Carrie said before she walked quickly through to the kitchen and grabbed a bottle from the fridge. Taking two wine glasses from the cupboard, she returned to the lounge and held the bottle up. "Here's one I prepared earlier!"

It was past midnight when Carrie eventually waved Jess off in a taxi, having told her all about the mind-bogglingly spectacular orgasms she'd been having at the hands of Bodhi and Dalton; she climbed into bed feeling lighter, happier, only then understanding what a toll Jess's meltdown had taken on her.

The sting of Jess's words hadn't completely worn off, but it would eventually, and in the meantime, Carrie was just happy to have her best friend back.

CHAPTER NINE

After spending Monday evening with Jess, Carrie devoted the rest of her week to work; she wasn't behind as such, but it was fair to say her mind hadn't been as on the job as she'd have liked. Now she'd come to an agreement with Bodhi and Dalton, and patched things up with Jess, she was finally able to devote all her attention to the lovely authors she was working with.

All of Saturday she'd been tossing up whether to see if Jess wanted to go out for a drink that night but decided instead to treat herself a night of pampering, starting with a mani-pedi at her favourite salon. It had been tempting to see if they could squeeze her in for a haircut, but what she really wanted was to get home and make good use of the deep, claw-footed bathtub. Some women looked for a dream kitchen; Carrie, on the other hand, had been all about the bathtub.

While the tub was filling up, she undressed in her bedroom, slipped into her towelling robe and went back into the bathroom to make the hardest decision of the day: pick a bath bomb from her extensive collection. Finally deciding on the heavenly citrus scent of Orange Grove, she dropped it in the water, giggling when droplets splashed her because she'd let go of it a little higher than she should have.

When the water was ten inches from lapping over the top rim, she turned the faucet off and placed her robe on the stool positioned beside the tub. The heat of the water lulled her immediately into a relaxed state as she lowered herself into the bath, and she let out a loud, pleasure-filled sigh. Was there anything better than luxuriating in a bath?

Yes, her brain told her, betraying the sense of calm that had rolled over her the moment she reclined against the back of the tub, a bath with Dalton and Bodhi would be even better than having a whole tub to herself to stretch out in.

Traitor.

It was all downhill from there. Inhaling the citrusy scent of the steam, Carrie was transported back to waking up in Bodhi's bed, met by the soapy, citrusy warmth of his skin. In turn, that made her think about Dalton and the masculine yet floral scent of the cologne he'd worn at the wedding; it went without saying that particular image made her remember what it had been like to be pinned up against the wall while he pounded her to a very public orgasm.

She'd been doing so well, not suggesting to Bodhi and Dalton that they should catch up during the week. *Catch up.* Everyone knew what that was code for. Now here she was, in the sanctuary of her over-sized bathroom considering inviting both men over to see if there was room in the bath for three people.

It had been her hope that time away from men would make her realise that she wasn't really that fond of them, and she had just gotten carried away because of the novelty of having sex on tap. Alas, all the distance had done was to make her look even more forward to the next time she saw them. Not going to their game the previous night was supposed to prove to herself she wasn't that fussed, but lying in the soothing warmth of the bath, her body was suddenly screaming for some very specific attention.

Even in the heat of the water, her nipples were hardening as if it was a bath of ice she was sitting in, and she couldn't resist plucking at the hard nubs, inhaling sharply at the resulting throb of her pussy. She plucked again, a little harder this time, and instinctively lifted her ass, intensifying the sensation between her legs. The next time she tugged, harder, and harder still, unable to stop the moans that accompanied each tug and throb.

She longed for the bigger hands of Dalton or Bodhi, knowing their skilled fingers would squeeze and tweak her nipples into the hardest of points, teasing her until she was a frantic mess, begging for more.

The great thing about living alone was the numerous places one could store sex toys. Reaching into the cupboard built into the wall just behind her, Carrie located the silicone dildo she kept especially for bath-time purposes and, gripping it in her hand like she might have Dalton or Bodhi, she immediately guided her hand, and the dildo, to where she so badly needed it.

Naughty as she was feeling, Carrie didn't try to suppress her moans of pleasure as she ran the tip of the dildo up and down her slit, using more pressure on each pass, willing the thick tip to go that little bit farther and stretch her open. She wanted it to last, to toy with herself for a little while before finally giving in, but even as it grazed over her clit, she could feel her orgasm developing and knew there would be no 'self-foreplay' that evening.

Taking a nipple between the fingers of her free hand, she squeezed it tightly while she pushed the dildo inside, crying out as it stroked all the hidden sensitive spots.

The heat of the water, the scent of citrus, the increasingly tight grip of her fingers on her nipple all combined in a way to that was torturous, causing tension to build instantly. Changing her grip on the end of the dildo, she was suddenly feeling more friction against her clit, and it intensified as she applied more pressure with her hand.

Her toes were curled tightly, the sounds of her pleasure echoing off the walls making it sound like it wasn't a solo pursuit she was partaking in.

The movement of her hands was creating waves in the water, which splashed over the end, splattering against the blue tiled floor. Harder and harder, she moved her hand until she was working her pussy at a furious pace, the muscles in her arm starting to burn and tire.

Needing something to take her over the edge, it was Bodhi and Dalton her brain automatically went to. They were all naked in her bedroom. Dalton was on his back on the bed and she had a hand either side of his head, riding his cock harder than she'd ever done before; behind her Bodhi was applying lube to her asshole with his fingers.

She felt the blunt head of his cock against her tight hole and, as he pressed slowly, pleasure like she'd never imagined rocked through her and she screamed as her orgasm hit.

It wasn't only in her fantasy she was screaming; her bathroom echoed with the sounds of her screams as her pussy clamped around the dildo, the power of her orgasm overwhelming her and causing her to shake violently, her skin burning all over.

She gasped for breath, inhaling water at the same time, which sent her sitting up and spluttering. As she got the coughing under control, she could imagine the headlines, *Senior editor for well-known romance publishing house drowns in bath after masturbation session*. Try breaking *that* news to her parents!

The water was no longer soothing, it felt soupy and had taken on a slight chill that was neither pleasant nor relaxing. Carefully, she removed the dildo from the tight clutch of her body and set it aside to be cleaned later; on shaky legs, she stepped out of the bath and stood onto the cool tiles.

Picking up her robe, she slipped it on and tied the belt, pissed off with herself for ruining what was meant to be a calming bath. She should have just kept her thoughts clean, and not given in to the urge to see if she could give herself an orgasm that came even close to the magic Bodhi and Dalton could perform.

Short answer, even though the orgasm was pretty good as far as self-induced ones went, it was nothing compared to the delights performed by the two men, and rather than curing the hunger, it had only served to leave her feeling starved.

What a silly thing to be upset about, but she was. The only cure—other than a visit to the house in Coogee—was movies and ice cream in bed, maybe even some chocolate.

Pity party for one, coming up.

Bridget Jones set the scene perfectly, and by the end of the first movie Carrie was starting to feel a bit less moody. Until Bodhi sent her a message.

'*Thought I'd let you know, Nova and Calum finally decided on a name for the baby! They named her Aurelia Harlow*'

'*Super cute name!*'

'*I know! What are you up to tonight?*'

'*In bed watching Bridget Jones, finished half a tub of chocolate ice cream and feel like a pig... if you must know, kind of... did stuff to myself tonight in the bath and it didn't live up to expectation so now I'm sulking*.'

'*Should have given one of us a call, or both... we would have helped out with that... very happily.*'

'*Figured I'd just scratch my own itch, but it just reminded me of how much better it is when it's not me doing it...*'

'*Tomorrow night?*'

'*I could be convinced*'

'*Get your butt over here when you're ready then...*'

'*What if I'm ready at 6am?*'

'*Just knock really loud on the door... always willing to help a lady in need*'

'*Seeing my aunty tomorrow for lunch, so I promise you'll get a decent sleep.*'

'*Well, if you change your mind...*'

'*See you tomorrow, Mr Hook*'

*'Already hard thinking about it... good night Ms
Lucas'*

If her stomach wasn't so bloated she looked eighteen-
months pregnant, Carrie would have already been in the
car heading in the direction of Coogee, but Bodhi didn't
need to know that.

***

Lunch with her aunt turned into lunch, shopping,
and afternoon tea and at 4 p.m. when she was driving
home, she decided at the last minute to take a detour to
Coogee. There was no point going home, only to go back
out an hour later.

At least that was how she justified it to herself,
pretending it had nothing to do with the fact she'd been
unable to think about anything other than the hours of
pleasure she knew awaited her.

Parking outside the house she ran up to the front
door and knocked, wondering which of the two ginger sex
gods would open the door. The bigger question was
whether or not she'd be able to contain herself long
enough to make it past the entrance before impaling
herself on the cock of whoever did greet her.

It was Bodhi who answered, looking surprised, but
happy to see her.

"You have no fucking idea how badly I want you
right now," Carrie gasped, gripping his t-shirt in her
hands and pulling him closer for a kiss.

The kiss wasn't as wild as she'd imagined it would be,
and when he pulled away, she noticed his cheeks were
red. Oh shit. He'd changed his mind, hadn't he? Then she
heard laughing coming from the lounge.

She clasped her hands over her mouth. "Oh fuck..."

"Nova and Calum are here," Bodhi informed her, the corners of his mouth giving away the fact he was trying not to laugh.

"I'm so embarrassed!" Carrie whispered, preparing to turn around and run straight back to her car, but Bodhi took her hand.

"No need to be," he finally laughed and nodded in the direction of the lounge. "Come on, you've gotta see how much Aurelia has grown!"

She had no choice but to follow him into the lounge, where Nova and Calum still looked highly amused, but at least they had the decency not to be laughing.

"Hi Carrie," Nova said politely. "You remember Calum?"

"Yes, from the wedding, it's nice to see you."

"You too!" and then with a wink he added, "sorry to have ruined your plans."

"Uh, sorry you had to hear all of that..."

This was the most awkward experience of her life. Nova and Calum had seen her at the wedding with Dalton and had probably presumed they were a couple, but now they'd heard her telling Bodhi in no uncertain terms how badly she wanted him. God only knew what they'd be thinking about her.

"We can just go for a run another day, if you want," Calum said to Bodhi. "Don't want to get in the way of far more exciting physical activity."

"No, I'll just come back later," Carrie said. "I insist. I didn't get in touch before I came over, so it's my fault."

"Me and Aurelia were going to go for a coffee while these two go for a run, you're more than welcome to come with us if you want to?" Nova said with a friendly smile.

"It would be nice to have some adult company while I wait for Calum."

Carrie could hardly say no, could she? "If you're sure you don't mind?"

"Not at all!" Nova smiled. "I can tell you all about Bodhi and what a little shit he was as a kid."

Carrie laughed and poked her tongue out at Bodhi. "How could I say no to an offer like that?"

"Whatever she tells you, it's lies! All lies!" Bodhi said, hands on his hips.

All the stance did was put his physique on display and Carrie felt her eyes being drawn to his crotch. Why did they make men's running shorts so... enticing? The outline of his cock was clear to her and she began wishing he'd taken Calum up on the offer of taking a raincheck on the run. She wouldn't even bother dragging Bodhi to the bedroom, the couch would do just fine.

She watched Calum crouch down to look at Aurelia, who was sleeping in her carseat. "Make sure you ring me if you need me, hun."

"I will," Nova said. "But I think between me and Carrie, we can wrangle this little one."

"I don't doubt it for a second," Calum said before standing up and kissing his wife.

Bodhi walked toward her, "I guess we'll see you when we're back," he said and kissed her on the cheek—an unexpected, sweet gesture.

"Have a good run..."

"Oh!" Bodhi turned as he was walking from the lounge. "Dalton is at his parents' house for dinner but will be back after that, in case you're wondering where he is!"

"I'll message him and say hello," Carrie said, her heart racing at the sound of his name and the idea of seeing him in just a few hours.

This not getting attached thing was working *so* well.

***

"How is life with a baby?" Carrie asked Nova as they sat at the beachside café, looking out over Coogee beach.

"Amazing and scary at the same time." Nova smiled down at Aurelia with such love in her eyes, Carrie felt as if she was intruding on special mummy and baby bonding time.

"I can't even imagine, it was scary enough when my cat, Tiger, was a kitten... and even then, he was still pretty self-sufficient."

"It's weird, you just do what you need to do without even thinking about it. I was so worried before I gave birth that I wouldn't know what to do, and that they wouldn't let me leave the hospital with her because I was so clueless... but then she was born, and everything just slotted into place."

"You look like a natural with her."

"I'm still working out the breastfeeding thing, but we're getting there slowly. I'm lucky Calum is such an amazing husband; he has been such a huge help, doing stuff around the house so I can focus on Aurelia. Yesterday she would only sleep on me, so I was stuck on the couch all day, Calum literally waited on me hand and foot, and then Kat came over and gave him a bit of a break, so he could go to the supermarket."

Carrie had almost forgotten about the woman who Nova had introduced as her girlfriend at the hospital, but curiosity got the best of her and she had to ask, "How long have you and Katrina been together?"

"Two years," Nova said. "I could see you got a bit of a shock the other day when I introduced her, I'm sorry, I presumed Bodhi would have told you about her."

"It was a surprise," Carrie admitted. "I've never met someone who is married and openly has a girlfriend as well. I work as a romance editor and have edited my share of stories with three or more in the bed but haven't come across it in real life."

She knew she sounded like an idiot blabbering away, but now the topic had been brought up, she was interested to find out how it worked.

"Aren't you living it yourself though?" Nova's question caught her off guard.

"Well... not really, I mean... it's just casual and... there's no relationship or feelings, it's nothing serious, just sex."

"I saw the way Bodhi and Dalton were looking at you the other day, trust me, you're living it."

Carrie laughed nervously. "Nah, it was just the emotion of the situation, you know, meeting a brand-new bubba for the first time... makes everyone go a bit gaa-gaa."

"The moment Bodhi introduced you I knew the three of you were doing it."

"Like I said, it's just a casual thing... they have needs, I have needs... friends helping friends."

"That's what I thought when I met Kat as well. Calum knew I was bisexual, and he was the one that told me she and I were both feeling something more than friendship. I denied it, of course, I mean, who wants to admit to their husband that they're attracted to someone else?"

"How did it eventually happen?"

"Calum invited Kat over one night for dinner. After we'd eaten, he gave me a kiss and told me he had booked into a hotel, that me and Kat had the house to ourselves for the night, and that he wanted me to explore what he could see developing between us, and that if that meant doing anything physical, I had his blessing."

"Wow! That must have been a shock."

"It was. I didn't think I would get up the courage to do anything, but that night we... well, let's just say things got very physical, and the next day, after Kat left, Calum told me that if I wanted to see where things went with her, he was happy to make himself scarce a few times a month." Nova smiled the smile of someone madly in love. "To start with me and Kat fooled around and had amazing sex, but then real feelings developed, and I was so ashamed. I confessed to Calum one night and expected him to tell me he was going to leave me, but instead he told me that he thought I should talk to Kat about starting a proper relationship."

"That's crazy, in an amazing way though. Not many guys would be secure enough to want that for their wife."

"It was awkward initially, but then we fell into a routine that made the three of us happy, and I can't imagine my life any other way now."

"How much time do you spend with Kat?"

"We have a couple of nights together a month, and usually spend time together one or two days a week. She understands my relationship with Calum comes first, and back when we started, she said that was how she wanted it to be."

"Do the three of you ever...?"

"Oh, god no. Calum and Kat are friendly to each other and they get on well, but there has been no desire on any side for us to have a threesome." She smirked. "apparently that's more my brother's forte..."

"You don't think it's... wrong?"

"I am of the opinion that as long as everyone is happy, and there is no cheating, who cares how many people are in a bed, or in a relationship? For that matter, who cares how the relationship is defined? Or the sexuality of the people in it? Seriously pisses me off the way society is so quick to point the finger."

Guilt clawed at her throat; she had always thought people who had threesomes were sexual deviants; that people in open relationships were just bored with each other. In her mind there had been a certain 'type' who got into situations that weren't 'normal' in the eyes of society.

Nova seemed very normal though, she loved her husband and seemed incredibly devoted to him, she didn't have twenty facial piercings, or a crazy hairstyle, and Carrie doubted she had a problem with drugs or alcohol.

She really had been a judgemental bitch, hadn't she? All of her life she'd been so quick to judge what was normal and what wasn't, and Nova's words had hit hard.

"You okay?" Nova asked, rocking Aurelia's car-seat with her foot.

"Just thinking about how judgy I've been in the past of people who were in relationships I didn't consider normal..."

"We've all been there, so don't feel bad... before I started dating Kat, I thought that even if it was all above board, if someone was in a relationship with two people, it was cheating."

"Thanks, that makes me feel a bit better."

"Look, I know you are just having some fun with Bodhi and Dalton, but how about we swap numbers, and if you ever want to chat about things, we can catch up for coffee or something? I know it can be confusing, regardless of whether it's casual or not."

"It's not weird for you, considering one of the guys is your brother?"

"Just don't go into any detail about him," Nova laughed. "I don't mind hearing about Dalton though... that man, he's like a big ginger Viking or something, especially when he hasn't shaved for a while."

Carrie was grateful she hadn't taken a sip of coffee because she'd surely have spat it out laughing, after hearing Nova's comment about Dalton.

The women swapped numbers, but before they could continue their discussion, Aurelia started crying and Nova automatically went into Mummy-mode. Thus, their trip to the café came to an end, leaving Carrie with a lot to think about, but at the same time, feeling less bogged down by the ethical dilemma of the current make-up of her sex-life.

With her sex-life in mind, she picked up her phone and messaged Bodhi.

'Don't have your shower until I get there... I have the sudden urge to soap you up... every single inch of you...'

CHAPTER TEN

"Thought they'd never leave," Bodhi said closing the door heavily behind him and stalking toward her like a lion with its prey. "Now... about that shower..."

Grabbing her waist, Bodhi marched her backward until her back was against the wall and kissed her with such heat Carrie lost her train of thought. The feeling of his hardening dick pressing against her brought her back into the here and now.

"I want you, rather badly... you need a shower, also rather badly—I figured we could combine the two in a very hot, soapy way."

He ran his tongue slowly across her top lip, an action that caused her eyelids to flutter and her heart to stampede.

"I think that is a brilliant idea." He took her hand and walked her quickly down the hallway to the bathroom.

Carrie watched as he pushed his shorts down until they dropped to the floor; she assisted him with his boxers, using it as an opportunity to wrap her hand around him and pump him a couple of times. A droplet of precum beaded on the tip of his cock and she wiped it off with her thumb, his eyes doubling in size when she put her thumb to her mouth and made a big show of licking it off with a slow swipe.

One taste of him and her vision for how the shower would play out completely changed. While he rid himself of his t-shirt and dealt to the shower, Carrie took her clothes off and followed him into the large glass-walled cubicle.

She kissed him lingeringly and the idea that he'd be able to taste himself on her tongue was more of a turn on than she'd expected. But first...

Carrie made quick work of soaping him up and washing away the lather, before her impatience got the better of her. No matter how badly she wanted to taste him, she had no desire to have sweaty man bits in her mouth.

She put the body wash down and wrapped her arms around his neck, so she could kiss him.

"I should go and get a condom..." Bodhi said against her mouth, looking unsure when Carrie shook her head.

"No, we won't be needing one this time..." She could see he was battling with a response, so casually added, "there is something I want, no, *need* to do."

"What are y—"

She dropped to her knees and smiled up at him briefly before taking him in her hand and this time instead of her thumb, it was her tongue running over the head of his cock.

His fingers made their way into her hair and a very loud inhalation was followed by a hissed, "Oh fuck."

Wanting to give him the full experience, Carrie took her time concentrating on the swollen head, swirling her tongue around and over it, licking with delicate strokes. The salty taste of him stayed on her tongue, proving a test of her willpower because the slight hint of him made her crave his cum in a way she didn't think possible.

Carrie opened her lips around him and Bodhi pulled on her hair, just hard enough to send a tingle through her scalp and down her spine. As much as she wanted to take him as far in her mouth as she could and suck greedily until he came, she resisted the urge to rush things, and took him in inch by slow inch, drenching him in the heat of her mouth.

She wasn't cruel though, not to mention too impatient to take any longer. Carrie took him in until she'd reached her limit and gave a long, deep suck, grinning around him when he moaned, "Jesus, fucking hell!" and gripped her hair tighter.

Moving her hands to the backs of his thighs she began moving her mouth up and down him, loving the way she could feel all the ridges of his cock against her tongue, and the way he lurched every time she moved her mouth back down his shaft.

His hands spanned the back of her head and, though she knew he was trying not to, he started moving his hips in time with her mouth. She'd never been one for deep-throating, but there she was, on her knees with Bodhi's cock hitting the back of her throat—and she wanted more of him.

Bodhi's groans were loud, even over the sound of the water, and she could feel the tension in his cock, a hint he was going to come soon. Knowing sometimes too much stimulation led to an anti-climactic orgasm, Carrie began sucking harder, allowing the thrust of Bodhi's hips to set the pace.

Heat scorched the back of her throat and she held his thighs tighter, her eyes squeezed shut, preparing herself for him to hit the moment of no return.

Harder she sucked, faster he thrust his hips; the bathroom filled with the symphony Bodhi's pleasure filled grunts and groans. Another taste of him. Hips moving faster, a long, deep groan announcing his orgasm two seconds before jets of his cum shot down her throat. She swallowed him down with ease, hyper aware of his cock contracting against her tongue as he emptied himself.

His hands relaxed on the back of her head, then fell away, the sounds of his ragged breath replacing the cries of ecstasy as he came down. Reluctantly, she let him slip from her mouth and took his hands, helping him as he slid down the wall of the shower, and sat on the floor beside her.

Bodhi eyed her with a spaced-out look. "You... fuck..."

Feeling immensely proud of herself for turning the man into a boneless mess on the floor, she ghosted her lips over his and stood up, picking up the bottle of body wash from the shelf in the wall and squirted some in her hands, prepared to give him a show while he recovered.

For someone who was in an incoherent heap on the floor, he did well to stand up and snatch the bottle from her hands. "Please, allow me."

Allow him, she did... but not before Bodhi had stroked *her* into a quivering lather using his skilled fingers.

... and then, not even five minutes later he dropped her —still wet in more ways than one—on his bed, spreading her legs and giving her a ravenous look seconds before burying his face in her pussy and devouring her.

***

Bodhi went to bed not long after Dalton got home, using the excuse of feeling completely drained because of what a particular woman's mouth had done to him in the shower. Carrie couldn't help but feel the real reason for him going to bed early was to give her time alone with Dalton and she didn't know how she felt about that.

They didn't have a fifty-fifty agreement, there was no promise she'd spend equal amounts of time with the men but given she hadn't seen Dalton since earlier in the week, it was nice to have the chance to enjoy his company. That was another cause of internal conflict; she shouldn't enjoy spending time with him in a non-sexual manner. Sex was the basis of their 'agreement', not spending quality one-on-one time together.

It shouldn't have felt right being curled up with him on the couch, and the way he was ghosting his fingertips up and down her arm shouldn't have felt relaxing. She willed herself to break the contact, to move away from him, but the simple fact was she didn't want to, because it felt so stupidly, perfectly right.

It wasn't Dalton making her feel that way, she convinced herself, comfort was a human need and in that moment her very human need was being satisfied. It was biology, instinct, nothing at all to do with the man fulfilling the need.

"My family were asking after you today... Mum was most disappointed I didn't take you over with me."

"And you put them straight, right?"

"Sure, I said 'guys, Carrie is just a girl me and Bodhi are both having sex with, sometimes together and sometimes individually, lay off okay!'" He laughed, and for a second she believed him, so she was glad when he added, "I just said you were a friend and why would I want to put you through the traumatic experience of a Kendry family dinner."

"What exactly happens at a Kendry family dinner?"

"Mostly me and my brothers doing a lot of name calling, and Mum telling us off," he said, and Carrie didn't doubt it. "The kids like dragging me outside and using me as a tackle bag, until one of us inevitably gets hurt—usually me."

"Poor, poor man," she said, voice dripping with faux sympathy.

"Then there is the actual food part, which is probably the only time there is any silence."

Though he was making it sound like a painful experience, Carrie could tell he lived for those days with his family, and she felt envious. Her own family was so small there was never any of the hustle and bustle he mentioned, none of the banter or loving chastisement from parents.

"It must be nice to have such a big family."

"Growing up, I used to wish I was an only child, or that I only had one brother, but now I wouldn't change a thing."

"I always wanted another kid in the house, but the only time that happened was when my cousins came to visit from America, which wasn't often."

"Must have been nice not having to fight for your mum or dad's attention though," he said. "That was one thing I hated about growing up with big brothers. Mum and Dad were always going to their sports or school events, and the twins were little shits, so they seemed to spend the rest of their time trying to keep them in line."

"I guess the attention was nice as a kid, but when I got a bit older, I wished they'd just leave me alone... they were always asking what I was doing and where I was going, who I would be with, what time I'd be home, blah blah blah."

She didn't tend to talk to anyone about being an only child because it was upsetting to think about the difficulty her parents had gone through trying to give her the little sibling she'd so desperately wanted. Even as a child, seeing her mum going through month after month of disappointment had been emotionally tolling. She would wake up to her mum crying, and overheard discussions between her parents, her mum asking what was so wrong with her, and suggesting her dad should leave and find a woman who could give him more kids.

Carrie didn't think her mum had ever truly come to terms with being unable to have any more children, and she remembered getting home from school one day to find her mum had packed a bag and gone away. A week later, her mother had returned, full of apologies, explaining she'd found out her sister was pregnant again and that she'd needed time to process it.

Simmering away in the back of Carrie's mind was the thought that she might not be able to get pregnant either. She knew there was a chance whatever prevented her mum getting pregnant was genetic and that, when the time came for her to start a family, she'd be unable to conceive. Carrie was lucky to live in a time where it was possible to obtain medical assistance for fertility issues, but even that didn't guarantee success.

All the more reason she was being stupid wasting her time with two men she had no future with. She should be out there trying to find her soulmate before it was too late to fulfil her dreams of getting married and having a family.

"Are you okay?" Dalton asked, concern written all over his face.

Carrie smiled sadly and nodded. "I'm okay, it's just that sometimes I get a little... not sad but, I don't know, reflective or something about growing up as a single child."

"I'm sorry, I didn't mean to upset you."

"You didn't. I like hearing about your family, and about Bodhi's. You are both really lucky and your families sound wonderful."

"Wonderfully crazy," Dalton joked, leaning in and kissing her tenderly. "I hope I'm not overstepping the mark, but you look really sad... and I was wondering..." Looking unsure he shook his head. "Never mind."

"What were you going to say?"

"It's just... my natural impulse seeing you like that is to take you through to the bedroom and look after you..." He gave her a nervous glance. "You know... hold you... so you're not alone."

It was the worst possible suggestion, and the obvious thing to do was politely decline his offer, because emotion would be a dangerous ingredient to add to their purely physical relationship.

"I- I would like that."

What the fuck was she doing? Him taking her up against the wall in a public toilet was fine, him holding her while she battled to hold back tears wasn't.

No, she should just tell him she'd changed her mind and was going to go home, or even go as far as telling him they should stop seeing each other in any capacity because she couldn't risk getting attached and experiencing the heartbreak that would come as a result.

Instead, she followed him to his bedroom and didn't protest when he helped her out of her clothes or got out of his own. Sliding between the sheets with him, she wasn't thinking about leaving, or about reminding him their relationship was just physical. After finding her way into his arms and burying her face in his chest, she didn't stop the tears from coming, nor did she resist when he tightened his arms and whispered that he was there for her and she should just let it out.

She should have, God knew she should have; but she couldn't.

It felt painfully right to be in his arms, and she had no idea what that meant for her, or for the three of them.

***

It was still dark when she woke and realised she hadn't followed through with her plan of going home after she'd stopped crying into Dalton's chest.

She was tossing up the idea of whether she should sneak out of his bed and go home, when his arms tightened, and he nuzzled his nose against her cheek.

"You okay?" he whispered, kissing her cheek and lightly caressing her lower back.

"I'm fine, go back to sleep, we don't need to be awake yet."

Rather than rolling over and going back to sleep, Dalton shuffled closer to her and pressed his lips against hers. She opened her mouth to him and smiled lazily at the sensation of his tongue gently moving against her own, the sleepy fuzz in her head clearing and making her all too aware of the glow of heat spreading through her body.

For all the heat building between them, they continued kissing like that, slow and sensual, hunger building so gradually Carrie wasn't aware of her need for him until she rolled on her back and opened her legs to him without conscious thought. When he moved on top of her, there was none of the usual haste to move things along; the kiss continued playing out, their tongues dancing together, exploring, enjoying.

She moved fluidly against him, each gentle roll of her hips increasing the hum in her clit as the length of his cock glided slowly up and down her slit, becoming drenched in the evidence of her arousal. Whereas usually there would be a rush for him to push inside her, this time there was no impatient need, both enjoying the way it felt to be moving together, to indulge in the hardness of him, gliding against the softness of her.

This time, their sounds of pleasure were kept for one another, soft moans, almost silent groans, shaky whimpers, the shallow inhalations and exhalations evidence of the effort required to maintain control.

After what felt like a lifetime, Dalton reached for a condom; settling back between her legs he guided himself to her opening and, after pausing for a few seconds to kiss her, he slowly sunk into her wet core, both of them shuddering as she clamped around him.

Carrie's legs automatically went around his waist holding him in place so tightly that, when he began moving his hips, his cock stayed buried inside her, placing intense pressure on her clitoris, stoking the heat burning brightly, just waiting to ignite. The friction was overwhelming, and she fought an internal battle between loosening her legs—allowing him to move out of her, therefore easing the friction—and keeping him right where he was.

Letting him pull out wasn't really an option because she was addicted to the constant pressure against the back of her pussy, so rather than releasing him, she pulled him more tightly against her, clamping her teeth on his shoulder as pleasure sparked inside her.

His hips moved harder, grinding against her clit, until she felt herself quaking around him, trembling as she began contracting... tighter... tighter... her clit burning, an inferno developing, threatening.

The heat inside her combusted her, consuming her whole body, rocking her with an orgasm so intense she couldn't scream, only fight against it, a strangled growl sounding as she bit down on Dalton's neck, riding wave after wave of violent ecstasy.

In a case of good timing, their orgasms had hit at the same time and the force with which Dalton had pressed inside her triggered aftershocks, drawing out her orgasm far beyond what could be considered safe. She struggled to catch her breath, or maybe forgot *how* to breathe; either way, when her climax finally petered off all she was capable of was lying boneless beneath him, the room spinning around her.

Dalton slumped on top of her, his breath harsh against her skin... they lay like that for a couple of minutes until he mustered the energy to move away and get rid of the condom. His absence from her body was noted, her pussy pulsating as if in protest.

Carrie might have protested too, but before Dalton had even pulled the blankets over them, she was slipping into a heavily sated, sexed-out coma.

CHAPTER ELEVEN

On Wednesday evening, Carrie had been home for all of five minutes when there was a loud knock on the front door.

She hadn't made plans with Jess, so it wouldn't be her at the door, meaning it had to be someone trying to convince her to change her phone/internet/electricity provider, or asking her to give them just a few minutes to explain why she should donate the price of just one coffee a day to their charity or cause.

Stomping down the hallway she pulled the door open, ensuring she was wearing a look that said, '*I do not want whatever you're selling*'... but instead of a salesperson on her doorstep, she was greeted by two tall, beefy men with hair in varying shades of red.

"Surprise!" Bodhi cheered, waving his hands animatedly.

"Surprise, indeed!" laughed Carrie. "Did we have plans I forgot about?"

"Nope, but the weather is so nice we thought we'd go to the beach for a couple of hours and wondered if you wanted to join us?"

"Sure, that sounds fun! Come in and I'll get ready... we're not going swimming, right?"

Dalton screwed up his face like she'd suggested going skinny dipping in a tank of piranhas. "You crazy? You can if you want, but I'd sooner not deal with shrinkage issues."

"We were thinking more of fish and chips and then some lazing in the sun, or a walk along the beach," Bodhi explained. "Make the most of the sun, because next week it'll probably be cold again and we'll have the damn heating on!"

He had a point there; spring weather was about as bipolar as it came.

Leaving the men in the lounge, Carrie went into her room and quickly threw a few things in a bag, changed from her jeans into a skirt, then swapped out her ballet flats for flip flops. She hated the heat of summer, but there was something so promising about spring time, which she put down to being able to feel the sun radiating on your skin, the warmth somehow penetrating your soul.

Speaking of penetrating... she put a change of clothes in her bag on the off chance she might not sleep in her own bed that night. It wasn't that she planned on sleeping over, but having work clothes on hand would make it a lot easier in the morning if she did.

Half an hour later, they were sitting at a wooden picnic table on the edge of the beach, opening the fish and chips they'd purchased from a shop nearby. There was a light breeze wafting the unmistakable smells of a barbeque in their direction, another part of the warmer weather she loved.

"You'll need to come to ours for a barbeque sometime," Dalton said.

"Yeah, it's getting to that time of year, isn't it?"

"Sure is. Last game of the season for us is Friday. Season has gone so fast!" Bodhi smiled. "You should come to the game. Nova is going to be there, seems to think Aurelia will sleep the whole game in the baby sling thingy."

"My crazy lot will all be there too," Dalton added. "Although that may be more of a deterrent than anything.

"I'll come, I'm just sorry I won't get to see you playing some more this year."

"We'll get tickets to you before Friday, you'll be sitting with all the families and friends of the guys on the team... hope you don't mind."

"Course I don't mind, we are friends after all."

For a few minutes, Carrie listened while the boys spoke about their season—at her prompting. She couldn't believe how much hard work they had to put in, and began seeing them, and rugby league players in general, in a whole new light. Just because it wasn't an office job they had, there was the impression they could slack off and only turn up for game day, but there was so much more to it.

The actual playing of the game was only a tiny part of what they did. When they weren't playing, they had video analysis, team meetings, time in the gym, cardio sessions, training on the paddock as a team doing various drills, preparing and planning for the next game, looking at which opposition players had which weaknesses or posed what threats in certain areas of the game. That wasn't taking into account nutritional and mental health factors, or the often lengthy periods of rehab after an injury.

Many players, Bodhi told her, studied whilst playing so they'd have something to fall back on when their career came to an end, whether natural or forced. Dalton explained he had a business diploma and wanted to work with kids in some capacity, so was considering a teaching degree at some stage. Bodhi was planning on getting into a coaching role and, when he had time, went along and helped coach some of the lower age grade teams at the club he'd played for as a kid.

There was far more to them than their size, and fancy footwork on the field. They had to work hard to make a living just like anyone else, the only difference was they weren't stuck in an office all day, though some days probably wished they were.

"On Saturday we've got a family and friends get together at the club," Dalton said, and she noticed he looked shy. "Did you want to come? My family will be there, Bode's will be too, you can even invite that friend of yours if you want..."

She'd told them about Jess's apology and had mentioned her reason for being such a bitch. Things were still a bit tense between the two women, but surely if she invited Jess to spend the day at the club, Jess would finally believe they'd moved on.

"Should I bring anything?"

Bodhi shook his head. "Just bring your gorgeous self."

She knew it was just a figure of speech but couldn't help the blush that sprinkled her cheeks in response to his words.

"When the family friendly part of the day is over, we usually hit a few clubs, you're welcome to stay around for that too," Dalton said.

Jess would certainly enjoy that part.

"You don't have to stay the whole time," Bodhi said. "People usually come and go throughout the day."

"Sounds fun, it can count as an early birthday celebration for me," Carrie said and instantly wished she hadn't.

"When's your birthday?" Bodhi asked.

"Next Saturday. October twenty-seven."

"Well don't make any plans for that day, we'll organise something," Dalton said.

"No, it's okay," Carrie said hoping she didn't sound ungrateful. "My birthday isn't a big deal."

Bodhi jumped straight in, "Uh, yeah it is."

No, it really wasn't. Now that her parents had moved to Brisbane, she didn't really celebrate her birthday. Jess usually took her out for lunch but other than a phone call from her parents, and her aunty if she remembered, that was the extent of the celebrations— and she was happy with the way things were.

"What do you do to celebrate?" Dalton asked.

"Nothing really. Lunch with Jess, that's about it. Past few years, I've treated myself to a weekend at my parents' little holiday home on Avoca beach. We used to go there all the time when I was a kid, so I like going back and getting away from everything for a couple of days."

"Sounds fun," Bodhi said and smiled wistfully. "My dream is to have a house on the beach but having a view of it will have to make do for now."

"The beach is where I go to do all of my thinking," Carrie said, looking out at the horizon, inhaling a deep breath of salty sea air. "Should we go for that walk?"

Putting their rubbish in the closest bin, they walked down onto the golden sand and started off in a southerly direction, toward the surf lifesaving club.

With every step, she could feel herself unwinding, the magical qualities of the sun and sound of the surf casting their spell and making her forget about all the stresses in her life. She became absorbed in her surroundings; the warmth of the sand at her feet, abandoned sandcastles decorated with shells telling of the fun that had been had earlier in the day, children playing, families lazing around together, couples and friends enjoying the last of the sun, and even a few brave souls testing the water.

Conversation flowed, and Carrie wished it was the middle of summer, so they could spend another few hours taking in the sights and sounds of what was one of her favourite beaches.

Given how good it felt to have the sand between her toes again, Carrie decided she'd make a point of getting out to Avoca Beach in the very near future. She could invite Jess and they could have a girls' weekend, work on their tans by day and drink a lot of wine while watching chick flicks by night.

Now the sun was hiding away to the west the air had a certain chill about it and Carrie hugged herself in an attempt to fight off the cool breeze. Noticing her attempts to warm up, Dalton put an arm around her and tucked her into his side, his body heat flowing like lava through her veins.

"Should we turn back?" Bodhi suggested. "It's getting a bit cold, huh."

Saddened by the prospect of leaving, Carrie begrudgingly nodded her agreement. "I guess so."

"We can always come back," Dalton said, stopping and smiling down at her. "The beach isn't going anywhere."

"I know," Carrie put her arms around his waist and rested her head against him. "It has been nice being out here tonight. I always feel so different when I'm at the beach, like I forget about everything else going on in life, and it's just me and the sand and the waves."

Dalton put a finger beneath her chin and tilted her head up as he dipped down and kissed her, the warmth of his body encompassing her, the chill of the breeze no longer bothered her.

Breaking off the kiss, she stepped away and walked the few steps away to where Bodhi was standing, looking out at the horizon. He smiled when she came to his side and after a couple of minutes transfixed by the ocean, they turned to face each other and even in the fading darkness she could see the beautiful green of his eyes sparkling.

Joining her hands behind his neck, she pulled him to her, capturing his lips in a featherlight kiss that made him whimper against her mouth. Compelled to hear that sound again, she kissed him with even lighter lips and was rewarded by another shaky whimper, and the feeling of his body quivering in response to her touch.

"Come home with us?" Bodhi whispered, the green of his eyes burning into hers.

She wished her response didn't come as quickly, or naturally. "Yes."

Walking back down the beach, Carrie was flanked by—and holding hands with—both men, trying to ignore the fact that eventually she was going to have to end this thing between the three of them. The thought was upsetting, and not wanting it to ruin the peaceful state of mind she was currently in, she locked it away to be dealt with at another date... when she was finally ready to say goodbye.

***

Much like Carrie had expected, Jess was thrilled with her invite to the Kings end of season get together and had insisted on a shopping trip to buy the perfect outfit, even though Carrie had explained it was a low-key, informal affair.

They met at the mall on Wednesday night after work and spent two hours going from shop to shop while Jess tried to decide on something to wear. Eventually she'd blown over three-hundred dollars on various items of clothing, explaining she'd decide on the day what she wanted to wear. It was her one chance, Jess had said, of 'bagging herself a rugby league hottie' so outfit choice was of the utmost importance.

Carrie was a little disappointed that for Jess the day was going to be all about the men who were present, rather than spending time with her best friend and, for the first time, this aspect of Jess's personality annoyed her. Usually she would laugh it off, because being man-hungry was 'so Jess', but all of a sudden it irked her.

In another typical Jess-move, she bought two bottles of wine at the supermarket and insisted they have 'a few drinky poos' after shopping. Feeling guilty for being irrationally annoyed with her best friend, Carrie agreed but knew she'd regret it the next morning when she had to get up early for work then wondered when she'd become such a judgemental bitch.

Jess's house was closer to the mall, so it was her lounge they wound up in, with Channing Tatum as Magic Mike on the big screen TV and the wine going down far too easily.

During the non-stripping scenes of the movie, discussion inevitably turned to Carrie's sex life. While she was reluctant to talk about it to begin with, after a couple of wines, she was all too happily telling Jess about the blow job she'd given Bodhi in the shower and, in more explicit detail, the way he'd repaid the favour afterward.

"So, you're just doing it with Bodhi now?" Jess asked. "He's way hotter than Dalton, I don't blame you."

Something protective billowed inside her and she frowned at her best friend. "Are you blind? Dalton is... ugh, he's this big, raw, animal of a man. You can't really compare them because they're so different."

"In what way?"

"Bodhi is energetic and playful and... god, it takes me hours to recover." Her pussy clenched as she remembered the shower. Moving on to Dalton, she explained, "but Dalton is so bloody intense and... I don't know how to explain it, like he's all consuming... I lose all concept of space and time when he's inside me."

"Christ, woman! How the hell are you even able to think straight? All that sex would wear even *me* out, and that's saying something!"

Carrie laughed at Jess's comment, it really was saying something, and she loved that her friend could joke about herself that way. "On Monday I had sex with Dalton at some stupid hour of the morning and it was so hard to get up when the alarm went off... he almost had to drag me out of the bed and force coffee down my throat."

Jess sniggered. "Sure he didn't try to force something else down your throat?"

That protective, defensive thing reared up again and she couldn't hide the disgust she felt. "He would never do that, neither would Bodhi. Just because we have some slightly weird agreement doesn't mean they don't respect me."

Holding her hands up in surrender, Jess frowned and looked at her like she had lost the plot. "Okay, calm down, I was just joking."

She wasn't usually so uptight with Jess, but her remark about someone forcing a cock down her throat – whether a joke or not – had really pissed her off.

Jess had the sense to change the topic of discussion and they spent the next couple of hours gossiping about who had broken up, who was pregnant, who was cheating, and who was being cheated on. She didn't take quite as much joy out of their gossip session as she used to, unable to help wondering if she was acting as gossip fodder for Jess and her other friends.

It was in good faith she'd spoken to Jess about her situation with Dalton and Bodhi, and at the time it hadn't crossed her mind that their private discussion might become public knowledge. How much of the information Jess had shared with her that night had been told to her in confidence?

Carrie knew she was being stupid. Jess understood the sensitive nature of her relationship with the men and there was no way she would tell anyone else, not when the information becoming public could have serious ramifications for both men. Surely, if there was any risk of the secret getting out, via Jess, it would have happened already because she had known for a couple of weeks by that point.

'*Calm the hell down,*' Carrie chastised silently and reminded herself, '*it's Jess, she's your best friend and would never do anything to hurt you.*'

When Jess was in the bathroom, Carrie saw the screen on her cell phone light up and as she'd predicted, the message awaiting her was on the group chat with Bodhi and Dalton.

Dalton: What are you up to?

Carrie: At Jess's... we had wine... too much...

Bodhi: A bit drunk, are we?

Carrie: No! Not at all! Not even a little. Okay. Maybe a little.

Dalton: You staying the night?

Carrie: Probably not, she's kind of bugging me but that's because I'm a stupid, drunk judgemental bitch.

Bodhi: I don't doubt the drunk part... but refuse to believe the rest of it.

Dalton: How are you getting home? Not driving yourself I hope?

Carrie: Will ring a taxi car thing soon...

Bodhi: Don't be stupid, we'll come and pick you up when you're ready. We're way cheaper than a taxi

Carrie: Her house is kind of out of your way, well, a lot out of your way

Dalton: It's not a problem, and if her place is out of our way that means it's out of your way too, meaning a taxi will be even more expensive

Bodhi: And don't argue with us, we're picking you up. Let us know when you're ready

Dalton: And the address

Carrie: Obviously... dumbass. Address is 222 Carlisle... just come now, message me when you are outside.

Bodhi: See you soon x

Half an hour later, when Bodhi messaged her to say they were there, Carrie didn't have to worry about breaking it to Jess because, after going to the bathroom, her friend had gone into her room and passed out on the bed.

If Carrie had been the one to fall asleep, Jess would have left her to it and the next day called her a party-pooper and reminded her about it for the next six months. But what did Carrie do? Put a bottle of water beside Jess on the bedside table and draped a blanket over her so she wouldn't get cold then locked the front door before leaving.

Once she sat in the car, Bodhi presented her with a bag of McDonald's and she was far more excited about seeing that big golden M than she should have been. Dalton laughed when she started shoving fries in her mouth, but she didn't dare. In that moment, those fries were the best thing she'd ever tasted, and she couldn't get enough. Or at least that was the case until she got started on the Big Mac, her appreciation for the meaty delight sounding much like she was in the throes of an orgasm.

In the front of the car, Bodhi and Dalton were in hysterics listening to her, but she couldn't blame them, if roles were reversed, she'd have been laughing too, and getting video evidence for future use.

"You guys wanna come inside at my house?" Carrie asked and snorted when she realised her double entendre. "I said come inside," she laughed, almost choking on her mouthful of Big Mac.

That would have been sad; *'Drunk woman dies choking on Big Mac while laughing at herself'*.

"We will walk inside your house with you to make sure you make it safely to bed," Dalton said carefully. "But I have a feeling you won't be quite up to the other thing."

"I'm always up for you!" She giggled like a sixteen-year-old, correcting herself, "well, you two are!"

Bodhi turned around and reached into the back seat, to put his hand on her knee. "So, you're a giggly, silly drunk then."

"And horny," Carrie said. "Very horny. So horny that you're lucky I'm not sitting on your lap in the front seat right now."

"I don't know about lucky," Bodhi said, his hand moving half-way up her thigh.

Her legs fell apart and she bit her lip, waiting in anticipation for the moment his fingers brushed between her legs. They didn't though, and looking at him, she pouted.

"You can move your hand up if you want."

He smiled softly. "Let's just wait until we get inside."

Carrie was going to protest when she realised they were at the top of her street and waiting until they were home no longer seemed like such a hardship.

Dalton stopped outside her house and, when Carrie got out of the car, she almost lost her balance. For some reason the world had started spinning, or was she the one spinning? Either way, walking straight was impossible without the support of Bodhi and Dalton, and when they got to the front door, she fished around in her bag for her keys but couldn't find them. Bodhi took the bag from her hand and found them instantly, unlocking the door himself.

Now her house was spinning, and she squeezed her eyes tightly together to try and make it stop, but all that did was make it worse.

"How about we take you to bed?" Dalton said in a way that told her she had no choice in the matter.

Carrie shook her head. "No! I need the bathroom!"

Shaking her head was the worst possible idea and if it wasn't for the men she'd have collapsed into a heap on the floor. Her stomach flip-flopped and.... oh shit.

A mad rush ensued with Dalton and Bodhi getting her into position over the toilet without a second to spare. Carrie didn't have time to tell them to get out of the room before the contents of her stomach came up, a sight and sound she knew must have been disgusting and would send both men running.

When she'd finished, much to her surprise, Dalton and Bodhi were still in the bathroom and helped her to her feet. Bodhi passed her a cold flannel so she could wipe her face.

She was led slowly to her bedroom where she sat on the bed and, after realising someone had filled up her drink bottle and put it beside her bed, promptly fell backward because of the way the room was suddenly tilted at a forty-five-degree angle.

"Feet," Bodhi said, and she tried to lift her feet up but couldn't and giggled at the hilarity of it. "Or I'll do it myself." Taking her feet in his hands, he removed her shoes, then undid the button on her jeans and wiggled them down over her hips, dropping them on the floor.

Carrie expected her panties would be next, but instead he put his hands behind her knees and lifted her legs, turning her so she was lying on the bed properly. Wiggling up the bed, she stopped when her head came to a rest on the pillow and she smiled sleepily, the way the pillow was cradling her heavier than usual head felt like bliss. Blankets were moved over her and, though she was seconds away from it, she refused to give in to sleep.

"Are you going to get in?" she mumbled.

"Do you want us to?" one of the men asked, but she couldn't determine which because the inside of her ears felt fuzzy.

"I'm horny, remember."

"How about we just sleep instead," someone said. "You're in no state for anything else."

"Are you not attracted to me anymore?" She wasn't upset, just curious.

"Even in a drunken stupor you're hellishly sexy," Bodhi's mouth was moving so it must have been him who said it. "But I'm not in a habit of having sex with girls who are so drunk they can't even get themselves inside safely."

"Hellishly sexy?" Carrie scoffed. "That isn't me. Maybe you're the drunk person."

"If you want us to get in bed with you, you need to move into the middle because I'm sure as hell not spooning Bodhi," Dalton said, causing Carrie to laugh more hysterically than she should have.

"Bodhi is nice to spoon though."

"For you, maybe."

"You're nice to spoon as well. You're both nice to spoon. You're both just nice," Carrie mumbled, inching to the middle of the bed.

"You're nice too," Bodhi said in that way people do when they're sick of the drunk person who won't shut up.

"I'm going to miss you both when we need to stop the sex... I wish we could just keep doing it, but we can't, because... because..."

Before she could finish, Carrie lost her battle against sleep, slipping into a deep drunken slumber between the two men she'd just unknowingly spoken the painful truth to.

CHAPTER TWELVE

Through the throngs of people heading toward the entrance of the stadium, Carrie waved as she finally picked out Nova and Calum walking through the crowd. Nova was wearing Aurelia in a sling while Calum was the designated baby bag carrier.

"We found you!" Nova sounded relieved.

Carrie laughed and smiled as she took a peek at Aurelia, who was sound asleep without a care in the world. "I was sure I would miss you. I didn't realise how many people would be here!"

"Mum and Dad are already in there," Nova said. "We were late leaving because Aurelia decided it was a great idea to have a nappy blowout, requiring a full change of clothes."

Calum chuckled and nudged Nova with his elbow. "You did jinx it by saying it looked like we were going to leave on time."

"Oh, bugger off you!" Nova said handing him a ticket. "Go and prove to Mum and Dad we're actually here, maybe then Mum will stop ringing me every two seconds!"

Calum kissed his wife and blew a kiss at baby Aurelia, then joined the crowd walking toward the entrance.

"Right, lady, tell me what happened."

Carrie had woken up on Thursday morning without any memory of what had happened the night before, except for the part when she had told Bodhi and Dalton she didn't want what they had to end, and she had been so ashamed she'd hid in the shower until the two men had left for training.

Nova had rung her that afternoon to let her know Bodhi had given her Carrie's ticket as well since they were going to be sitting together, and Carrie had told Nova something had come up and that she wasn't going to be able to go. The other woman had called bullshit and refused to let her skip the game, promising they'd talk beforehand.

"Got horribly drunk the other night at my best friend's house. Bodhi and Dalton picked me up to take me home and had to help me inside... they put me to bed and at some point, I told them that I wished we didn't have to stop having sex and that I'd miss them when we did."

"And?" Nova prompted.

"And that's it..."

"You're freaking out about *that*?"

"Remember the part where what I have with them is just casual? Telling them I don't want to stop is about the worst thing I could have done."

"Why is it so bad?"

Carrie had a feeling Nova was trying to make her come to some grand realisation but refused to play along. "Missing someone means feelings, not wanting it to end means feelings, casual sex is all about *not* having feelings."

Nova put a sympathetic hand on her shoulder. "You're a human, feelings come naturally."

"They shouldn't though, not in this scenario! I need to end things now before someone gets hurt."

"End it then."

"But I—"

"Uh huh, you don't *want* to end it. So... don't end it!"

"It is all such a clusterfuck though, Nova. I like them more than I thought I would, to the point I have to force myself to stay away."

"Don't fight it then, just let whatever it is that's going to happen, happen." Nova said, like it was the easiest thing in the world. "Let me ask you, if you felt that way about one guy, what would you be doing?"

She had her there. The answer in that case was simple.

"I can't, though... I want to get married, I want babies, I want a future... I can't have that with Bodhi *and* Dalton."

"Why not?"

"Because there are three of us, not two. It's just not realistic. In a fantasy world, sure... but not in my world."

"Look, the only people who can decide on the terms of your relationship—whatever form it takes—are the three of you. Just because casual relationships for someone else means no feelings, doesn't mean that is the way it has to be for you guys. My advice is to just enjoy what you do have and don't worry too much about what might or might not happen in the future."

"I *am* enjoying myself... and the idea of just cutting myself off isn't something that appeals."

"That's your answer then," said Nova. "Just enjoy it. You'll know when it's time to sit down with them and talk more seriously about it."

"Thanks, Nova. I know you've probably got other crap to worry about, but I've got no one else to talk to and—"

"Don't apologise! I told you I was here if you wanted to chat, I really don't mind." Her phone buzzed and looking at it she rolled her eyes. "My mum, on the other hand, does mind that I'm not sitting in my seat right this second, so she can coo over her grandbaby. We better get up there."

Nova's mention of her mum brought with it the reality she was about to meet Bodhi's parents, something Carrie didn't feel prepared for. She didn't feel prepared for much of anything these days. Walking into the stadium, Nova promised Carrie their parents had no idea she was anything more to Bodhi than his friend and assured her there would be no awkward questions.

Lining up to enter the stand, Carrie told herself it was time to stop worrying about what might or might not happen, and that she was there to support her friends, and their teammates, as their season came to an end.

They took their seats minutes before the game got underway, and the moment she saw Bodhi and Dalton run onto the field she forgot all about her anxiety and confusion. The sight of the men took the breath from her lungs and she needed to remind herself to inhale as she was attacked by a bombardment of flashbacks—of the naughtiest kind. Her abdominal muscles tensed to fight the physical response taking place between her legs, but it was useless.

One look at the two men and she'd gone from tense and wanting to avoid them, to wet and throbbing, impatient to get the two men home so they could take turns making her scream.

Things would need to come to an end eventually, but Nova was right, in the meantime she should just enjoy herself... which wasn't a hard ask when Dalton and Bodhi were concerned.

***

"You're coming inside, right?" Nova asked when the game had finished, and they were making their way from down the stairs to where the players were milling around talking with fans.

"I thought I'd just make my way home... Tonight is about the guys and their families, and I'm neither."

"You're more family than you realise," Nova said, motioning with her finger for Carrie to turn around.

Turning, she saw Dalton's mum walking in her direction, a huge smile on her face and her arms wide open for a hug. For a moment she thought Dalton must have been behind her, but nope... it was her his mum enveloped in a brief, but tight hug.

"Lovely to see you, Carrie!"

"You too, Viv," Carrie smiled, noticing the rest of Dalton's family hovering a few metres back, watching them.

"Clara—Harlan's little girl—was dying to come and say hello to you during the game but we told her she could wait until afterward when we were inside with her Uncle Dolldoll."

"I... well, yes, of course!" She smiled and waved at Dalton's niece, who waved back enthusiastically. There was no way to get out of it now, was there? It looked like she'd be crashing the party and going into the inner sanctum.

"We'll meet you in there then, love," Viv said and walked back to the rest of the family.

"Not family, my ass!" Nova laughed. "Come on, we'll go say hi to Bodes and Dalton and then I'll take you inside."

Bodhi was deep in discussion with his parents, Jill and Mike, so Carrie went to Dalton first, having to restrain herself from jumping into his arms, which seemed the natural thing to do.

"Hey, you," Dalton said with a warm smile, his eyes focused solely on her.

Carrie stood before him with a goofy grin on her face and, while she probably should have said something a bit more coherent, simply said, "Hey yourself."

"I'm glad you came."

Beside her, Nova snorted. "I'm going to leave this one in your capable hands, Dalton... should probably go and say congrats to my bro."

"Subtle, isn't she?" Dalton laughed.

Pursing her lips and shaking her head, Carrie rolled her eyes. "Very."

He smiled shyly at her and looked down at his feet as he spoke. "It's okay for a player to hug a fan, right?"

"You have no idea what this fan wishes this player would do to her right now... but yes, a hug would be appropriate."

They hugged and the feeling of his firm body against hers made it harder to fight the urge not to jump into his arms or push him down onto the ground and straddle his face. "Wanna come home with us after this, for a little three-way celebration?" he whispered huskily, her mouth instantly going dry. Unlike another part of her anatomy.

She nodded in reply and stepped back from him, afraid she would forget where they were, and start kissing him or slip her hand inside those tight shorts of his and—

Carrie was grateful for the reprieve given to her, by the sound of children wildly screaming '*Uncle Dolldoll! Uncle Dolldoll!*', and after telling him she'd see him soon, she walked over to where Nova and Calum were standing with Bodhi and his parents.

Bodhi's eyes brightened when he saw her and without thinking, he put his arms around her waist, lifting her up for a brief kiss. There was nothing romantic about it, but it wasn't the type of kiss a man gave a friend, and when her feet were planted back on the ground, she noticed his parents looking at them in surprise.

"Mum, Dad, this is my friend Carrie. Carrie, these are my parents, Jill and Mike."

"Your sister introduced us before, you idiot," his mum laughed.

"So, friend, huh..." his dad said with a raised eyebrow.

"Friends, Dad. A man and a woman can just be friends, y'know."

"I married my best friend," his dad said with a look of satisfaction. "Just so y'know."

The situation was made all the more awkward when Dalton came to stand beside Bodhi, with his family following soon after. The Kendrys and Hooks greeted each other and the compliments for Bodhi and Dalton were soon flying, giving Carrie a chance to catch her breath, briefly.

"Carrie," Nova said sweetly. "How about you give me your phone and I'll take a photo of you with Bodhi and Dalton."

With all eyes on her she didn't have the opportunity to say no, so she handed Nova her phone and stood in front of the two men.

"Stand between them," Nova said, holding the phone up and sneaking her a devious look.

"Come here," Dalton laughed, taking a step sideways, allowing room for her to fit between them.

The proximity was a painful tease and she wished instead of standing together in a very public place they were in the privacy of a bedroom—or a house at least, where they could shed their clothes and she could be pinned between them in a far less innocent way.

Slipping an arm around both waists, she smiled for the camera and had a feeling Nova took her time on purpose. The longer she stood between them, the more she was imagining getting very sweaty with them, the words Dalton spoke earlier, '*three-way celebration*' ringing in her head. It was more of an insistent screaming actually, one she didn't think would disappear until that three-way celebration came into being.

Nova's game came to an end when Aurelia began crying in the sling, requiring the devoted attention of her mother. "Come on, we better get inside before this one screams the stadium down."

"We'll see you inside," Dalton said and leaned down as if to kiss her but stopped himself. "Soon. We'll see you inside, soon."

"I want a cuddle when I get in there," Bodhi called after them and Carrie turned, giving him a warning look, then realised he was talking about Aurelia.

Beside her, Nova was sniggering and as they walked away from where Bodhi and Dalton were standing with their families. "That wasn't half obvious."

Carrie cringed and looked at her new friend. "Fuck up."

"Love your wallpaper, by the way."

"Thanks, it's the view from the holiday house my parents have on Avoca Beach."

"Is it?" Nova asked, struggling to stifle a laugh.

Looking down at her phone, Carrie immediately saw what Nova thought was so funny. Her wallpaper was no longer the view of Avoca Beach, it was the photo that had just been taken of her and the two sweaty, but happy looking men.

"Bitch," she cursed, much to Nova's amusement as she put her phone back in her bag.

She'd change the wallpaper later.

***

Being grouped with all the families and friends after the game wasn't as nerve-wracking as Carrie had expected, in fact, she'd completely surprised herself by enjoying it.

The players she'd been introduced to had all been lovely and didn't treat her like she didn't belong, like she'd gone into it thinking they would. Everyone else had been just as nice and not one person looked at her in that curious 'what the hell are you doing here?' way, and a few had even said they hoped to see her at the get together the following day.

She was treated as if she belonged, but she knew the truth; she was a big ol' fraud who was only there because she couldn't wait to give Bodhi and Dalton their second workout of the evening.

Nova and Calum went home after they'd had a chance to talk to Bodhi and congratulate other team members on the win, at which time Dalton's family took her under their wing. His nieces and nephews seemed almost obsessed with her, but it worked to her advantage because it meant she could avoid discussion of a more adult nature, based primarily around what it was she wanted with their son/brother/brother-in-law.

Before leaving, Bodhi's parents stopped to say goodbye to her, saying it was lovely to meet her and they hoped to see her again. Carrie could tell they were curious about the nature of her relationship with their son and she was relieved they were kind enough not to broach that particular subject.

Though she'd enjoyed her time amongst the friends and family, Carrie was more than happy when Dalton told her they were ready to leave. She'd taken public transport to the stadium and her plan had been to take it back home but given her change in plans, she followed the men out to the carpark.

The trip only took fifteen minutes, but as far as she was concerned it might as well have taken fifteen hours, such was her impatience to get the men into a bedroom and take Dalton up on his highly inappropriate suggestion of a threesome.

The one-on-one bedroom time she'd been having with the men had been—she didn't want to say special because that suggested emotion, but she'd enjoyed it. A lot. The idea of being caught between both men as they writhed and ground against her? She was already mentally halfway to orgasm.

Bodhi and Dalton went into the lounge and Carrie stood in the doorway, looking at them. "You guys can chill out for a while if you want, but I am just *sooooo* tired, I think I need to get naked and lie in one of your beds... I'm a little horny so I guess without you guys there, I'll need to touch myself."

The lights in the lounge went off and two delicious hunks of man chased her down the hallway and into Dalton's bedroom, the room containing the nearest bed.

"We're tired too," Bodhi said, taking his top off and dropping it at his feet.

"So, so tired," Dalton agreed, his t-shirt already off, fingers working the button on his pants.

"We should probably all get into bed," Carrie said and tilted her head putting a finger to her mouth as if working out a problem in her head. "But... this horny thing, I don't know if it will just go away, and I don't know what to do about it." She sighed and made a sad face. "If I was at home, I'd just use my vibrator and squeeze my nipples until I came, and if I was really greedy, I'd keep fucking myself with the vibrator until I had another orgasm..."

A pained groan sounded from where the men were standing and was followed by a cough as one of them cleared their throat. It was Bodhi who spoke. "I'm sure between the two of us, me and Dalton can fuck the horny out of you..."

His words made Carrie scowl at how effectively they were playing her at her own game, and the way his words were causing such a physical response between her legs.

Dalton bridged the gap between the two of them and, with slow hands, helped her out of her top, at which point Bodhi stepped in behind her and ran his fingers up over her hips and waist, following her ribs to her spine, ghosting upward until he reached the clasp of her bra which he undid at the same time as Dalton popped the button of her jeans.

She was close to hyperventilating as Dalton pushed her jeans down her legs, while Bodhi's hands slipped around to her front and he cupped her breasts, tormenting her nipples through the lace with the tips of his fingers.

Her panties came down and she stepped out of them as Bodhi's fingers slipped inside her bra. She arched her back, urging him to take her nipples between his fingertips, while at the same time she widened her stance in invitation to Dalton, whose hands were moving up her inner thighs.

Nothing had prepared her for how overwhelming it would feel to have Bodhi rolling her nipples between his fingers at the same time Dalton was spreading her wet folds. It was hard to breathe and nearly impossible to concentrate, with the tension developing in her body. She was leaning against Bodhi now, unsure she would stay upright if it were up to her to keep her balance. Between her legs, Dalton's fingers were gliding through the wet slick, purposely avoiding her hole and her clit, stirring an ache she thought would never be relieved.

Two agonising minutes later, Carrie shuddered at the welcome intrusion of two fingers into her body, almost dropping to the ground when his thumb found her clit and began rubbing in light circles. It was then Bodhi added a second hand to the mix, both of her nipples now being squeezed tightly between the firm grip of his fingers.

She couldn't control the shuddering response of her body and it only got worse when Dalton slid his fingers out, pushing back in with the addition of a third finger. The pressure on her clit was increasing and a sob tore from her throat as she realised she was about to come before she'd even seen, let alone touched, a penis.

Bodhi applied more pressure with his fingers, her nipples caught between his vice-like grip, and Dalton's thumb worked her clit faster, harder, his fingers working in a come-hither motion, stroking all the spots that usually went neglected. It was too much, too fast, and she screamed as her orgasm hit; Bodhi's teeth dug into her neck and only added to the wild energy wracking her body.

A second before her legs gave way, Dalton's fingers left her body and Bodhi picked her up, carrying her to the bed where he lay her down. The men had rid themselves of their pants and boxers before she'd even moved to the middle of the bed and it wasn't until Bodhi gave her that smile that she realised who was in front of her and who was behind.

Dalton pressed up against her and she was briefly disappointed she could feel the latex barrier between them; she wanted to feel him, *really* feel him, but those thoughts were shunted from her mind when she felt his hand on her thigh and moved her leg back over his hip, as he lined himself up.

"Oh fuck," she gasped before he'd even pressed inside her,

There was nothing slow about the way he entered her; he pulled her into him as he forcefully pushed his hips forward and began pounding into her so hard she expected pain to follow. But it didn't, and rather than asking him to be a bit gentler, she started pushing back into him, *wanting* it harder, willing him to fuck her with all he had.

Teeth were tugging on her nipple, and as with Dalton's cock, she waited for the discomfort, but it didn't come, and she instinctively moved her hand behind Bodhi's head applying pressure, so he'd understand she wanted more.

Faster. Harder. The personification of fucking.

Carrie had only just had an orgasm and while she'd thought she'd have a couple, hadn't expected them to be so close together... and this one that was building. Fuck. She wasn't going to survive it, there was no way her body could cope with what was building inside her.

And then Bodhi had to make things worse by moving his hand between them and start rubbing her clit. He didn't start out light either, instead going straight for the firm, tight circles that made the pleasure coil tightly, and tighter still until she was rigid all over, her body trying to fight the heat screaming through her veins.

Tighter, and tighter, it was too much; her body gave in and she screamed until her throat was raw, her body convulsing with each pulse of the orgasm the men were dragging out of her. Dalton's hips kept slamming, Bodhi's fingers working her clit furiously. It kept coming. There was no end to the tsunami that had engulfed her, so completely.

She didn't just come down from that orgasm, she crashed.

Her body felt hypersensitive and she smacked Bodhi's hand away, only to find he was no longer touching her; she tried to pull away from Dalton, who was still filling her to the hilt, but realised he had already rolled away and currently had his back to her, removing the condom.

"I-that—"

"Shhh baby, just go to sleep," Bodhi whispered, his voice a soothing sing-song.

Carrie melted into him, loving the way their bodies slotted neatly together like two pieces of a jigsaw puzzle. She felt so protected, so cared for... her brain far too full of the glorious post-orgasm haze to care that she shouldn't have been feeling either of those things. Dalton slid in behind her and the way his body cupped hers so completely and perfectly made her chest ache in an indescribable way. Something was happening, and she had no control over it; but there, in that bubble of serenity, she didn't want control.

CHAPTER THIRTEEN

The weather couldn't have been more perfect for the end of season get together; there wasn't a cloud in the sky and as if to make up for the shitty weather of the past few days, the sun was shining brightly and throwing off summer-esque heat.

Bodhi and Dalton had picked her and Jess up an hour earlier, but since arriving at the stadium, Jess had hardly spoken to her. It was, after all, hard to talk to someone who was more interested in mingling with the single men on the team. Not that Carrie minded, it was nice to see Jess—ever the social butterfly—doing her thing.

A bouncy castle had been inflated down one end of the field and it was covered with children; she'd expected a gathering of rugby league players to be loud but hadn't thought the noise would be courtesy of all the kids in attendance.

As she took a look around the field, it struck her how family orientated the whole get together was. Down the opposite end of the field a group of the players was having a game with some of the kids and she wasn't sure who was having more fun, the children or the adults.

Bodhi and Dalton were amongst that group, along with Dalton's brothers and Calum, and Carrie was finding it hard not to be distracted by the sight of her two men acting like clowns. She'd never seen either smile more broadly and it was with sadness she realised that before long, Dalton and Bodhi would each find a woman to settle down with and start a family of their own. They'd be such good daddies, something that was only adding to the list of reasons whatever it was they had had to finish sooner rather than later.

"You okay?" asked Nova, who was sitting beside her.

Carrie smiled sadly. "Just... thinking."

"Do I need to ask what about?"

"No..."

"Try not to worry about the future, hun. Things have a way of working themselves out."

What would that entail? Either Bodhi or Dalton finding a woman to settle down with, leaving her free to look more seriously at a relationship with the other? That would solve the problem of being excessively fond of two men at the same time, but... the idea of seeing either man with someone else made her feel queasy.

"Is Kat coming today?"

Nova laughed, "definitely not, she isn't really a fan of big social things like this."

"That's a pity."

"You are so transparent," Nova said. "It's almost painful. I meant it when I said everything will work out in the end, so *please* stop fretting. Just enjoy it, remember?!"

"Being able to enjoy it isn't the problem… it's enjoying it *too* much that I'm struggling with."

"Can't help how you feel, trust me. The harder you fight it, the more miserable you'll be."

"Why must you be so wise?" Carrie sighed and found her eyes drifting back to the cluster of men spread out on the southern end of the field.

Though there must have been thirty-odd men and at least as many kids playing, her eyes instantly picked out Dalton and Bodhi. There was no ignoring the way her stomach flip-flopped as she drank them in, her skin flushing hot and cold when she remembered the orgasms they'd treated her to the night before.

It wasn't much of a step to imagine what else they could have done in that bedroom. She'd never had anal sex and it hadn't been something she'd cared to experience, but since meeting Bodhi and Dalton she'd found herself wondering what it would be like to have both of them inside her at the same time, often fantasising about it late at night. A tiny part of her had been hoping it might be brought up in conversation before they wound up in Dalton's bedroom the night before, but she sure as hell wasn't going to be the one to mention it.

Not yet, anyway…

A light tap on her shoulder was followed by the lispy English of a young child she quickly identified as one of Dalton's nieces. "Cawwie, you want to pway wif me?"

"Uh, sure." Carrie smiled. "What is your name?"

"My name Lucia Gwace Kendwy." She looked at Nova and whispered, "What is your baby name?"

"Hi Lucia, I'm Nova and this is Aurelia."

"Auwewia can pway too if she wants," Grace said, and Nova gave her a big smile.

"That is so kind of you, Lucia. Aurelia is a bit little to play, but we will come and watch you and Carrie if you want?"

"Yes pwease!"

Giggling quietly, and quite taken by little Lucia, Carrie and Nova stood up and followed her in the direction of the bouncy castle. After a few metres the little girl stopped and waited for them, before putting her tiny hand in Carrie's, something about the gesture bringing tears. Would this be what it was like when she was a mum? *If* she ever became a mum.

"Going to introduce me to your friend?" Jess's voice came from behind her, giving Carrie a fright.

"Shit! You scared me!"

"My Mummy said dat is a bad bad word," Lucia interrupted.

"I'm sorry, Lucia. Your mummy is right, it is a bad word and I shouldn't have used it."

Lucia pointed at Jess. "Who dat wady?"

"This is my best friend, Jess. Jess, this is Dalton's niece, Lucia."

"On babysitting duties already, huh," Jess said with raised eyebrows, completely ignoring the child.

"No, Lucia asked me if I wanted to play with her, so I believe we're going to have a little jump on the bouncy castle."

Jess sniggered. "Fun."

"Hey, Lucia, if Carrie will take Aurelia for me, can I come and play with you?" Nova asked and Carrie couldn't help but think it was a dig at Jess.

Speaking of Jess... "Nova, this is my best friend, Jess. Jess, this is Bodhi's sister, Nova."

"Bodhi's sister, eh," Jess said bitterly. "Really is becoming a family affair." The hearty laugh that followed her bitchy comment was by no means a friendly one.

"Any friend of my brother is a friend of mine," Nova said with a warning tone in her voice that sent Carrie into action.

"Right! Give me that little cutie and you two kids can go and have fun," she said, holding her arms out for Aurelia, who as usual, was strapped to Nova's chest in a baby carrier.

Nova loosened the straps and with delicate movements took Aurelia in her arms and placed her in Carrie's. Removing the sling she placed it on the ground and toed off her sandals, inspiring Lucia to do the same.

"If she starts fussing, just wave me over," Nova said and took Lucia's hand. "Come on munchkin, let's go and get our bounce on."

"Bye, Cawwie!" Lucia waved as she took Nova's hand and they ran in the direction of the bouncy castle.

Carrie turned to Jess and frowned. "That was a bit rude."

"What?"

"The passive aggressive bullshit toward Nova."

"You need to stop being so sensitive, Carrie. I wasn't being passive aggressive, I was just pointing out that you're friendly with both of their families, which is odd for someone who is just sleeping with a guy, sorry, guys."

Had they been in a more private place, Carrie would have continued the discussion, but a bitch fight in front of people she hardly knew wouldn't be a good look, so she swallowed her words and changed the topic.

"Looks like you had a captive audience over there." She motioned to the group of men Jess had been speaking to.

A self-satisfied smile spread across her face. "Looks like I may have my pick tonight."

"Any front runners?"

"Well, remember the guy from the gala that made eye contact with me? Jed? Anyway, he's been smiling at me a lot in that dirty way guys do when they're imagining what it would be like to fuck you."

Carrie laughed. "Sounds very promising."

She may have laughed, but inside she felt uncomfortable with the discussion. The two women had spoken like that plenty of times before, but that day it felt... dirty, to be listening to her friend talking in a way that showed how little self-respect she had. Jess often joked that all a guy had to do to get in her pants was smile, and it occurred to Carrie the comment wasn't so much a joke as it was fact.

Who the fuck was she to judge though? Bodhi and Dalton were proof she didn't have a moral compass, and to be thinking that way about her best friend was shameful.

But... the older they got, the less Jess's habit of sleeping with whoever took her fancy seemed like an amusing personality trait. The one-time Carrie had brought it up with her, Jess had explained that having sex made her feel attractive and wanted, which made her feel good about herself. Carrie had not brought it up again, after all, who was she to question the way her best friend lived her life?

Sure, Jess took risks and Carrie couldn't count the number of pregnancy scares there had been, or the times her friend had confided in her about receiving treatment for a sexually transmitted nasty; but she was an adult and was in charge of her own life, and more importantly, her own body. Somewhere in the back of her mind Carrie had envied Jess and her ability to take what she wanted without caring what anyone thought.

Had being the operative word.

With the exception of the shared barbecue lunch, Jess didn't talk to Carrie for the rest of the time they were at the stadium. Carrie sensed her best friend didn't want anything to do with her for the time being and, given the tension between them, the distance wasn't necessarily a bad thing.

It was late afternoon when Jess finally approached Carrie, only to inform her she'd no longer be needing a ride home because Jed was taking her back to his house to kill some time before they all met later in the evening at a club.

Carrie forced a smile for her best friend and, with a knowing wink, told her to enjoy herself. Who knew, maybe having sex would make Jess forget about whatever it was that was causing her to be such a bitch? Wasn't it what she'd wanted, after all—to be able to tell the world she'd fucked a professional sportsman which, in her eyes, would give her instant social status.

"Hope she realises that guy is a fucking snake when it comes to women," said Austin, one of the players Bodhi and Dalton got along with well and whom she'd been introduced to after the game the night prior.

"I get the feeling she'll be more than capable of handling him," Bodhi said.

They were sitting on the grass in a group, the setting a lot quieter now most of the children had been taken home and only a few stragglers remained—mostly the single guys and the ones who didn't have kids.

"He might have met his match," Carrie said, trying to sound light-hearted but unable to keep the strain from her voice.

Austin laughed and leaned back, propping himself on his elbows. "Good luck to both of them in that case."

Dalton was lying flat on the grass with his hands resting above his head and Carrie found herself distracted by the trail of ginger hair running from his belly button to down beneath the waistband of his shorts. She forced herself to look away from him when she began picturing herself kissing said trail, down, down, down, following the smattering of hair until her lips came in contact with his penis, which would, of course, be rock hard and too tempting to ignore.

Looking up, she caught Bodhi just as he looked away and wondered what it was he'd been thinking about; judging by the way he'd casually put his hat over his crotch it didn't take a genius to guess.

They weren't meeting at the club until 8 p.m., leaving ample time for... what was it Jess had said, 'killing time'? It was currently 4 p.m. meaning if they left soon, they could kill time repeatedly before needing to leave the house to meet everyone at the club.

"We should go," Bodhi said, beating her to the excuse making. "If you want us to... mount... that TV... in your room, we should probably do it now."

It was a pitiful excuse and she fought not to laugh as the three of them stood up and said their goodbyes. Something told her everyone saw through the excuse and knew it wouldn't be the TV getting mounted, but she didn't care. Like Nova had said, why shouldn't she enjoy it? It was just a little fun and she had nothing to be ashamed of.

***

It was 9 p.m. when they walked into *Surge*, offering up the excuse of their taxi being a no-show to explain their lateness. Whether people believed them or not, no one suggested there was another reason behind their delayed arrival—except Jess, who drunkenly made a blowjob motion with her hand.

For a split-second, Carrie was worried Jess was going to say something, instead she stumbled over to where Carrie and the boys were standing and hugged her.

"I'm so glad you're heeeeere!" Jess screeched. "I missed you!"

"Missed you too," Carrie said, not sure whether either of them meant their heartfelt declarations.

"Jed is suuuuuuuuuuch a good lay!" Jess whispered loud enough for Bodhi and Dalton to hear.

"You been here long?"

"Long enough to have a few vo'ka limes!"

That Carrie didn't doubt.

"I'm going to go get us some sodas, do you want one, Jess?" Bodhi asked, frown lines interrupting what was the face of a god.

Jess laughed, loud and obnoxiously. "Soda? Nooooooo, I'll take a vodka and lem- lime though, thanks Bo-Bo."

The man Carrie had been briefly introduced to but didn't have any inclination to get to know well put an arm around Jess's shoulder. "Don't worry, babe, I'll get you a proper drink."

"Thanks Jed, you're the best." Jess kissed him like there was no one else in the room. "And you give the best orgasms." More kissing. "Wanna go to the bathroom so you can give me another one?"

"Enjoy your sodas," Jed scoffed and squeezed Jess's boob roughly. "Come on, sexy."

Carrie was left speechless, much like everyone else in the group, all watching Jess and Jed as they made their way through the crowd in the direction of the sign indicating the bathrooms.

Dalton was first to speak. "That was disturbing."

"Putting it mildly," Bodhi agreed, looking perplexed. "It was like... a sex show, or something."

"How about a drink and some dancing?" someone called out.

"Anyone got some bleach for my eyes?" someone else joked and everyone laughed.

"Can't offer bleach, but this round is on me! Shots for everyone!" Dalton shouted and was met by much cheering. "To the lounge we go!"

Because they were the Kings, and were seen as local royalty, they were admitted to the VIP lounge, allowing them access to the dance floor as well as their own bar and big cushy booths and couches to lounge around on.

When the barman came over with the tray of shot glasses full of tequila, Dalton made a toast to the team and a season that, although it hadn't gone as well as they'd hoped, had been an improvement on the last one. Next year would be their year, he proclaimed, and everyone drank to that.

A bottle of tequila was brought to the table, courtesy of the establishment, but Carrie limited herself to another two shots, enough to get a buzz on, but not so much that she'd be likely to act in a way that she'd regret in the morning.

Bodhi and Dalton also limited their intake and even though she told them she didn't mind if they wanted to drink more—it was their celebration after all—but they, for similar reasons to hers, opted for non-alcoholic drinks after three or four shots. To her surprise, there were a few that limited themselves, going completely against the stereotype of the booze-loving league player.

Of course, there were some who did keep throwing the drinks back, quickly reaching various levels of intoxication.

The group was getting rowdy and even though she was essentially sober, Carrie was having a great time being in a party atmosphere. She always found she had more fun when she wasn't completely trashed, partly because she got to watch everyone else act like idiots and had the pleasure of laughing at them. Drunk people were entertaining, that was for sure.

"Oh shit, Austin is off," one of the guys from the team laughed and pointed down to the dance floor where Austin could be seen dancing closely with a woman.

"She looks old enough to be his mum!" Carrie giggled.

"That's Austin's thing," Bodhi said. "He has a thing for the older ladies... for a while he had a bit of a thing for Nova, which was pretty funny. Think he died the night he was at my place and Nova was there with Kat and they kissed in front of him."

Carrie rolled her eyes. "Every man's dream, isn't it?"

"Not every man," Dalton said.

"And definitely not when it's my sister," Bodhi laughed.

At their own little seat for two away from the rest of the group, Jess and Jed were back from their bathroom rendez-vous but looked to be getting close to a repeat, judging by the way she'd straddled him and the way his hand had disappeared up her skirt.

The beat of the music was calling to her, but there was no way she was going to hit the dance floor alone.

"Either of you want to go dance?"

Bodhi stood up. "I'm keen!"

Standing beside Bodhi, Dalton smiled at her and nodded. "Count me in!"

They walked down the staircase leading to the dance floor and quickly got lost in the throngs of people dancing to music from the '90s and early 2000s.

How the hell was music she'd grown up with now considered old school? That was implying *she* was old. Though, compared to Bodhi and Dalton who were aged twenty-five and twenty-six respectively, she was ancient. Not that they seemed to have a problem with her advanced age.

Given all the sex she'd been having, it was a miracle she hadn't broken a hip!

She quickly got swept away by the thrum and beat of the music and struggled to remember ever dancing as much or enjoying herself so immensely. It helped she was plastered between Bodhi and Dalton, the heat of the crowd making them sweaty, reminiscent of the condition they found themselves in after having sex.

Mmmmm, sex.

The closeness of the men became too much and Carrie, lost in the music and the atmosphere, pulled Bodhi down until their lips met in a passionate kiss, while they moved their bodies in time with the beat. Dalton was pressed against her with his hands on her hips, his cock a ridge against the small of her back which she couldn't resist rubbing against. His breath tickled her skin with each exhale and when she felt the tip of his tongue run down the tendon in her neck, she moaned into Bodhi's mouth.

Bodhi tugged on her bottom lip with his teeth and in response she rolled her hips against Dalton, who, in what was a domino effect, bit down on her neck.

Fuck. If she hadn't bagged Jess earlier for rushing off to the bathroom with Jed, that was where she'd have been dragging Bodhi and Dalton in the next minute or two. Burying her face in Bodhi's neck she screamed with frustration. She was having a tantrum over not being able to have sex. Maturity plus.

When Usher's hit, *Let it Burn*, came on, Carrie knew she was doomed; with its slow, sultry beat, the song had always made her think of sex. Dancing between Bodhi and Dalton as she was, sex was already at the forefront of her mind and the song only amplified the frustration torturing every cell in her body.

Pulling Bodhi down by the collar of his shirt, Carrie put her lips to his ear and asked, "How long until we can go home?"

"A little horny, are we?"

Carrie grimaced, his words going straight to her clit. "Your fault. And Dalton's. You're both awful teases."

Bodhi said something to Dalton and she scowled at him, wondering what he was plotting. No doubt something that would cause her to leave a trail of horny juice wherever she moved. Bloody men and their stupid, irresistibly wicked ways.

Her sulking ceased the moment two pairs of lips caressed her neck. Bodhi trailed wet kisses from crook to ear, while Dalton grazed with his teeth, the heat of his breath setting a fire beneath her skin.

Without any thought Carrie's hand made contact with their cocks, massaging and squeezing as if they were the only people in the room.

But they weren't. Shit.

"We're going. Now," she ordered with a stern voice that didn't belong to her.

"You bet your fucking ass we are," Dalton growled into her ear, slapping her ass for good measure.

"Your house is closer," Bodhi said breathlessly.

Not bothering to say goodbye to the people they were meant to be with, they pushed through the sea of writhing, dancing bodies toward the exit. People were pointing at Bodhi and Dalton in a way they were probably very accustomed to but was foreign to her. From discussions they'd had, she knew both men liked to take the time to fans who stopped them, but that night both seemed to have tunnel vision and, much like her, had only one thing on their mind.

By some miracle, a taxi was waiting outside the club and as they all piled into the back—Carrie in the middle, of course—she gave the driver her address.

Before the driver had even manoeuvred the car into the stream of traffic Carrie's fingers were dipping into the waistbands of Bodhi and Dalton's pants, unable to wait a second longer to finally feel the throb of steel against her palm.

CHAPTER FOURTEEN

Why was Bon Jovi singing to her? And just why was he living on a prayer? Those were the first thoughts to cross Carrie's mind as she was wrenched from sleep. Bon Jovi hadn't snuck into her room, she realised, it was her cell phone ringing.

Reaching over Dalton she picked it up and saw it was Nova. What on earth was she ringing her for so early? Okay, 10:30 a.m. wasn't technically early, but considering she'd only fallen asleep around 5 a.m. it was early to her.

She answered the phone and, with a dry mouth, greeted Nova. "Hey..."

"Sorry to ring you but this is important. Are the boys with you?"

"Yeah, they are. What's wrong?"

Had something happened to Aurelia? Even if it had, why would she be ringing her and not Bodhi?

"You better put this on speaker," Nova said.

Carrie shook Bodhi and Dalton, "Nova is on the phone, something is wrong."

Bodhi sat up, panic on his face. "What is it?"

"Sorry to wake you guys up like this," Nova said. "But shit is going to hit the fan, in fact it probably already has."

"What do you mean?" Dalton asked, suddenly alert.

"The *Telegraph*—there are photos of the three of you taken last night."

Dalton cradled his head in his hands. "Oh fuck."

Bodhi cringed and asked, "What sort of photos? Bloody hell, please don't tell me they're from the taxi?"

"What? No, not from a taxi. From the club last night, photos of the three of you looking very intimate..."

"As in?" Bodhi prompted.

"Five photos. One of Carrie and Bodhi kissing, one of Carrie and Dalton kissing, one of Carrie kissing Bodhi while Dalton bites her neck, one of Carrie pressed back into Dalton, and one of you guys both kissing Carrie's neck at the same time."

"Oh fuck. Anything other than the photos?" Dalton asked, picking up his phone and holding it out to show Carrie and Bodhi his four missed calls from his mum.

"No, just a caption, '*Kings players Dalton Kendry and Bodhi Hook celebrate the end of the season with the help of a mystery woman*', and then something about a source who wished to remain anonymous that had seen the three partying together at *Surge* on Saturday night."

"Could be worse, I guess," Dalton sighed. "I've got missed calls from mum, so I should probably go and call her..."

Carrie watched Dalton walking from the bedroom and felt the room closing in on her.

"Sorry to have to ruin your day waking you up like this," Nova said. "It will blow over though, don't worry. It's just a few photos."

Just a few photos? Carrie knew she'd gotten carried away at the club but hadn't thought for a second there would be this type of repercussion. At the most, she'd expected Bodhi and Dalton to get a ribbing from their teammates who'd been there, but now those photos were public property and would be seen by hundreds of thousands of people.

She wasn't named, but Bodhi and Dalton were, and it was their careers most at risk from something like that going public. No one cared who she was in the grand scheme of things, but the media were going to eat Bodhi and Dalton alive—she'd seen it happen before when high profile people were outed for doing something or someone they shouldn't. It was all her fault; if she had suggested they go home earlier, like she was going to, they wouldn't have been on the dance floor in front of everyone.

The next question was, who the hell had leaked the photos? Who would do something like that? It wasn't like they'd been breaking any laws, and any night in a club you could find men and women kissing and grinding and groping on the dance floor. The difference was, no money could be made from photos of 'normal' people getting kinky in the club, and whoever had shared those photos was a lowlife piece of scum who obviously didn't have anything better to do with their life.

"I'm so sorry," Carrie said, swallowing back tears. "I didn't mean for this to happen."

"Hey, don't cry!" Bodhi put an arm around her and held her against his side. "This type of shit happens when you're in the public eye and you just have to roll with it."

"But what if you guys get in trouble with the club?"

"They'll talk to us about it, for sure, but it's only some photos and we were all fully clothed. It will blow over."

"How can you be so sure?"

"Because this type of crap happens all the time. Hasn't happened to me before, but I know enough people it has happened to, to know it'll blow over soon enough." Bodhi said, rubbing her back. "Come on, let's get up and get some coffee into us."

She felt so stunned by what had happened that she didn't even point have a witty comeback about there being something else she'd like to get into her.

***

After fielding calls throughout the morning from various people they knew, Bodhi and Dalton had eventually been called in to have a meeting with someone from the club at midday.

They'd left with promises it would be okay and that they weren't going to get in any trouble, but it didn't stop Carrie from feeling awful. She'd never be able to forgive herself if Bodhi and Dalton's careers were impacted because of her stupid lack of self-control and she found herself wondering if the whole incident was maybe a message from the universe that it was time to end things.

She didn't want to end things though. Not yet. Their ability between the sheets wasn't even the main selling point, she genuinely liked both men and enjoyed spending time with them. They treated her with the type of respect and courtesy she'd always dreamed of, and she hadn't once felt pressured by them to do anything, or to act in a way that wasn't being true to herself, and that was a rare find.

A little after two, her phone started to ring and, without looking, Carrie knew it was her parents. They were going to be so disappointed in her, and she considered not answering... but that would be like saying she was ashamed of what she had with Bodhi and Dalton, so with shaking hands, she picked up.

"Hi Mum."

"Hi love," her mum said, her voice tense. "Carrie, I saw those photos. What the hell is going on?"

"Oh, Mum. I'm so sorry," Carrie said, her lip quivering with the effort of fighting back tears. "I-I didn't me-mean for it to h-happen."

"Who are those men? How do you know them? Do you even know them? What were you thinking?" Her mum sounded flustered and Carrie could just picture her parents sitting in the lounge, her dad rubbing her mum's back, or stroking her hand, not wanting to believe their sensible daughter could have done something so irresponsible.

"Their names are Bodhi and Dalton, I have known them for about a month now. They are good friends of mine."

"Carrie, it's Dad here," her dad finally spoke. "Didn't you realise people would see you if you were fooling around like that in public? Especially with two men who I understand are in the professional league competition?"

"I'm so sorry," was all Carrie could get out. "I know I've disappointed you."

Her dad's sigh was loud and long. "You're old enough to run your own life now, Caz," he eventually said. "But it was a hell of a shock to see those photos online this morning."

"It wasn't fun for me either," Carrie said bitterly, knowing she had no right to take that type of tone with her parents; they weren't the ones who'd gotten her in this situation.

"Look. We love you, okay? If you want to talk, you know where to find us…" It was the most emotion she'd heard from her dad in years.

"Love you guys too," Carrie said. "And I am sorry."

"We don't want to keep you, we're sure you're probably not in the mood to talk about it, but we had to say something."

"It's okay, Mum."

"We love you," her parents said at the same time and Carrie half-smiled.

"Love you guys as well. Bye."

She was bawling hot, salty streams of tears before she'd even put the phone down. How had she made such a mess of everything? Instinct told her to reach out to Bodhi and Dalton, but she'd already done too much damage where they were concerned, and it was best for all of them if she stayed away for a while, or maybe forever.

The idea of the photos being a sign from the universe shuffled through her mind again and she wondered if it was time to blow the whistle on their arrangement. Or perhaps what she needed was to choose one to be with, if that was even possible. Truth was, she didn't like one over the other, didn't get on with one better, didn't have a stronger connection with one; if Bodhi and Dalton could somehow be combined together the result would be her perfect man and then she wouldn't have anything to worry about.

Couldn't go making it too easy on herself though.

She was contemplating having a bath when she heard a knock at the door. Excitement and relief bubbled; if Bodhi and Dalton turned up, it was completely out of her hands and wasn't the same as her reaching out to them.

"I'm in the kitchen!" she called, leaving out the part that she was in there to get a glass of wine to drink in the bath.

But it wasn't Bodhi or Dalton who walked into the kitchen, it was Jess and judging by the smile on her face, she'd missed all the scandal. Lucky her.

"How are you on this fine day?" Jess asked, dropping her bag on the bench.

Carrie handed her a wine glass. "Crap..."

"Aaah yes, that feeling when your world starts crumbling around you and there is nothing you can do to stop it."

So, she had heard?

"A little sympathy would be nice," Carrie sighed, filling the two glasses.

"Sympathy? Why? Because you're realising even your perfect little life can be tipped on its head?"

She paused mid-pour. "Excuse me?"

"Oh, Carrie. Sweet, innocent, *perfect* little Carrie." The look on Jess's face was full of venom. "I've been waiting so long to see you fall, just didn't think it would happen quite so sensationally."

Was she mistaken, or was Jess's voice painted with glee? "Jess... what's going on?"

The woman who'd been her best friend for over half of her life simply rolled her eyes. "I did warn you that it was a bad idea to carry on fucking Bodhi and Dalton." She shrugged. "As usual you thought you knew best, you are Carrie Lucas after all, and you're far better than the rest of us, especially your best friend."

"What are you saying?" The hairs on the back of her neck were standing on end. "Did you have something to do with the photos?"

Jess laughed in a way that made Carrie nauseous. Surely she was wrong...

"It was too easy," Jess said. "The three of you were dancing for everyone to fucking see, so I did what anyone with half a mind would do and took some photos." She narrowed her eyes and continued. "A quick email to my friend Mark at the *Telegraph* and boom!"

Carrie gasped and felt the floor moving under her feet. She put her hands on the counter to steady herself. "*You* leaked the photos? Why?!"

"You've always thought you were so much better than me, Carrie. You got better marks at school and university. You were always getting awards for your writing and for being a member of this or that society... and then your fucking dream job fell into your lap and suddenly you were a big career woman. You got the house, you got the car, you went to gorgeous parts of the world... and then you came to the gala with me and it was *you* who hooked up with not one but two men. We all know you only stayed friends with me so you could lord it over someone."

Jess was so fucking off the mark it was unbelievable and, for the first time in their friendship, Carrie wondered about the stability of Jess's mental health. She had always been the one envious of the life Jess led. Jess had never once said she envied a single thing Carrie had—the opposite in fact, she spoke at length about how boring it was to be a responsible adult, and that she'd never swap their lives for anything.

"What the fuck Jess? That is so—"

Jess raised her hand and interrupted. "Hold on honey, I'm not finished. You see, I've known for a long time about all the money you've got stashed away for your grand round the world trip, and I knew if I put up with you, the time would eventually come that I could cash in on the bore-fest that has been this friendship."

Carrie was devastated. "How can y—"

Jess pointed to her own mouth. "Still talking. Where was I? Oh yeah, cashing in. See, I'm not as stupid as you think I am so when you began telling me all the dreary details of your sex life with Bodhi and Dalton, I was clever enough to record every single word you said."

"You—"

"Every single word. The threesomes, the blow jobs, hard and fast in the disabled toilet, the hand jobs, the fingering... all of it, Carrie—recorded on my phone and backed up on a USB, because as I'm sure you know from your line of work, only an idiot doesn't back up the important stuff."

"Why are you doing this? What do you want from me?"

"See, I'm sick of living in Australia and, through connections at work, I have a job lined up in Los Angeles. I just need the money to relocate... around twenty thousand should do it."

Carrie couldn't believe what she was hearing. "Twenty-you're-you expect me to give you twenty thousand dollars, so you can move to LA?"

"Pay me the twenty thou and I will delete the voice recordings I have... I go away and your little problem goes away."

"And if I don't?" She was almost afraid to ask.

"If you don't?" Jess laughed. "Oh honey, if you don't, then in a week people the world over will be reading a juicy piece of journalism about a boring but morally corrupt woman named Carrie who is having sex with two men waaaaaaay out of her league." She giggled. "Ha, league, see what I did there?"

"You—"

"Oh yes, yes, I would. I'm sure the voice recordings will make it online quickly and then no amount of denying it is going to work... Bodhi and Dalton's reputations will be ruined, they'll lose sponsorship and the club will decide against renewing their contracts. I don't think your boss will be very happy with your name getting out there either. That type of scandal doesn't look good in the business world..."

"This is a joke, right? Please tell me it's a joke."

"It's not a joke by any means." Jess said. "I know you're good for the money, so don't try and use that as an excuse."

"Most of that money was left to me by my grandma! Are you really so cruel that you'd expect—"

"In case you couldn't tell, yeah, I really am that cruel."

"This is absurd," Carrie said angrily, her hands tensing as she imagined punching the smug bitch in the face.

"Much as I love the look on your face right now, I'm going to have to love you and leave you. You've got my bank account number, if the money doesn't show by Saturday morning... well, you know the deal."

Carrie stood rooted to the spot watching Jess walk away. When the front door slammed, she began shaking uncontrollably, unable—and not wanting—to believe what had just happened. Had her best friend really just threatened her with the destruction of three careers if she didn't cough up twenty thousand dollars?

Her best friend was blackmailing her.

She'd never felt so betrayed in her life and the idea that it was her best friend who'd treated her in such a way? It was too much. Nausea exploded in her gut and she ran for the bathroom, knocking her glass of wine over on the way causing it to shatter.

Lurching over the toilet bowl she felt dizzy and found it hard to stay balanced while the contents of her stomach were expelled.

When her stomach had finally settled down, she slumped against the wall, tears like acid falling uncontrollably, her breath coming out as huge wracking sobs, shaking her to the core.

Whenever the tears let up, she would think back to the words spoken by her so-called best friend and the tears would resume. After what had to be over an hour on the bathroom floor, Carrie stood up and made the mistake of looking at her reflection in the mirror; her eyes were swollen and red, making it look as if she'd been punched. She felt as if she'd been punched—only by words rather than a closed fist, which considering the trouble she was now in, would have been desirable. Bruising would heal, but what Jess had said, the threat she'd made? How was she meant to recover from that?

Repulsed by her reflection in the mirror, Carrie walked into her room and threw herself on her bed. Maybe if she went to sleep, she would wake up and find it had all been a dream. Yeah, who was she kidding? This was about as real as it got, and it was going to get worse before it got any better.

***

She was by no means asleep, rather in a catatonic state, and could hear someone calling out to her. In her head, she was calling back, but the action didn't translate into real action.

A weight on the end of her bed was followed by a circle of warmth moving back and forth against her calf.

"Carrie," the voice was saying. "Carrie. Honey. Are you okay? It's me. Nova."

Nova?

Gradually the paralysis melted from her brain and things started making sense again, but only just.

"What are you doing here?"

"I called you to see how you were holding up, but you didn't answer... and then I called again, and again... I got worried, so here I am."

Before she could tell Nova to leave, because she didn't deserve anyone's sympathy, the bank of tears broke again, but at least this time she wasn't by herself, sitting on the floor of her bathroom.

She couldn't tell Bodhi and Dalton about Jess's threat, but if she didn't tell someone she was going to lose the plot, and she feared that would happen literally, not metaphorically. Could she tell Nova though? She was Bodhi's sister; what if she told him, or their parents? It was her own fault Jess had this ammunition on the three of them, and it should be her problem alone to solve it.

Wiping the tears from her eyes she sat up and faced Nova, who she was surprised to find, really did look concerned. "Nova, can I tell you something?"

"You know you can..."

Carrie gulped for breath, the emotion of the words to come already crippling her. "This is so hard."

"Shit, you're not pregnant, are you?"

She actually laughed. "Oh, god no. That would actually be a relief, well, it wouldn't be a relief to be pregnant, but it would be a relief if that was what I have to tell you."

Nova really looked puzzled now. "What is it then? Why are you so upset? I mean, I know the photos coming out isn't a great thing, but surely it's not what has you *this* upset?"

"My best friend, Jess? She was the one..." Carrie took a deep breath and forced herself to continue. "Jess is the one who leaked those photos."

Anger licked at Nova's mouth, a scowl quickly absorbing her pretty features. "She *what*?!"

"It's so much worse though, Nova, and I need to know you won't tell anyone, especially not Bodhi or Dalton. I need you to promise me." Carrie hated feeling so desperate.

"I promise."

"She came over earlier and she-she—" A deep, calming breath. "She has voice recordings... of me talking about Bodhi and Dalton, in detail..." Her throat tightened, and it hurt to swallow, but she forced the words out. "She wants twenty thousand dollars, or she is going to go to the media with the recordings."

Nova laughed. "Okay, nice joke. Let me guess, Bodhi and Dalton are in on this as well?" She looked around as if expecting the two men to jump out and yell 'got ya!'. "Oh shit. You're serious... aren't you?"

All Carrie could do was nod and cry. It felt even more real now that she'd told someone about it, and she realised she wasn't going to wake up to find it had all been a nightmare. It was as real as it got.

"Why would she do that?" Nova asked, her fists clenched at her side.

"Apparently I have the perfect life and look down on her and she's been waiting for years to make me tumble." Through tears, she added, "All those years she was using me, everything we went through together and she was just waiting for her chance to say, 'fuck you'. Now she has, and it isn't even me who has everything to lose, it's Bodhi and Dalton."

"You need to tell them," Nova said, her voice like silk. "They wouldn't want you to be coping with this alone."

"No!" Carrie said firmly. "I'm not telling them. I'm going to pay Jess the money and she's going to use it to relocate to the States. Like she said to me, I pay for her to leave and this problem leaves with her."

"I don't know a lot about blackmail, but I'm pretty sure they always come back for more. What's to say she won't demand more if you do pay her off?"

"She won't," Carrie said, unconvinced. "She just wants the money to leave the country... I've got money put away for travel, I do have the funds there. It seems like the easiest solution. She leaves, and I never have to see her again, and Dalton and Bodhi's careers remain intact."

Nova sat with her head in her hands for a minute, and when she finally looked back at her, Carrie could see resignation in her eyes. "Fine. I won't tell them, but I think it's a bad idea for you to pay her, *and* for you not to mention it to my brother and Dalton."

Relief flooded her. "Thank you... I feel bad asking you to keep it a secret, but I just need to deal with this in my own way. I'm the one that got us in this shitty situation so I should be the one to get us out of it."

"Will you at least tell them after it's all over, when the wicked bitch of the east is safely in the States?"

"I'll think about it... that's the closest I can come to a promise."

Nova nodded. "That's good enough for me," she said, adding, "Look, I need to get home to Aurelia, why don't you come with me? You can have dinner with us, I can drop you back later?"

It was a lovely offer, but Carrie knew she wasn't going to be good company for anyone. "I would, but I think I just need to be on my own for a bit. I do feel better now that I've told someone though, so thank you." She offered a smile. "I don't know if I'll go into work tomorrow, if I don't, did you and Aurelia want to do something? Coffee, or the beach maybe?"

"I need to run it by Aurelia," Nova winked, "But I'm pretty sure her social calendar is empty tomorrow, so yes, that would be perfect."

"I'll text you in the morning and we can make a plan?"

"Okay," Nova said, and frowned. "You sure you don't want to come home with me?"

"I'm sure," Carrie confirmed. "But thank you..."

She walked Nova out to her car and when she went back inside felt vaguely happy for a few minutes, and then she remembered every single one of Jess's words and her world came crashing down around her, again.

***

It was just before seven and Carrie was sitting down to eat after coming to the realisation, she'd not eaten a bite all day, when there was another knock at the door.

For a moment she contemplated not answering, in case it was Jess but she came to the conclusion that avoiding Jess was no way to live her life. Even so, it was with much caution she opened the front door, only to find Bodhi standing on the other side.

"I hope you don't mind me turning up unannounced," he said. "I was worried about you though, after what happened this morning, and I had to come and check on you."

"Come in," she smiled, wishing the urge to tell him everything would go away.

Regardless of her reasons, it felt wrong to be keeping something so big from Bodhi and Dalton—and even harder when one of them was standing right in front of her.

"How did the meeting go?" Carrie asked as they sat together at the dining room table while she ate her boring dinner of rice and sweet chilli sauce.

"Don't worry," Bodhi laughed. "We're not in trouble. Everyone agrees it will blow over quickly, we've just been told not to talk to the media if we're asked any questions about the photos."

At least that was some good news to come out of the day.

The longer she sat talking with Bodhi, the more paranoid Carrie became that any minute Jess might walk in and find the two of them together. Who knew what her ex-best-friend would do then, blackmail Bodhi as well? Snap a photo of them together and send that out into the world as well? What if she was waiting until late at night when she knew they'd be in bed? There was nothing to say she hadn't followed Bodhi and she was biding her time just waiting for the perfect opportunity to make things a hell of a lot worse.

"I need to get out of this house for a bit," Carrie started. "Why don't we go back to your place and when Dalton gets home, we can watch more of *Banshee*?"

With all the sexual content and graphic violence, it was sure to distract her from the clusterfuck that her life had become.

"If you want to!" Bodhi smiled. "Or we could get Dalton to come around here with the USB?"

"Let's do your house," Carrie said. "I'm feeling a bit claustrophobic here at the moment."

"Been getting phone calls?" Bodhi asked sympathetically.

"No... well, my parents rang, but other than that, no."

"How did they take it?"

"They were confused, worried... as you'd expect, I guess."

"When Mum rang, she asked what the hell was going on and said that she'd thought me and you were together because I kissed you at the game. She was confused more than anything, told me that what we do is our business, but that we should probably try and keep it out of the media for now."

"No arguments here," Carrie sighed, swallowing back a few rogue tears.

"Dalton's mum was pissed with him for doing something stupid like that in public, and, as you can probably guess, his brothers all rang to offer their opinions and offer their varying degrees of sympathy and/or jealousy."

Hearing the reactions of both families only solidified in Carrie's mind the importance of not telling Bodhi or Dalton about Jess blackmailing her. It wasn't just the three of them who would be shamed if the whole story got out, it would be everyone associated with them. She couldn't put Bodhi or Dalton through that, and certainly not their families.

Carrie packed a bag and she followed Bodhi over to his house in her car. She'd decided not to work out of the office the next day and, when she left their house, would treat herself to a trip to the beach and see if the fresh air could clear her head.

Dalton didn't get home from his parents' until late, by which time Carrie was well beyond having the attention span required to watch anything and so the three of them retired to Bodhi's bed. The mood was more downbeat than usual, without the slightest suggestion made by any of them that they could see the day out with an orgasm or three.

It wasn't an orgasm she needed though, and long after Bodhi and Dalton had fallen asleep, Carrie lay perfectly still focusing on the two bodies pressing against hers, and feeling, for the first time that day, like the world wasn't coming to an end. *That* was what she needed. *They* were what she needed.

CHAPTER FIFTEEN

On Monday night, after her catch up with Nova in the morning and spending the rest of the day at the beach, Carrie didn't feel as mentally refreshed as she'd expected to.

She'd thought she had a few days to make up her mind about whether or not to give in to Jess's demands, but while enjoying a triple shot coffee with Nova, it had dawned on her that her bank would have a daily limit she could transfer. After checking with her bank, it was confirmed she could only transfer five thousand dollars per day, meaning she'd need to pay Jess in installments, and, to meet the Saturday deadline, the first lot of money would have to be transferred the following day. Her decision needed to be made ASAP.

Who was she kidding? She had no option but to pay Jess. Carrie couldn't risk the damage a scandal like that could do to Bodhi and Dalton, or their families. She was an insignificant part of the equation, but Bodhi and Dalton? There was no way she could do that to them.

What she needed to do was pay the money and get out of their lives for good. She'd been kidding herself thinking it could just be a bit of fun; sex, as fun as it was, complicated everything. So far it had ruined her friendship with her best friend, but that was a minor issue in comparison to what would happen if she didn't pay Jess.

So she would pay Jess, then spend one final weekend with Bodhi and Dalton, since they were insisting on taking her away for her birthday. The following week, she'd get to the hard part, physically breaking it off with them, the idea of which was enough to make her want to run away and never come back. Had it really only been a month since she'd met them? It felt like a lifetime ago, and she had to admit, since Bodhi and Dalton had entered her life, she'd been the happiest she could ever remember.

Did she need to cut them off completely, or would they be able to form a friendship that didn't include sex? The thought of not having anything more to do with them wasn't pleasant, but the idea of seeing them on a regular basis and not being able to touch them... that was just as bad, if not worse.

Carrie wondered if she should take a leaf out of Jess's book and leave town, move far away from the dual temptation of Bodhi and Dalton. It wasn't a realistic option though, she loved Sydney and had no desire to move away to try and start over in a city where she didn't know anyone.

The tiniest part of her wanted to say 'fuck you' to Jess and not pay her a cent, and it seemed the longer she took to make her decision, the bigger that part was going to get. Unable to take that risk she pulled up the banking app on her phone and through a blur of tears made the first payment to Jess. It was done now. She was obligated to pay the remaining fifteen thousand, otherwise her sex life would become public property and she'd be down five thousand dollars.

Nova had told her to let her know what she decided, so Carrie messaged her, *'Paid Jess the first $5,000...'*

'Sorry you feel you need to do this... keep some money aside because if I ever see that smug little bitch again, you're going to need to bail me out of jail'

'Thank you for not telling Bodhi about this... him and Dalton don't need the stress'

'And you do?'

'You know what I mean'

'Yeah, I know... I just hate you are going through this alone when there are two very capable men who would be by your side in a second if they knew'

'It's best I don't get dependent on them for any of that emotional crap...'

'Far healthier for the three of you to pretend it's just sex, right? Even if I can see they're as crazy about you as you are about them?'

'It is just sex...'

Carrie took Nova's lack of reply as an indicator she'd been called to the aid of the far cuter Aurelia and tried to ignore the idea that her new friend might be banging her head against a metaphorical brick wall that very moment.

It was just sex, and soon it wouldn't even be that. She knew she should tell Bodhi and Dalton of her decision before they celebrated her birthday, but she needed to be selfish and allow herself one final, magical weekend with her men, and she didn't want the weekend tainted by the mutual understanding it would be their last time together.

While out with Nova that morning, Carrie had told her she wished she'd only met one of the men, because she could have happily entered into something more serious if it was just her and Bodhi or her and Dalton. To test her, Nova had asked whether she wished she'd met Bodhi or Dalton, and Carrie had been unable to provide an answer. It felt wrong to even hypothetically choose one over the other.

Picking one was an option, but as with leaving Sydney, it wasn't realistic. If she couldn't have both, then she couldn't have either, it was as simple as that.

***

It wasn't until early Friday evening, when they arrived on her doorstep to whisk her away for the weekend that Carrie saw Bodhi and Dalton again.

She'd been downright avoiding them, under the guise of being horrendously busy at work, but the more the week progressed, the harder it had been to not just turn up on their doorstep or invite them over. It was a weaning process, she needed to get used to life without them and it had been harder than she'd expected.

Her resolve completely betrayed her the moment she opened the door and saw them standing on her doorstep; she launched herself into Dalton's arms, kissing him with all the pent-up frustration of the past week and then moved on to Bodhi, losing herself in the heat radiating from his body.

"I've missed you, guys," Carrie said without putting an ounce of thought into it.

Stupid fucking brain!

"Missed you too," Bodhi said, kissing her gently.

The men followed her inside and she turned to them. "So, where are we headed?"

Dalton reached out and took her hand, leading her into him. "We thought maybe you'd like to go out to Avoca Beach? To the beach house you were telling us about?" He suddenly looked unsure. "We don't have to though, actually, it was probably douchey of us to even think you'd want to go there with us, we can j—"

She shut him up with a kiss. "No, Avoca sounds perfect. I haven't been in a while, and you guys will love it."

"You could always invite Jess out too, if you wanted? You mentioned you usually see her on your birthday, and we don't want to keep you from her!" said Bodhi.

Carrie felt weak at the mention of Jess's name. During her lunch break that day she'd transferred the final five thousand dollars and hoped that would be the end of it. She really didn't like lying to Bodhi and Dalton, but it was the only way. "Jess and I had an argument, I'm not too sure where our friendship stands, so no... it will just be me and the two of you this weekend." '*The way I like it*,' she added silently.

"Sorry to hear that! She didn't get all high and mighty about us again, did she?" Bodhi asked, the sympathetic look he gave her almost too much to bear.

"No, nothing to do with you two." A blatant lie. "Just boring old girl stuff... it happens. I think we've been drifting apart for a while now."

Carrie excused herself to include a couple of beach-necessary additions to the bag she'd packed, and after taking the keys for the Avoca Beach house from the hook in the kitchen, she gladly followed the men out to Bodhi's car, ready to escape the world for a couple of days.

Rather than following Clovelly Road as was her usual route to get into the city, Bodhi turned at Burnie Street, going in the direction of Bondi. She thought he might have been taking a scenic detour, but he continued out toward the coast, refusing to tell her where they were going as they drove past *Icebergs*, *Bondi Ink*, and the *Bondi Pavilion*, eventually coming to a stop just past the surf lifesaving club.

"Thought we'd get some dinner before we hit the road properly," Dalton said, and Carrie eyed him suspiciously.

"Where did you have in mind?"

"Booked a table at *North Bondi Fish*," Dalton shrugged, like it was no big deal.

"Are you kidding?"

"You mentioned you loved seafood, so we were going to originally cook you something when we got to Avoca, but decided actual proper seafood cooked by a legit chef might be more birthday-celebration worthy."

Carrie just stared at the two men, mouth gaping.

"And before you mention paying for your own meal, dream on," Bodhi said. "It's your birthday, this weekend is about you, so let us spoil you."

"Something tells me you'd ignore me if I refused to let you..."

"Damn straight," Bodhi laughed and put an arm around her waist. "So come on, let's get this birthday of yours officially started.

Soon after walking into the restaurant, they were taken to their table, which happened to have a fantastic view of the waves of Bondi crashing against the shore. It was one of those places she'd always wanted ago, but never got around to, mainly because she didn't have anyone to go with. Her main birthday dinner companion in the past had been Jess who was allergic to seafood, making that particular restaurant a no-go.

Now here she was, sitting across from the two men who'd brightened her life over the last month, about to enjoy what was bound to be the best seafood of her life. It was easy to forget this was their 'goodbye tour', so to speak; that the following week she'd be putting an end to all of it and moving on with her life, sans Bodhi and Dalton.

The thought threatened to ruin the whole weekend for her, so she put a stop to those thoughts once and for all, refusing to allow herself to think about it for the rest of the weekend.

They started their meals with a serving of oysters and as could be expected, many jokes were made about the aphrodisiacal effects of the oyster. Not that she was in need of an aphrodisiac to get in the mood, all she needed was to look at the men and she was ready to go. Dalton mentioned something of that effect himself and had they not been at such a lovely restaurant, Carrie would have suggested they skip dinner and get out to Avoca Beach as quickly as they could.

For the mains, they each ordered something different. Carrie opted for the mussels, while Dalton ordered the beer-battered flathead and Bodhi the Moreton Bay bug linguini. When the food was delivered,

Carrie couldn't resist snapping a photo to post on Instagram—food porn was, after all, the in thing. Were you even on social media if you didn't post photos of food?

She could have happily stayed there all evening, looking out over the ocean and enjoying the natural beauty that was all around them, but there were other things she wanted to do, things involving nakedness, something not generally accepted in public. Knowing they still had a close to two-hour drive before they made it to Avoca, they decided against dessert and got back on the road with bellies full of what had been spectacular food.

The sun had gone down by the time they re-started their journey and as they drove through the city, Carrie marvelled at just how beautiful the place she was lucky enough to call home really was. The Harbour Bridge was a sparkly beacon which, on her trips to Avoca Beach, had always symbolised freedom and leaving the world behind, and on that particular trip it was more of a relief than ever before.

Finding herself in the rare position of being a passenger, Carrie was able to sit back and relax, something she'd been unable to do all week. With each five thousand dollars she'd put in Jess's account, the more tense she'd become and the worse she'd slept at night. It had reached the point in the early hours of Thursday morning that she'd considered turning up on Bodhi and Dalton's doorstep, knowing one or both of them could fuck her into a blissful state of peaceful sleep.

She'd resisted, just.

On the upside, she'd managed a lot of work during those sleepless hours and could now enjoy the weekend, with the knowledge that when she was back to the real world, she wouldn't have to worry about catching up on work. At least something was going well for her.

Considering it was the first time she'd relaxed all week, Carrie quickly felt the true extent of her exhaustion and fell asleep at some point going over the Brooklyn Bridge, as they headed toward Mooney Mooney. It wasn't until they reached the outskirts of the township of Avoca Beach that Dalton woke her to ask for directions. That single hour of sleep was the best she'd had all week, and even better, when she woke up from it, she was with Bodhi and Dalton and the promise of the perfect last weekend together.

Last weekend together. Well, that was a mood kill. Carrie pushed the thought away and directed them through the streets until they came upon the simple three-bedroom weatherboard cottage her parents had bought before she was born. It looked out of place now, amongst all the new houses that had gone up in recent times, but for Carrie there was no house more beautiful than the little cottage of her childhood.

They unpacked the car and Carrie led them to the front door, down the winding path she'd loved so much as a kid. Flanked with thick bushes and trees, it cast an almost eery feel at night and she used to pretend it was haunted; during the day with the sun streaming through at odd intervals it had been an enchanted forest. She'd almost spent as much time in the front garden as she had at the beach across the road.

Once she'd unlocked the door, she stepped inside, and flicked on the hallway light before she turned to

Bodhi and Dalton. "Welcome to my humble beachy abode."

"It's great!" Bodhi said, following her down the hall.

"I can see why you like it so much," Dalton said. "It feels so homely."

Carrie flicked the light on in her bedroom as she walked into the room and sat on the edge of the king size bed her parents had decided to replace her old bed with a couple of years earlier. Thank goodness they had, there was no way the three of them would have fit in the ancient double bed that had been in there since her early teens.

Thinking about bed made her yawn and it was with sadness she realised all she wanted to do was slide between the sheets and turn her brain off for ten hours. While still in Sydney, she'd been looking forward to the opportunity to catch up on what she felt was lost time with Bodhi and Dalton, considering their lack of contact that week, but now they were near a bed, it was only sleep that appealed.

"What's wrong?" Bodhi asked as he sat beside her and took her hand.

"Oh, nothing really," Carrie said, casting him and Dalton an apologetic half-smile. "I just... I haven't slept very well this week and I'm exhausted. All I feel up for tonight is sleeping, and I know that goes against everything I've been hinting at up until now, but—"

Bodhi put an arm around her waist and leaned in, dropping a kiss on her cheek. "If you want to sleep, you sleep. Me and Dalton will sort out the food we brought then we'll lock up and join you."

"I'm sorry, I know the whole point of this weekend is—"

"For you," Dalton said. "The weekend is for you to spend in whatever way makes you happy. Sleep all weekend if you want to. We possibly brought the X-Box to keep us entertained if you decided you want some boy-free time at some point, so don't worry about us."

Bodhi stood up and pointed at the bed. "Yeah, get your ass in bed now or there will be serious repercussions, young lady."

"What type of repercussions?" Carrie grinned, knowing full well the so-called repercussions would be sexual in nature. "Because I'm sure I will be fine after a good sleep tonight, so y'know, I'm all up for repercussions tomorrow."

Bodhi shot her a devilish grin. "If you insist."

"Oh, I insist."

"Right, get yourself sorted for bed then and we'll be back in a few minutes," Dalton said, then paused. "Do you want us to sleep in the bed with you? We can always sleep in one of the other rooms if you want the bed to yourself."

"You kidding? Of course, I want the both of you in bed with me. I like being the meat in a Dalton and Bodhi sandwich."

"Well, we like you being the meat as well," Dalton said and opened his mouth as if to say something but closed it again. "We'll go and get that food put away."

Unexpected tension filled the air and Carrie wasn't sure where it had come from. It could have been she was imagining it, she was after all, almost asleep on her feet.

Bodhi and Dalton walked out of the room and, after using the bathroom, Carrie undressed and slid into the middle of the bed, sinking into the pillowtop of the mattress, feeling like she was on a cloud. She closed her eyes and willed herself to stay awake until she'd, at least, had the chance to kiss Bodhi and Dalton goodnight.

When the men came back in, she was flitting in and out of sleep. Dalton joined her in bed first and in a move that came as naturally to her as breathing, she cuddled up to him – and for the first time that week everything felt right; when Bodhi joined them soon after, his body protectively moulding into hers, it didn't just feel right, it felt perfect.

"I wish I could go to sleep like this every night," Carrie mumbled, the words jumping around in her head and slipping out without thought.

"You're not the only one..." Bodhi.

"Maybe we could..." Dalton.

Carrie surrendered to sleep, willing it to take over immediately before she gave any thought to what had just been whispered.

***

The sun was pouring in the kitchen window as Carrie danced around the kitchen to the hyper vocals of her favourite guilty pleasure, the Spice Girls. On the stove top, bacon was sizzling away, the sausages were cooking in the oven, and the button mushrooms were diced and waiting on a chopping board, while fresh tomato wedges were piled on another, all waiting to be consumed.

She'd awoken far too early and had gone for a stroll along the beach, leaving a note for Bodhi and Dalton to let them know she'd be back soon. When she got home,

Carrie had been surprised to find the men were both still asleep and, after a happy birthday phone call from her parents, she had decided to treat the men to a cooked breakfast. They were still asleep, but she knew when the smells of food wafted through, they'd be in the kitchen faster than you could say 'wake up!'.

A high pitched scream came from the bedroom. "Bodhi! What the fuck are you doing?!"

"I didn't mean to, you dick!"

"I hope not!"

After turning the stove off as a safety precaution, Carrie walked to the bedroom where she found Dalton and Bodhi were out of the bed, standing on opposite sides of the room, looking alarmed.

The sight made her laugh, and she couldn't wait to hear what had caused them to act so oddly. "What's going on here?"

"*He rubbed my nipple!*" Dalton screeched, pointing an accusatory finger at Bodhi.

"I didn't mean to!" Bodhi said, hands on hips, cheeks flaming red. "I didn't realise it was you! I thought Carrie was still in bed and it was *her* nipple I thought I'd rubbed!"

Carrie started laughing and there was no chance of her hiding it. She laughed until her ribs hurt and her eyes watered, and just when she thought she'd stopped, she'd look at the sassy way Bodhi was standing and start all over again.

"If you guys want more alone time, I can go to the beach or something." Carrie snorted, the looks on their faces sending her into a fit of giggles again.

Dalton cracked a smile. "Didn't you think it was weird there was a lack of boob attached to the nipple?"

Bodhi didn't hesitate to retaliate. "Didn't you notice the boner pressing against your ass?"

Carrie was laughing uncontrollably, her laughter only intensifying when Dalton pretended to throw up and ran from the room like a sixteen-year-old wailing the world was unfair and he hated everything.

"How long have you been up, birthday girl?" Bodhi asked.

She sidled up to him and put her arms around his waist, playfully licking his nipple, enjoying the resulting gasp from him. "Woke up at seven. Tried to get back to sleep. Couldn't. You two looked so cute sleeping so I thought I'd sneak out and let you sleep in."

"You should have woken us up! We were going to make you breakfast in bed, but it smells like you've beaten us to it."

"It's almost ready, just need to do the mushrooms."

"Coffee, anyone?" Dalton called from the kitchen.

"Come here first, there's something you need to see!" Carrie called and when Dalton came back into the room, he looked at her questioningly.

Rather than answering straight away, Carrie slipped out of her dress and stood with her hands on her hips. "You said this weekend is about me and I want to get it started in the right way..." She sat on the edge of the bed and spread her legs, splaying herself and leaving no question about what she wanted.

It was later, *much* later, when they finally sat down and ate breakfast so late it could have been considered early afternoon tea.

CHAPTER SIXTEEN

When they finally got dressed and left the house the sun was at its highest in the sky and for the first time that spring, it actually felt hot. Carrie considered suggesting they brave the water, but after watching a man running in and then running straight back out—screaming about shrinkage—she decided against it.

Instead of going into the water, they walked along the beach until they found a relatively private spot and set themselves down beneath the obnoxiously large umbrella her parents kept at the house. Carrie made no secret of the enjoyment she took out of watching the men taking their tops off, and similarly, when she stripped down to her tankini bathing suit, there was no missing the metaphorical drool running down Bodhi and Dalton's chins.

A woman could get used to being looked at like she was a goddess, Carrie decided, or at least she could if she didn't have to end things with the two men looking at her with adoration and appreciation.

She did have to finish things, right? Ever since hearing Bodhi and Dalton's words as she was falling asleep the night before, the word 'polyamory' had been running through her mind.

The idea of being in a relationship with more than one person felt not so much wrong as... abnormal. When she got married, she wanted it to be a forever thing and she didn't know if a polyamorous relationship held that same potential. Wasn't it inevitable that someone would end up getting hurt? That the relationship between two of the people would strengthen to the point it pushed out the third and a trio would become a duo?

Marriage wasn't even an option in a polyamorous relationship, so let's say she did pursue something long term with the two men, she would never be able to get married. She'd always placed so much importance on getting married that she'd never considered being in a committed relationship that didn't contain an '*I do*'.

Was it specifically marriage that was so important to her, or rather, was it the idea of a life-long commitment? It wasn't something she'd thought about before and she realised marriage may have held so much appeal because it was what society depicted as the only legitimate option for a '*one person forever*' relationship. You got married, you had kids—it was just what you did.

Society wasn't exactly understanding of alternative relationships, and if she entered into something beyond what she already had with Bodhi and Dalton, she'd forever be a social outcast. People would naturally make judgements because, in the eyes of the world, polyamory wasn't appropriate... it was for sex addicts and people who couldn't be monogamous, a way for men to get the sex they wanted without having to sleep around.

"Sunblock?" Dalton asked, holding up the bottle of SPF50 she'd brought with her.

"Please!"

"Lie down."

She did as he asked and when he straddled the top of her thighs, she found herself drifting off to a very naughty place where clothes didn't exist. He pulled up the back of her top and did her lower back, then moved higher to do her shoulders, which entailed him leaning forward and brought his cock in contact with her butt.

Suddenly, she could imagine him putting an arm beneath her hips and pulling her so her ass was sticking up in the air. It wouldn't be a bottle of sunblock in his hand, but a bottle of lube, and she could picture him squirting some onto his finger and gently rubbing it in circular motions. He'd use a bit more and this time the tip of his finger would spread her, she'd have to bite back a cry of pleasure as she pressed back against him, silently begging for more. His hands would leave her body and she'd feel more lube being applied, and this time instead of the tip of a finger rubbing against her, it would be the tip of his cock. He'd press carefully against her, patiently allowing her body to grow accustomed to him, pushing in millimetre by millimetre until—

"Better be careful with those hips of yours..." Dalton's words pulled her from her fantasy just before he took the final plunge.

She shook her head and cleared her throat. "Uhhh..."

He leaned until he was almost flat on top of her and whispered in her ear, "What were you imagining me doing to you?"

Dalton was getting hard against her ass and it was more than she could handle.

"Nothing, well... something... but nothing beach-appropriate," she said quickly and the moment he was off her she sat up, trying to ignore the way her asshole was pulsing as the remnants of her fantasy wore off.

"Thought we got it out of your system earlier," Bodhi teased.

"I don't know what it is, the two of you turn me into some sort of constantly horny sex monster."

"Now you know how it feels to be a man," Dalton joked. "Welcome to our world."

"You two lying there all shirtless and muscly and growly certainly doesn't help." Carrie pretended it was a complaint.

Looking at the sight of manliness before her, she grabbed her phone from her handbag and took a photo... she was only human after all, and there was no denying her appreciation for the two men stretched out on their towels.

"You're a pervert," Bodhi said.

She shrugged. "It's my birthday, I'm allowed."

Dalton chuckled. "Can't argue with that."

"You're just lucky I didn't take a photo of the two of you cuddled up in bed earlier."

"You're gonna pay for that!" Dalton growled and, faster than a man of his size should be able to, he was on his feet, diving for her.

Carrie jumped to her feet a split second before he made contact, dropped her phone on her towel and ran toward the water's edge, her laughter morphing into a shriek when she turned and saw both men were chasing after her. She hadn't planned anything beyond running away so when they got closer her only option to escape them was to run into the water. Or at least that was how she saw it, figuring the men would stop before they entered the cold abyss.

But they didn't stop, and she ran through the waves, the men inching closer and closer until she felt arms around her waist, as well as her knees and *splat*! she was tackled into the water, half screaming and half laughing as she gasped for breath.

"I give up!" she screeched. "This water is *freezing*!"

"I can tell," Bodhi bit his lip, his eyes focused on her nipples.

"And you called me a pervert!" Carrie laughed as Dalton pulled her to her feet.

"You okay?" Dalton asked, and Carrie nodded.

In a moment that could only be called devious, she used his kindness against him, taking the chance to push him into the water, laughing at the tangle of arms and legs as he gripped Bodhi's arm and pulled him down with him.

If she thought she was getting away, she was sadly mistaken, a hand closing around her ankle brought an end to her escape and she only added to the tangle of arms and legs as she collapsed on top of them.

Cold lips kissed hers and Carrie shivered partially from the cold, partially from pleasure, as a tongue plunged inside her mouth and toyed with her own. It was

Bodhi, whose green eyes were now looking deep into hers in a way that suggested their public outing was over.

"I could do with a shower," Carrie said, her voice dripping with suggestion.

They hauled themselves out of the icy water and ran up the beach to collect their belongings. From there it was a quick two-minute walk to the house, and the moment the front door was closed behind them, the bathing suits came off.

"So, shrinkage is a myth, huh," Carrie said, thoroughly impressed looking from one cock to the other before making eye contact with Bodhi and Dalton.

"I call it the Carrie effect," Bodhi joked. "I could be naked in Antarctica but if you were within eyesight, I'd be hard as a pole."

"I can vouch for the Carrie effect," Dalton said following her into the bathroom and she purposely stopped in her tracks, so he bumped into her, at which time she put her hand behind her and ran her palm up his length.

"Seems you can."

The shower was a lot smaller than Bodhi and Dalton's, making three people quite the squeeze, but rather than being a hindrance, that worked in their favour. Within a minute of getting in, Carrie had two cocks in her soapy grip, enjoying the chorus of gravelly moans and groans as she gripped and tugged both men until hot bursts of cum shot against the shower wall.

Being that the shower was so small, there was no room for the men to slump to the ground like they'd have been able to in their own shower, and Carrie hoped there would be no falling over. The last thing she needed to explain to her parents was why the glass walls of the shower cubicle had been smashed; worse would be any resulting injury and the scenario had to be explained to ER staff.

Bodhi and Dalton stood still, huffing and puffing, as they tried to recover from the magic performed by her fists. While they did that, Carrie washed herself, enjoying the way both men watched her as she paid particular attention to her boobs.

The recovery was quite miraculous, one minute Bodhi and Dalton were standing like statues, the next they were taking the lead, her boobs a soapy treat in their hands. Fingers rubbed and squeezed her nipples while a hand drifted down over her belly, between her legs, two fingers easing inside her.

"Not fair," Carrie gasped. "There's two of you!"

"I can tell you hate it," Dalton said and kissed her, breaking it off so Bodhi could do the same.

Carrie moaned as a thumb pressed on her clit. "So much…"

"What were you thinking about at the beach?" Dalton asked.

Carrie's legs almost buckled when her pussy stretched as more fingers entered her. It felt different though, not like it usually did when one of the boys had three or four fingers there… almost as if—

Looking down, she found her suspicion was confirmed. There were not one but two hands between her legs. She looked at them, incredulous, her head falling backward as two sets of fingers worked the sensitive flesh of her pussy.

"Fuck," she exhaled loudly, "that feels—" someone parted their fingers, sending bolts of pleasure screaming through her. "Fuck! Don't stop!"

"Tell us what you were thinking," Dalton prompted.

"I was thinking..."

"Yes?"

"It's kind of embarrassing."

"Well, you certainly seemed to enjoy your embarrassing thoughts at the time." Bodhi reminded her.

Fingers slowed down.

"Don't stop!" Taking a breath, she looked nervously toward the roof. "I was kind of thinking about what it would be like if, uh... if one of you.... well—"

"Sounds interesting, don't stop," Bodhi said and kissed her neck.

The fingers moved faster. Her legs shook.

"Fine. I was imagining what it would be like if one of you was fucking me up the ass."

Fingers harder, faster, deep. Body quaking, burning.

She screamed as her orgasm hit, making her forget all about the embarrassing confession she'd just made. Waves crashed and rolled over her, the orgasm feeling as if it was coming from two places... it was an orgasm unlike any she'd had before.

Collapsing against Dalton's chest she struggled to breathe, and if it wasn't for his strength holding her up, she'd have hit the floor, of that she was certain.

"About what you were saying before we so rudely made you come..." Dalton said, the mention enough to make her bite her bottom lip as his hand cupped her bottom. "We could always give that a go, if you wanted..."

"Maybe," she whispered, still too strung out after her orgasm to commit to anything, not verbally, anyway. The way her pussy was clenching at the idea, one could have been forgiven for thinking one of them was already inside her and she was seconds away from an orgasm.

They had the Carrie effect, she had the Bodhi-and-Dalton effect.

When she dressed after the shower, Carrie checked her phone for only the second time that day, her stomach jumping into her throat when she saw she had a message from Jess. She didn't even bother imagining it might be an apologetic, 'here is your money back, sorry I'm a bitch' type message, and only hoped it was confirming the money was all accounted for.

Happy birthday Princess Carrie! Hope you're having a lovely day skanking around with those two losers. Yeah, I noticed the three meals in your photo on Instagram last night, I'm not stupid. The twenty thousand is all there so for now your sex life remains private property. I have, however, done some recalculations and realised I actually need thirty thousand to move from this shit-hole country. You have until next Saturday to deposit the remaining ten thousand. If you don't, you know the deal. Have a happy fucking birthday.

Just like that, it all came rushing back. The past week had been hell and she'd been an idiot to think it would be over after she'd paid the money. Nova had been right, Jess was after more and once again she was dealing with the possibility her stupidity could ruin Bodhi and Dalton's careers, while creating a scandal for three families.

Needing to be alone, she walked into the lounge where the men were enjoying a beer and made up the excuse of needing a nap to hide out in the bedroom for a while. Chances were she was going to cry soon, and if Bodhi and Dalton were there when that happened, there was no way she was going to be able to keep up the lie, and their weekend would be ruined.

Closing the door to the bedroom, she undressed and got in the bed. She could smell the faint scent of both men on the pillows and that in itself was soothing, until she remembered the part where it was their last weekend together... and then she really did start crying.

She smothered her sobs with a pillow, taking it off when she started feeling dizzy, so she could take a breath and get more oxygen into her system. How tragic would it be if Dalton and Bodhi came in to check on her and found her dead? Not the way she wanted the weekend to end. She didn't *want* the weekend to end.

Needing to vent, she messaged Nova, '*You were right. Jess messaged me and is demanding another ten thousand. I have no choice but to pay... and now I'm afraid she'll demand even more until I have no money left and it becomes public anyway.*'

'*Oh shit, I'd hoped she wouldn't do that. I'm sorry. Presuming you still haven't told Bodhi or Dalton?*'

'*No, they don't need to know, it's my problem*'

'*They'd want to know, but I get why you feel you can't tell them. I'm sorry she's ruined your weekend like this*'

'*I'm doing that all by myself*'

'*What do you mean?*'

'*I decided after this weekend I can't see Bodhi and Dalton anymore. It's getting too complicated; I like them*' *both far too much for it to go on and I forget for a while but then I remember and it makes me sad*

'If it makes you sad maybe it's not what you really want?'

'It's what I have to do... want has nothing to do with it'

'Talk to Bodhi and Dalton – you're going to drive yourself nuts if you don't'

'Already feel like I am'

'Meet me on Monday for a coffee? Or just come and chill with me and Aurelia? We can talk about all of it, okay?'

'Okay...'

'Now go back and enjoy those bloody men'

'... let's just say they deserve the break they're currently having...'

'Haha, good on you. Enjoy your weekend hun, see you Monday xxx'

After speaking to Nova, Carrie felt a little better, or at least good enough to face Bodhi and Dalton without breaking into tears at the drop of a hat.

With only a day and a half left together, Carrie felt she owed it to them, as much as herself, to have a good time and not get bogged down by everything else bumping around in her mind.

***

Carrie spent the rest of the afternoon watching Bodhi and Dalton battle it out on the Xbox. She had no idea what the game was, it was just your run of the mill shoot-someone-or-get-shot type of game, and the commentary provided by the men was hilarious. If anyone had been listening outside, the police probably would have been called, given the 'I'm going to kill you!' and 'Die, bitch!' comments, mixed with the sound of fake (but real sounding) gunfire.

Dinner was low-key compared to the seafood extravaganza the night before, but just as delicious. She'd always had a weakness for the burgers sold at the takeaway shop down the road so when Bodhi and Dalton had asked what she wanted for her birthday dinner, it had been a no-brainer.

Instead of going inside to eat, they walked over to the beach. It was a lovely, calm night so there wasn't a huge risk of getting a mouthful of sand with your burger or chips, something that tended to destroy the ambience of such an idyllic setting.

While they sat and ate, Carrie spoke at length about the time she'd spent at Avoca Beach during her childhood. To their credit, Bodhi and Dalton seemed genuinely interested in her stories and not once did their eyes glaze over, nor did they attempt a change of subject.

"Must have been lonely growing up without siblings," Bodhi said. "Must have been nice coming here and finding other kids to play with!"

"Looking back, it was lonely, but at the time it was normal." Carrie said and for some reason she felt compelled to continue, rather than change the subject like she'd usually do. "My parents tried for a long time to give me a sibling, Mum had six miscarriages after I was born and, toward the end, it was taking a toll on her and Dad... their relationship really suffered."

"I'm sorry, that must have been horrible for them, and for you."

"I actually had an older sister, Becky..." Carrie said, surprising herself by opening up about something she'd never told another soul. Not even Jess. "She was born prematurely and back then they didn't have the technology they have now... Mum said she was a fighter, but after a few hours she just couldn't fight anymore, and she passed away."

"Crap, I'm sorry, Carrie, I shouldn't have brought the subject up," Bodhi said. "But while we're at it, Mum had a couple of miscarriages between Nova and me, which is why there is such a big gap between us."

"Lachlan and Emily needed to do IVF to get pregnant with Kingston. With him, they tried for eighteen months to get pregnant before the doctor told them it wouldn't happen naturally. With Greyson, they went straight to IVF and it took four cycles," Dalton said. "I feel bad for them because my other brothers seem to get their wives pregnant just by looking at them."

"The older I get the more I worry I'm going to have problems like Mum did," Carrie said, wishing she could shut up... like the boys wanted to hear about *that*.

"You're not the only one," Dalton said. "With Lachie and Emily, it's his sperm that is the problem, so it's always in the back of my head that maybe I'll have the same issue. I'm a lot like Lachie in other ways, so why not in that way."

Carrie sighed and leaned her head on Bodhi's shoulder, taking Dalton's hand and putting it in her lap. "This being an adult thing really sucks."

They sat in a state of reflective silence and Carrie grabbed for a new conversation starter but came up empty handed. She didn't know why she'd chosen that night to finally open up about Becky but doing so had put a real dampener on the weekend. One day she'd learn to shut up, but apparently today was not that day.

"I'm going to go and get a jumper," Bodhi said and stood up. "You two want anything?"

"No thanks," Carrie replied and took the keys from her bag. "You may need these though.

Bodhi leaned down and kissed her. "I won't be long."

"My admission was a bit of a mood kill, wasn't it," Carrie said.

Dalton shook his head and pulled her closer, "No, it wasn't a mood kill... it's life, and just because we're doing the casual thing doesn't mean we can't have discussions about serious stuff."

"I've never told anyone about Becky."

"I'm honoured in that case," Dalton kissed the top of her head. "It can't be easy to talk about."

"Mum and Dad don't talk about her a lot, so I guess I grew up not feeling like I was allowed to talk about her, and it just became a habit not to."

"It's sad that people feel they need to keep that sort of stuff to themselves," Dalton said. "One of my cousins had a little boy who was stillborn a couple of years ago... she had a funeral for him and everything. My aunty got really upset afterward and eventually blurted out that she'd lost her first baby the same way and that her ex-husband had refused to let her talk about it, so she'd pretended like it never happened and felt she never had the chance to say goodbye."

"How awful!"

"The baby, Taylor, is in a part of the cemetery especially for babies, and whenever my aunt goes to visit, she leaves two lots of flowers, a blue bunch for my cousin's boy, and a pink bunch for the little girl she lost."

"I can't imagine going through anything like that." Carrie sighed. "Becky's ashes are at Mum and Dad's, but other than her birthday they're kept in a drawer. It used to upset me, made me think Mum was ashamed, but I understand now it's just the way she copes with her grief."

"Everyone has their own way, I guess."

"Sorry, I know this is a morbid topic, especially for what's supposed to be a weekend of fun."

"It's not morbid. It's part of life, and I don't see any point in keeping all of that stuff inside." He pat the sand between his legs and Carrie moved so she was sitting between them, resting against him, he put his arms around her and she instantly felt emotionally lighter. "If you ever want to talk about your sister... you know where to find me."

"Thanks," Carrie said, glad he couldn't see her tears.

Soon, she'd no longer have the chance to talk to him about anything.

"You're also allowed to cry, so you know," Dalton whispered, giving her a gentle squeeze.

She felt like a fraud, he thought she was crying about the older sister she'd never had the chance to meet, when in reality, it was the prospect of cutting him and Bodhi out of her life that had her so upset.

"I'm back!" Bodhi said, plonking down beside her. "One, two, three!"

Carrie wiggled from between Dalton's legs and looked at both men in shock as they sang 'Happy birthday', and from a box she'd presumed contained beer, Bodhi pulled out a birthday cake.

"Oh my god!" Carrie laughed and suddenly she didn't care that her face now felt as if she'd been sunbathing on the sun. "You guys!"

"Couldn't let our favourite birthday girl go without cake!" Dalton said and high-fived Bodhi. "Very smooth work, Sir. Your idea to keep the cake in a beer box was a stroke of genius."

"You really didn't have to do this."

Dalton smiled sheepishly. "We were going to buy a store-bought cake, but Nova threatened to kick our asses and she helped us bake one before we picked you up yesterday."

She sat between the two men who moved so close there wasn't a millimetre between her and either of them. "Store-bought would have been fine. You're both far too sweet... and way too good to me."

"You're a special woman..." Bodhi said, matter-of-factly. "You deserve to be spoilt, whether it's your birthday or not."

Words from the previous night rang in her head... '*You're not the only one*'. '*Maybe we could*'.

God, she wished it were true... but the reality was, their time had almost run out.

CHAPTER SEVENTEEN

For the second day in a row Carrie woke up having done nothing in bed but sleep.

Unlike the previous morning, Bodhi and Dalton were awake before her, but thankfully still lying beside her, and the last thing she wanted to do was get out of bed, for the simple reason it would mean the official start of their last day at the beach, not to mention their last day together, full stop.

She envied the men, who were blissfully unaware of the true meaning behind the day.

"We can come back another weekend, you know," Bodhi said when she pouted at his suggestion they get up.

"It has just been a nice weekend, getting away from all the Jess stuff."

"What do you mean the Jess stuff?" Bodhi asked. "The fight you had?"

"Yeah..."

Carrie hated lying to Bodhi and Dalton and the more she did it, the worse she felt. Why couldn't she just tell them what had happened? When the time came, it would help them to understand why she had to end things—*or* it might make them decide to end it before she had a chance, meaning she wouldn't feel so bad. If calling time on what had been the most magical month of her life was the right thing to do, why did it leave such a bitter taste in her mouth, and more concerningly, in her heart.

"Are you okay?" Dalton asked.

"I-I feel sick," Carrie said. A blatant lie.

"Can we get you anything?" Bodhi looked concerned and it made her feel like shit.

There she was, lying, while Bodhi and Dalton looked ready to call for an ambulance.

"I'll be okay." Another lie. She wasn't going to be okay after doing what she had to do. "I think the best place for me is my own bed though. Would you mind if we went back to town now?"

Why was she asking to leave when it was the last thing she wanted? It made no sense, but at that moment, nothing did.

"That's fine," Bodhi said. "You sure you're okay?"

"I'm..." Not fine. At all. "Fine, probably just coming down with a virus or something."

Not even half an hour later, they were in the car on their way back to Sydney, and Carrie—like the fucking wimp she was—was pretending to sleep in order to avoid conversation that she knew would result in something along the lines of '*do you want to do something next weekend?*'.

Next weekend didn't exist for them. It existed for Bodhi and Dalton, it existed for her, but not for *them*.

"I wish every day could be like that," she heard Bodhi say quietly.

"Me too... but it's like Nova said, if it's meant to be more, it'll happen by itself."

They'd spoken to Nova about her? About the possibility of more?

All this time, she'd been worrying about how hard it would be on her when all was said and done, but the way Bodhi and Dalton were talking, and some of the things they'd said over the weekend... what if it was just as hard on them?

The point of saying 'no more' was to assure no one got hurt, but what if it was too late for that?

She couldn't have those sorts of feelings for two men, she just couldn't. Feelings would lead to love and if she reached that point, she would really be in trouble. It was one thing to think fondly of someone and enjoy their company, but when the L word came into the equation, there was no going back. That was when people would *really* get hurt. She couldn't do that to them, or herself.

Two hours later, they arrived at her house and, as much as it pained her, Carrie didn't invite Bodhi and Dalton in.

They made her promise to call them if she needed anything, and she reassured them she would, but as with most things she'd said that day, it was a lie. The only contact she was going to have with them after that was when she completed the god-awful task ahead of her and officially ended their month of... sex. It had been a month of sex. Nothing else. Certainly not something she'd been longing for her entire adult life.

Who was she kidding?

She was in love with Bodhi and Dalton, but it was a love she'd have to take to the grave.

***

After a night of fitful tossing and turning, totalling less than an hour of sleep, Carrie came to a realisation on Monday morning.

She had to end it that day or she'd run the chance of a mental breakdown.

Luckily the meeting she'd scheduled for that morning was rescheduled, the notification coming through just before she was set to leave. The last place she wanted to be was work and so she touched base with her boss and got permission to work from home.

Much as she didn't want to be at work, she was happy to have the distraction at home and worked through, finally stopping for a break at three o'clock. She'd been completely immersed in her work and hadn't been conscious of anything going on around her, including the messages from Bodhi and Dalton checking to make sure she was okay.

At five thirty she patted herself on the back for a good day's work and was about to treat herself to a glass of wine when her cell phone rang. It was Dalton.

'Thanks universe', she thought as she stared at her screen. Clearly it was a sign to go for one last visit to Bodhi and Dalton's and do what she had to do.

Because she couldn't stare at the phone all day, she clicked accept. "Hi Dalton."

"Carrie, oh, thank God" He sounded out of breath and instantly she got the feeling something was wrong. What if he and Bodhi had had a fight – over her? She'd never forgive herself if—

"Nova just rang me, Bodhi's been in a crash. He's in the ambulance now and—"

"Is he okay? What happened? Is he-is it bad? Is—" she gulped for breath, each forced inhalation like needles being driven into her lungs. "I-I—" No words, only tears. And shaking. Uncontrollable shaking.

"I'm on my way to your house now, wait out front."

The phone went dead, and Carrie stared at it clasped in her hand for a couple of minutes, not too sure what had just happened. She must have imagined the panic-stricken words Dalton had spoken to her; surely it was a misunderstanding.

And then she watched from outside her body as she raced into her room and got her handbag, throwing in her phone charger (why did that seem so important?!) and an extra tube of lip balm because the dry hospital air always made her lips dry. She fumbled with the keys hanging on the hook in the kitchen and dropped them three times before making it outside. Locking the door, she walked on wobbly legs to the gate and was grateful for the cinder block fence; had she not sat down that moment, she'd have collapsed.

When she noticed Dalton's car coming along the road, the tears started falling and after clambering into the car she fell into Dalton's arms, not caring that the steering wheel was digging into her or that she was likely breaking his ribs.

"Nova rang a minute ago, he's being assessed now," Dalton told her as they got on the road. "He knocked his head pretty bad and there was a lot of blood, so he needs a CT scan to rule out a brain injury."

"How can you be so calm?" Carrie snapped. "I'm sorry, I'm just..."

"It's okay." Dalton reached for her hand and clasped it in his. "I'm freaking out too."

"Do you know what happened?"

"Someone ran a red light, smashed into his passenger side."

"Thank god it wasn't his side of the car."

Just imagining that scenario brought tears to her eyes and she looked away from Dalton, so he wouldn't see, but there was no fooling him.

"It's okay, baby. Bodhi will be okay. Probably a bit battered and bruised, but he'll be okay."

"Promise?"

"Promise."

Before she could read too much into his innocent use of the word 'baby', the hospital came into view and Carrie felt a conflicting mix of relief and anxiety knowing they'd soon be able to see him.

"Nova said she'll meet us outside the ED entrance."

She didn't care that his parents might be there, or that people would see her rushing to his bedside; all she cared about was seeing for herself that he was okay.

Miraculously, Dalton found a park a few rows away from the entrance to the hospital and, the moment their feet hit the ground, they were running; had she not been so terrified, she'd have taken time to boast that she was out-running him. When they entered the hospital, Carrie forced herself to slow her pace to a quick walk, though the closer they got to the ED, the faster her steps became, until she was essentially running again.

As promised, Nova was waiting beside the large sign which screamed 'Emergency Department' in bold red letters. The two women rushed toward each other and hugged tightly. Nova's eyes were bloodshot and for a minute Carrie wondered if she was about to give them the worst possible news.

Luckily that wasn't the case.

"He's going to be okay." Nova almost trembled with relief, her voice shaking as she continued, "He's got a concussion and they are sending him through to CT soon to make sure there is nothing more sinister going on. Other than that, he has a pretty nasty gash on his head and has what they think is just a bruised cheekbone, but they'll look for facial fractures when he has the CT."

"Are you holding up okay?" Dalton asked, giving Nova a quick hug.

"Better now that I know there are no serious injuries. They're confident the CT will come back clear but need to do one just in case."

"Thank god," Carrie said, closing her eyes and exhaling deeply.

"He asked about you just before I came out here." Even with the shock of what had happened to Bodhi, Nova still had it in her to smile smugly at Carrie. "He'll be glad to see you. Both of you."

"Feeling is mutual," Dalton said and put a hand on Carrie's shoulder. "You ready?"

"No, but yes. Mostly yes."

Nova swiped a key-card against a sensor on the wall and the door opened. "Come on."

They walked down a long stretch of corridor—or at least it felt long—and Nova halted outside a room toward the end. "He's just through there. I'm going to go outside and try to get hold of Mum and Dad. They're on the Gold Coast at the moment..."

Nova gave Carrie one more hug and walked back down toward the entrance/exit.

"You ready for this?" Dalton asked.

"Yes." Carrie took a deep breath and bit back tears. Bodhi couldn't see her crying, he couldn't see how scared she'd been at the thought of losing him.

Crossing the threshold into the room of cubicles she peaked through the closed privacy curtain and finally laid eyes on the man she so badly needed to see. Bodhi's eyes found hers and the tears she'd been so determined to hide slid down her cheeks as she rushed to his side, with Dalton following behind her.

"Hey," Bodhi croaked, a faint smile quickly turning into a wince.

"Bodhi... I was so..." She tried to finish but the tears made that impossible.

"Shhh." His voice was a ragged whisper. "Don't cry, sweetheart. I'm okay."

"Nova said you need a CT? That it might be a brain bleed?"

"Doctor doesn't think..." he took a laboured breath. "Just wants to check."

"Are you in much pain?"

"A bit... they gave me something before and it has taken the bite off." This time he gave her a proper smile. "My lips aren't sore though..."

Cautious of hurting him or bumping any of the wires connecting him to machines and equipment, Carrie brushed her lips against his, not appreciating the way her throat swelled with emotion as she did.

"I'm sorry if I scared you."

"Don't ever do that again," Carrie's voice was tight as she struggled to maintain composure

"Yeah," Dalton's voice boomed behind her, "Next time you want to do the groceries just say something, don't feel like you need to scare me half to death."

"Guess I could do that," Bodhi grimaced.

A woman in a white coat entered the cubicle and after introducing herself as Doctor Polson, told them they were going to get Bodhi organised to go up to CT, explaining that as they weren't next of kin, they'd need to wait until he was moved to a ward to see visit Bodhi again.

"I'm sorry, when Nova said we could come in, we thought it was okay," Dalton said.

The women smiled kindly. "It's okay, Mrs Ives cleared it with me first. If everything goes okay, in a couple of hours, Bodhi should be set to move up to the ward for what is hopefully only a night of observation."

"Thank you for letting us see him," Carrie said and wiped tears from her eyes. "It means a lot to both of us."

"Good luck, mate," Dalton said. "We'll see you when you're a bit more comfortable."

"I'm glad you're okay," Carrie said, her voice watery.

"Take care of her," Bodhi aimed at Dalton. "If it didn't hurt so bloody much I'd be frowning right now."

Blowing him a kiss, Carrie turned and walked out of the cubicle, making her way as quickly down the corridor as she could before she broke down again.

Dalton pushed the button to open the door and they walked through the hospital foyer and out the main entrance where they found Nova sitting on a wooden bench taking deep breaths. She gave them a tearful look.

"Well, that was a really fun phone call."

Dalton sat beside her and put an arm around her shoulders. "Jill and Mike okay?"

"Mum was a mess. Dad was trying to be strong, but I could tell he was just as worried as her. They're getting the first flight back. Calum is going to pick them up from the airport and bring them here." She began openly crying. "Aurelia is due for a feed and Calum has to give her a bottle and my boobs are aching because they are so damn full, and I just want to hold my baby girl and never let her go."

"I'm sorry, Nova. Look, the doctor said we had to go, but if you need us to stay with you, we will," Dalton said, the look of compassion on his face as he spoke to Nova making Carrie's heart melt.

"It's okay. Kat is on her way. She brought me in, but I sent her back home to get my breast pump for me because I need to express before my fucking tits explode."

"Want us to stay until she arrives?" Carrie asked.

Nova shook her head. "No, I'm going to go back in now. Make sure my baby bro isn't making any trouble in there."

"They were getting him ready for CT when we left."

"I better get back in then." Nova stood up and hugged both of them. "I'll be in touch as soon as I hear anything."

They watched Nova walking quickly toward the entrance and then turned in the direction of the car.

Dalton took her hand in his and much slower this time, they crossed the carpark.

***

After the hospital Dalton had asked Carrie where she wanted to go, and when she said she didn't want to be alone he told her he'd hoped that would be her answer, because he didn't want to have to leave her in the state she was in.

They'd been home three hours before Nova rang with another update, this time a good one; the CT had cleared Bodhi of a brain bleed and had confirmed it was just bad bruising to his cheekbone. He'd been admitted to the ward for at least one night of observation, and they'd make up their minds the following day as to whether he needed a longer stay. Her and Bodhi's parents had just arrived and were in with him, officially leaving Nova free to go home to her baby girl.

Carrie hadn't expected the relief that followed Nova's phone call and, this time, when she cried, the tears weren't full of fear, they were an emotional release.

"I'm taking you to bed," Dalton said, his voice as soft as butter.

"Okay." There was no point arguing.

He stood up then took her hands and helped her to her feet, keeping her hand in his as he led her from the lounge and down the hallway into his bedroom.

"I'm going to go and lock up," he whispered. "I'll be back in a minute."

She shed her clothes, slumping over as she pulled the sheets back and flopped down, happy to be in bed after what had ended up being one of the most stressful days of her life. When Dalton returned, he undressed and got in beside her, letting out a long, loud sigh as his head hit the pillow, clearly feeling the effects of the day as much as she was.

"How are you feeling now?" Dalton asked, taking her in his arms.

"Exhausted. Relieved. Still in shock."

"That about covers it."

"Hope you don't mind me staying, I just needed the company."

"I wouldn't want you being anywhere else."

Carrie looked up and their eyes locked. She breached the gap between them and brushed her lips against his, a warm tingly sensation filling her body as he kissed her back.

He cupped her face and kissed her, not so much harder, as with more emotion, causing her to whimper against his mouth, her tongue darting out and licking the inside of his upper lip.

Dalton's fingertips grazed up and down her side, their tongues lightly brushing and tangling, in no rush, just exploring, enjoying. After the day they'd had, it was as if they'd developed a new-found appreciation for each other, or simply that they were reminding one another what it was to be alive.

Needing more contact with him, Carrie rolled on her back and guided Dalton on top of her. In other circumstances it would be a dangerous position to be in, but that evening, there was no risk of getting carried away. That wasn't what this was about.

The kissing became more heated, but it was still slow and sensual, a kiss of delight rather than need. Her legs were loosely around his waist and while there was no mistaking the feeling of his erection against her belly, that night she was in no rush.

His lips found their way to her neck and she tilted her head to the side, allowing him easy access. It was with slow, lazy kisses that he made a path from her ear down to her collar bone, before retracing the path even more lazily, the combination of the heat of his mouth and wetness of his tongue causing breathy, barely-there moans to come from the back of her throat.

The magic of his mouth against her neck triggered a gentle rolling of her hips and she took a tighter grip around his waist, pulling him closer and creating more heated contact between their bodies.

Dalton moved his hips back and she felt the very tip of him against her entrance. He smiled, his eyes slowly closing with delight, but his hips remained still.

"You feel beautiful, like I knew you would." His voice was full of calculated control, and she knew he was fighting some very intense urges.

Dipping his head, he grazed her lips with his and pulled his hips back. Instantly, Carrie missed the pressure of the blunt head of his cock against her and wished she had it in her to throw caution to the wind and give him no choice but to sink inside her without a barrier of latex between them.

Dalton reached for the condoms but before he had a chance to open it, she sat up and, taking it from his hand, she removed it from the foil wrapper, taking great pleasure in sheathing him and feeling the solid throb of his erection under her fingers.

Lying back down, she pulled Dalton down with her, her legs automatically joining around his waist again, tighter this time. She held her breath as he guided himself into her, her exhalation coming out as a moan in time with him sinking inside her. He stilled when he was enveloped by her walls and smiled down at her.

"Hi."

She giggled quietly. "Hi."

He smiled again and pulled slowly out of her, sinking back in all the way and stilling briefly to drop a kiss on the tip of her nose.

Carrie's legs tightened of their own accord, and Dalton began moving in earnest, his thrusts slow and gentle, but deep. Because of the slow pace, his pubic bone rubbed against her clit with every thrust of his hips, causing her to clench and swell around him.

His lips never left hers, the kiss creating a constant stream of pleasure which seemed to pulse directly into her clit.

Where she'd usually be moaning loudly, the sounds of her pleasure were hushed, a gift for Dalton's ears only. His breathing was becoming ragged, but much like her, the voice of his pleasure was a lot quieter than usual, the room almost untouched by the groans and grunts made against her mouth.

Under normal circumstances her orgasm seemed to build and hit out of nowhere, but this time she could feel it slowly and steadily brewing, building with each passing minute, tension on top of tension on top of tension. Delicious heat blossomed in her belly, stoked by each rhythmic contact of his cock against the back of her pussy.

He felt enormous inside her, but was moving with ease, her pussy sopping with arousal, welcoming each and every thrust with a contraction that moved her closer and closer to the abyss.

Closer and closer, his thrusts slow and deep, but with more power to them, and each time he pulled out he dragged over her clit, coaxing, willing the torrent of pleasure inside her to escape.

When Dalton pulled out slower than usual, the extended friction against her clit was what set that pleasure free and she screamed against his mouth, her legs constricting his waist, allowing him to hit deeper. His face was contorted, and she could see the second he lost his fight, the final thrust powerful and emphatic, a strangled, deep-seated growl tearing from the base of his throat as he emptied himself.

When he slumped on top of her, Carrie's hand moved automatically to his back and she began ghosting up and down his spine, loving the warmth of his skin, damp with sweat beneath her hands. He was so relaxed against her and it felt natural to be soothing him, to feel his heart beating frantically in time with her own.

The spell was broken when he moved away to dispose of the condom, and she was faced with the stark reality she'd just made life so much harder for herself. What she and Dalton had just done - it wasn't sex, and it certainly wasn't fucking. They'd made love and there was absolutely no going back from that.

She'd tried not to let emotion come into it and now it had bulldozed her and as a result, when she ended things, she wouldn't just be sad because she'd not see them again, she was going to be heartbroken over losing the two loves of her life.

CHAPTER EIGHTEEN

For once she didn't sleep well in the arms of Dalton. In part because she kept having nightmares where Bodhi and Dalton were in a car crash and died horrible, bloody deaths. Jess had caused the crash on purpose and laughed like the Joker as Carrie collapsed between both men and hollered with grief. Sometimes the car went on fire, sometimes they drove off the end of a pier and into the ocean, but the end was always the same.

Worse than the nightmares were the thoughts swamping her brain when she was awake. It felt as if she'd been waiting her whole life to meet someone who made her feel the way Bodhi and Dalton did, but now she'd found it, she wasn't allowed it and it was being wrenched away from her out of necessity.

Yet again she toyed with the idea of choosing one, but the longer she knew them, the more impossible that seemed. She didn't want Bodhi or Dalton, she wanted Bodhi *and* Dalton. In a perfect world, she could have both, but it wasn't a perfect world they lived in. The reputations of the two men were more important than what she selfishly wanted, and for reasons she'd gone over what felt like fifty-thousand times, a relationship built on three people would have an expiry date, a messy one at that.

Even if Bodhi and Dalton wanted to be with her, she knew they'd soon grow sick of it. She was seven years older than Bodhi and six older than Dalton—sooner or later that age gap would come between them in some way or another. Her biological clock was ticking and if Bodhi and Dalton didn't want to start having children until they were in their early thirties, that would mean Carrie would be close to forty and, considering the problems her mum had had conceiving, she didn't hold out much hope if she waited that long.

They wouldn't want to be tied down by a woman and a baby. Both were young with so much ahead of them and, though she hated to admit it, she would just hold them back and they'd end up resenting her.

If they wanted what she did. They were probably happy with the status quo, regular sex and blowjobs, without any of the drama of a relationship.

Lying in the dark, Carrie tried to convince herself Bodhi and Dalton were just using her for sex and there was nothing more to it for them. Any chance she had of coming close to believing it was dashed when Dalton tightened his arms around her and whispered, "I love you."

Tears stung her eyes as she silently mouthed 'I love you too', her heart breaking with the knowledge she'd never be able to say those words to his face.

He and Bodhi could never know how she felt about them.

***

Even if she'd wanted to spend the day with Dalton, she had that rescheduled meeting to attend first thing and after lunch was a meeting with an author they'd recently signed. The longer she spent with Bodhi and/or Dalton, the harder it was going to be when she had to say 'sorry, this isn't working out', so having to work was a blessing in disguise.

Nova rang when Carrie was on her lunch break and ice-cold fear ran through her veins. What if Bodhi had taken a turn for the worst? Or maybe worse, he was gone?

"Hey hun!" Nova sounded happy and Carrie was finally able to breathe again.

"I was sure you were ringing with bad news."

"Nope, no bad news today. Just letting you know Bodhi will be going home at some stage this afternoon."

"That is great news!" It really was.

"Now I have a favour to ask you..."

"Oh?"

"Would you mind staying with him tonight? Just to keep an eye on him? I think he'd probably be happier with you being in his room all night than Dalton, which is my other option."

"Yes, of course I will." She'd had her last night with Dalton, now was her chance to do the same with Bodhi, just minus the sex.

"Mum was insisting he go to their place for a couple of nights, but he really didn't want to do that... he's already sick of mum fretting over him."

"As long as he knows I'll be doing the same thing."

"I have a feeling he won't mind you smothering him with attention."

"Let him know I'll be over after work… and tell your mum I'll take good care of him."

Usually one to hope the day would fly by, Carrie was disappointed when she was able to leave earlier than normal. She wasn't ready to see Bodhi, knowing the sight of his battered and bruised face would send her into full mothering mode and she wouldn't want to leave his side, making the inevitable even harder.

Carrie knew it was cruel to even consider breaking it off so soon after what Bodhi had been through, but if she left it any longer, she would be leaving a trail of destruction in her wake. After this one night with Bodhi, it was over. She couldn't risk waiting another day.

That morning she'd put five thousand dollars into Jess's account and the next day she would transfer the remaining amount. It would all be over, she could move on.

If only she could decide how to tell Bodhi and Dalton it was over. She'd played the conversation in her head many times, but nothing sounded right, and she was ashamed to admit it, but she was thinking about leaving a letter for them instead. It was the wimp's way out, but if she wrote a letter, she could get all of her feelings out without having to contend with the emotion in the room.

She'd be able to explain herself properly and wouldn't stumble over her words. Bodhi and Dalton wouldn't see her crying, but more importantly, she wouldn't have to look into their eyes as she spoke the words she really didn't want to say.

All she could think of were stupid clichés to try and lessen the blow of what she needed to do; 'you have to be cruel to be kind', 'if you love them set them free', 'one door closes, another opens'. The letter would come across like a bloody sermon at the rate she was going.

The door was open when she got to Bodhi and Dalton's and she walked inside to find Bodhi lying on the couch, a bandage around his forehead, his right cheek a nasty shade of purple. His eyes lit up when he saw her and he shuffled closer to the back of the couch, holding his hand out to her.

Seeing him looking so still and almost lifeless was a shock to the system and as she carefully planted herself beside him, she wiped a few sneaky tears away.

"Looks worse than it is, babe."

"I was so scared, Bodhi!"

"I know, and I'm sorry." Bodhi held his arm out to her. "Come, lie down."

Somehow, they managed to fit on the couch together, just. It felt good being wrapped in his arms and Carrie wished she had the ability to pull away from his embrace, but physically and mentally she couldn't. It was as if she was paralysed.

The irony was, she'd almost lost him and now she had him back she couldn't let go, but that was precisely what she'd be forcing herself to do the following day. It went against every instinct, yet she refused to look into why it felt so wrong, afraid she might lose the strength to do what was right for Bodhi and Dalton.

"Is there anything special I need to do while I'm looking after you?"

Bodhi grinned. "Well you could give me a bl—"

"As far as your concussion goes," Carrie laughed.

"The doctor said a blowjob is the best treatment."

She knew he was joking around and would never demand a blowjob... and that kinda made her want to give him one. "You're an idiot."

"Other than a blowjob, the doctor did say I need to be woken every two to three hours and be asked an easy question... on the table there is a list of symptoms to look out for and when to call a doctor or to go back to the ED."

A noise in the doorway made her look up and she was greeted by Dalton looking wet and dishevelled, standing in a towel.

"Must be getting sick of the place," Dalton said light heartedly.

What she'd never get sick of was the sight of him in his towel, tied perilously low on his hips, putting his raw strength on display. The trail of ginger hair caught her attention, as it always did, and, in her mind, she walked over to him, removed the towel and dropped to her knees, giving him a long hard suck. Looking up she'd realise there was now a second cock in her face just waiting to be sheathed by her mouth...

"Do you?" Dalton was asking, and Carrie stared blankly at him.

"Uhhh..."

"Earth to Carrie," Bodhi laughed. "Since I'm not allowed to do anything too strenuous, we were going to watch a movie, that good with you?"

"Oh, yeah, of course. Good idea."

Not quite as fun as the double blowjob, but probably the safer idea.

With his near-nakedness still distracting her, Dalton continued where Bodhi had left off. "We were thinking a Die Hard marathon, but we can watch something else if you want."

"Die Hard is good," Carrie said. "Anything with Bruce is good!"

"Yippee ki-yay, motherfucker!" Dalton called loudly as he walked back down the hallway, making her and Bodhi laugh.

Carrie sat up and put her hand on Bodhi's hip. "Can I get you anything?"

"I'm due for some more meds actually, and I need to fill up my drink bottle."

"You stay there, I'll go and do it."

"Regardless of what my mum and Nova probably told you, I'm not an invalid, I can do things for myself."

"I know you can," Carrie said. "But you also need to rest up, and that is where I come in."

Without giving him a chance to argue Carrie picked up his bottle and went into the kitchen to fill it up, taking two pills from the box beside the information sheet about concussion. In the lounge Bodhi was now sitting up but looked uncomfortable. She handed him his bottle and pills and excused herself, returning a minute later with the comforter from his bed and a couple of pillows.

"Are you a mind reader or something?" Bodhi asked.

"No, I just know what I do when I'm sick and a big part of that involves curling up on the couch with blankets and pillows."

Dalton entered the lounge wearing clothes this time and much to her amusement he also had the comforter off his bed. He looked at her and blushed. "What? Isn't a grown ass man allowed to enjoy a bit of comfort?"

"I'm not judging! Why do you think I got Bodhi's for him? It's like a necessity when you're having a movie marathon."

She watched as Bodhi got himself into a comfortable position leaning against the arm of the sofa with his head resting on two pillows. He patted the space beside him and Carrie sat down, his arm quickly going around her shoulders, holding her close.

As scared as she was of hurting him, she couldn't resist how natural it felt to melt into him, asking, "Is this okay?

Bodhi kissed the top of her head. "Perfect."

When he'd closed all the curtains and put the USB into the TV, Dalton sat beside her and she changed positions turning slightly toward Dalton and resting her legs on his lap. It was a cosy set up, especially with the addition of the comforters, both of which she was under. Luckily it wasn't the middle of summer, or such a configuration would never have worked!

Because she'd seen the Die Hard movies so often Carrie didn't need to concentrate on what was happening on the screen, leaving her far too much time to think.

It was the last night she'd spend with the men and they had no idea. It felt as if she was keeping an awful secret from them, and she knew she was going to struggle to forgive herself after all was said and done.

How would her nights be spent from here-on out? Alone. That was how they were going to be spent. She no longer had a best friend to spend time with, Bodhi and Dalton wouldn't be an option, her parents were hundreds of kilometres away, and as much as she liked her colleagues, she'd not struck up a real friendship with any of them.

She was pathetic and was going to die old and lonely.

She managed to hold off the tears until they were well into the second movie, by which time the room was dark enough that if Dalton looked at her, he wouldn't be able to see the misery in her eyes

Why was she putting herself through such agony? She should make up an excuse to leave and Dalton would just have to be the one to check in on Bodhi throughout the night.

But Carrie couldn't bring herself to do it. Breaking that final contact was going to kill her and, if anything, she clung more tightly to what she knew were the last moments she'd ever spend with the two men she'd stupidly fallen in love with.

***

Climbing into bed after watching the third movie, Carrie turned to Bodhi and for what was probably the fiftieth time that day, asked him if he needed anything.

"No, I'm good," Bodhi said stretching out. "It's nice to be in my own bed, even nicer to have you in it with me."

For the last time.

"You probably won't be saying that tomorrow morning after I've woken you up every two hours!"

"Can't be any worse than last night... then again, I'm lucky to be alive so probably shouldn't complain."

"That's definitely the important part," Carrie said. "I don't know what I would have done if..."

"Well I didn't... so you don't have to worry." Bodhi turned and looked at her. "Made me realise a few things though, like how important it is to appreciate the people in your life."

Please don't go saying anything emotional. Please.

"Yep." Carrie hated to give a one-worded answer when Bodhi was so clearly processing what had happened to him, but it was all she could commit to.

"I'm not just talking about my family, either." Bodhi cupped her face. "You've made the past month one of the best of my life, and I'm so glad we met."

Oh fuck.

"I am too."

He kissed her gently. "Funny how someone can become such an important part of your life so quickly."

"I'm just going to use the bathroom," Carrie lied and got out of bed. "Won't be a minute."

No, she wasn't a minute. Half an hour later she tip-toed back into Bodhi's bedroom, relieved to see her suspicions had been right and he'd fallen asleep. What a fucking sore excuse of a woman was she? A guy was pouring his heart out to her and she'd run away, too afraid to hear him say the words she'd had a feeling were coming. Three little words that would tear through her heart like a bullet shot at close range.

Whether she'd had to wake Bodhi up every couple of hours or not, Carrie would have had one of the worst sleeps of her life that night. There was only one period of two hours between checks that she actually went to sleep and even then, she'd woken up three times before her alarm went off.

Bodhi had been able to answer her questions and other than being sleepy, didn't show any of the warning signs she needed to look out for. That was a relief, at least. She'd be leaving with the knowledge he was on the mend and hopefully wouldn't spend too much time worrying about him. Missing him would be a different story, but at least she wouldn't be worrying.

Hearing movement in the other end of the house Carrie knew it was almost time and pushed the tears that threatened *waaaaay* down. She couldn't let emotion rule her that day, not when she had something so important to do. Important and cold-hearted. Was she really going to say goodbye, walk out the door and never turn back?

It was made worse when Bodhi rolled over and kissed her sweetly before putting his arms around her and holding her against him. "Thanks for last night."

"It's okay."

"I hope you got some sleep."

"I did."

"Are you okay, Carrie?"

"I'm fine," she lied. "I've just got a busy day coming up at work and it's been playing on my mind a bit."

Something was certainly playing on her mind, it just wasn't work.

"Leave whenever you're ready, Dalton is home and Mum will be over at some point this morning."

There was a hint of disappointment to his voice, and Carrie came horrendously close to suggesting she could come over after work, but remembered that would no longer be an option.

A letter was going to have to do. There was no way in hell she was going to be able to say what she needed to say and remain on top of her emotions. She was going to have to say goodbye to Bodhi and Dalton in a way that seemed natural and didn't give away the pain she was feeling inside. For all her planning, there wasn't going to be a chance to say goodbye properly.

Ten minutes later and dressed, she tried to sound upbeat when saying goodbye to Bodhi while taking a final look in those dreamy green eyes. She'd kissed him softly, longingly, her throat closing over as she struggled to keep her emotions at bay.

"See you later," Bodhi said.

It took all her strength to smile at him and say, "Sure."

She walked into the kitchen and politely turned down Dalton's offer of a coffee, telling him she needed to get to work. As with Bodhi, she kissed him goodbye, the pain in her chest threatening to bring her to her knees as she took in the overwhelmingly beautiful sight of the man who made her feel so protected and safe.

"Have a good day!" Dalton called behind her.

Walking down the hall she managed a croaked "Uh huh", as her vision fogged over and her throat closed tight, she felt like she couldn't breathe. The pain in her chest surged, sorrow streaming through her veins as she walked down the front steps, refusing to look back for fear of what might happen.

She opened the driver's side door and got in her car, managing to drive for an entire thirty seconds before waves of grief caused her to pull over before she crashed and killed someone.

After a few minutes of bawling on the side of the road, earning her confused looks from passers-by, Carrie made it home safely. The tears held off until she'd closed the door behind her and leaned against it. She wasn't sure if she slid down to the floor on purpose or if she collapsed, but she wasn't going to be moving any time soon.

Taking her phone out of her handbag, she called her boss, feeling like a deceptive bitch for what she was about to do.

"Angelique," Carrie didn't give her a chance to speak. "I hate to do this but I need to take some leave, I have a family emergency and I can't go into any details right now b—"

"Oh shit, I'm sorry Caz. Don't worry about explaining, I can tell by your voice that you're in no state to discuss whatever is happening. You do what you need to do, okay? Ring me when things have calmed down a bit and we'll go into specifics about the amount of time you'll need."

She sobbed loudly. "Th-thanks An-Ange."

"Let me know if I can help in any way."

"I w-will. S-sorry."

"Don't apologise, you go and be with your family. I'll email you later okay?"

"Okay, b-bye."

Hanging up Carrie felt ashamed of what she'd just done. She'd flat out lied to her boss and used her family as an excuse for the state she was in, which was her own doing. It was bad, bad karma to lie about something bad happening in your family and knowing her luck something really bad would happen now, and it would be all her fault.

She needed to act quick if she was to carry through with what needed to be done so she forced herself to her feet and went into her bedroom to prepare. Not only was she leaving Bodhi and Dalton without talking to them, she'd decided the grown-up thing to do was run away from her problems and sitting on the edge of her bed, with tears irritating her cheeks, she booked a one-way flight to Brisbane, departing in four hours.

While she was at it, she opened her banking app and paid Jess the last five thousand dollars, wondering when she was going to get a call from the bank because of suspicious activity on her account. What would she say? *'No, no, nothing suspicious, just paying off blackmail demands.'* That would go down really well.

She pulled her red suitcase out of her wardrobe and started packing, having no idea how many days she was packing for. Could be one day, could be forever. Did she really think she could just bugger off to Brisbane and start over again? Her parents would be happy to see her, but they'd think she was crazy just turning up on their doorstep unannounced. It occurred to her she was going to have to tell them something, but she could think about that when she was on the plane.

There was a more pressing matter requiring her attention. The letter.

She sat down at the dining room table with pen and paper and after scrapping many attempts, finally signed off on the letter she hoped would explain her feelings and justify her actions.

Dear Bodhi and Dalton

I hate doing this to you via a letter, but no matter how hard I tried I just couldn't find the strength required to say this to you face to face. Let me start by saying the past month has been the best of my life... and that is kind of the problem. Back when we started doing what we've been doing, we agreed that if one of us didn't feel right about it, we'd end it. I thought that when it eventually came to an end it would be because we'd gotten it out of our systems and the novelty of having three in the bed had worn off, but I now realise how wrong I was. I feel like a piece of scum for doing this in a letter, but I can't see either of you again. My feelings have got in the way and I've come to the conclusion that what I feel for you both goes far beyond merely liking you. I stupidly fell in love with two men, who deserve so much more than what I can give them. You're both young and amazing and sweet and caring and hellishly sexy, and you each deserve to find that one person you want to spend the rest of your life with. You deserve weddings and babies, you deserve all the happiness in the world and I don't think that happiness can come from this 'thing' we have. It might work to begin with, but you'll eventually want more from life than sharing me. I don't want to hold either of you back from doing the things you want to do because I'm at the age where I want to settle down and for my dreams of a family to come true, that's something I need to get onto sooner rather than later. I don't want to tie either of you down because my biological clock is ticking. I am so sorry. I know this letter is me taking the easy way out, but it was the only way I could get my feelings out and say what needed to be said. I love you both and my heart is breaking as I write this, but it's what I need to do to set you both free, so you can have the happiness and love you deserve. Thank you for the amazing 32 days you gave me, I will never forget it, or you. Especially you.

Love,
Carrie xxxx

CHAPTER NINETEEN

Swinging the door open, Nova smiled.

"Hey stran—"

"It's all so fucked up," Carrie sobbed.

"Oh fuck, what's happened?" Nova took her hand and led her inside. "What did those boys do?"

Carrie shook her head and covered her face with her hands. "They didn't do anything, it was m-me."

"What do you mean?"

Unable to explain, Carrie took the letter from her handbag and handed it to Nova. "This."

She couldn't look as Nova read the letter and picked at a loose thread on her jeans, as if it was the most interesting thing in the world.

"Bloody hell, Carrie."

"I can't do it, Nova. I just can't."

"I don't get it. You love them, why does that suddenly equate to needing to end it?"

"It's like I explained in the letter, I can't hold them back, I can't tie them down, they deserve so much more than I can give."

"Honey, they are both crazy about you. I doubt they'd see it as you holding them back or tying them down."

"Whether that's true or not, I would always see it that way."

"I get the feeling nothing I can say is going to make you change your mind."

"It's not." Carrie swallowed back a lump of tears. "And now I need to ask you a favour."

"What?"

"Could you take the letter over to them? I don't want to leave it in the mailbox in case it somehow goes missing or there is a downpour and it gets saturated and they can't read it."

"I don't want to." Nova sighed. "But because I can see how tough this is on you, I will do it. I think you're making a mistake though and, as soon as they read it, they'll be on your doorstep."

Carrie looked away and knew guilt was written all over her face.

"If you're going to be at your house?"

"I-I need to get away for a few days. Clear my head. Let the dust settle. Any of those clichés that people throw around when they're running away from their problems."

"Where are you going?"

"Away. Just... away." Her lower lip trembled and no matter how hard she tried to force the tears away they came, fat drops rolling down her cheek and tumbling from her chin.

Nova smiled sadly and put her arms around her, rubbing her back soothingly, not bothering to tell her to stop crying, which Carrie appreciated. She needed this release badly and made the most of being able to share her sorrow, rather than having to keep it all to herself.

When time came for her to leave Nova hugged her and made her promise to keep in touch while she was away. Carrie promised she would but refused to tell her where she was going for fear her friend would tell the men where she was.

If Bodhi and Dalton felt so inclined there was a chance, they'd go out to Avoca Beach expecting to find her there, and she felt a bit guilty she'd be sending them on a wild goose chase. She didn't think they'd try to find her though; they'd probably read the letter and move on to someone younger and far more enjoyable.

Driving toward the airport Carrie didn't feel as relieved as she'd expected she would. All she could think about was Bodhi and Dalton and how they'd react to her letter, hoping it wouldn't be as hard for them to read as it had been for her to write. Who was she kidding? Of course, it wouldn't be! They would probably think they'd been let off the hook and soon enough she'd be a vague memory in the deepest recesses of their minds.

Knowing long term parking at the airport would cost her an arm and a leg, she parked in the Blu Emu carpark and managed to catch the free shuttle bus to the airport five minutes later.

Was she really doing this? Just running away?

Later, as the plane was taxiing down the tarmac, she hung her head in shame, because running away was precisely what she was doing. She'd turned her phone off when leaving Nova's house so even if they wanted to, no one would be able to contact her.

How had it come to this? How had she stooped so low?

***

The weather in Brisbane was hot and sticky and a temperature gauge outside the airport told her it was thirty-two degrees, ten degrees hotter than it had been in Sydney when she'd left. Gross. She hadn't dressed for the conditions and before finding a taxi she went back inside and changed her jeans and long-sleeved t-shirt for a skirt and short sleeved tee, wishing she'd thought to pack sunblock because after a minute in that heat she'd be as red as a lobster.

The taxi driver made small talk as they drove the fifteen minutes to her parents' house, but she wasn't much in the mood for discussing the weather, or the latest political debacle, and certainly not the reason for her trip. '*Just visiting my parents*', she'd explained adding another person to the list of people she'd lied to that day.

Driving through the suburb of Nudgee, Carrie felt detached from the city her parents now considered home, and already found herself missing Sydney and her quaint little house.

Without thinking she took her phone from her bag, putting it away just as quickly when she remembered she couldn't message Bodhi and Dalton to tell them how hot and stupid Brisbane was. She couldn't even contact Nova because that would require turning her phone on, the thought of which made her nauseatingly nervous.

Speaking of nervous, when the taxi pulled up outside her parents' house, she was suddenly worried what they would think of her arriving unannounced. They'd know straight away something was wrong, and how could she possibly explain it to them? It was likely they'd think it had something to do with the photos of her, Bodhi and Dalton – and that wouldn't be entirely wrong, but it wasn't the full story either.

As she walked up to the door she considered turning around and racing after the taxi which had just pulled away, but where would that leave her?

Carrie knocked on the door before giving herself a chance to chicken out and could hear the tap-tap-tap of high heels growing louder, her mum, Lindsay, no doubt wondering who was knocking at the door.

The door opened, and her mum actually squealed when she saw who it was.

"Carrie! Darling! What are you doing here?" Lindsay laugh-cried. "What a lovely surprise! I was just saying to your dad yesterday that we should fly down to visit you, and now here you are!" She wiped her eyes. "Oh darling, it's so lovely to see you."

"You too, Mum," Carrie said, wiping her own eyes. "I hope you don't mind me turning up like this."

"Of course not! Come in, come in! Do you want a cup of tea? Coffee? A wine?"

"Coffee would be great."

"How are you?"

"I'm... I'm..." The rest of the words stuck in her throat.

"Darling? Are you okay?"

Carrie shook her head and blinked back tears, hoping her mum wouldn't see she was crying. Her mum, of course, knew her daughter better than anyone and led her straight through to the lounge and sat her down on the couch, putting her arms tightly around her and rocking slowly from side to side like she'd done when Carrie was four and had woken up after a nightmare.

"Sweetheart? What's wrong?"

"You're going to think I'm horrible if I tell you. I've fucked things up so badly, Mum."

"I would never think you were horrible, Carrie. I'm your mum and I'll always love you regardless."

This wasn't how it was going to go. She was meant to have a nice week with her parents, escaping the aftermath of what she'd left behind in Sydney. No part of her plan had included breaking down minutes after arriving, prepared to tell her mum everything.

"I've made a horrible mess."

"Do you want to talk about it?"

"Yes, but no."

"You know what they say, about a problem shared..."

"I'm in love, Mum." She spat the words out.

"What is so wrong with that?"

"I'm in love with..." A deep breath. "With two people."

"Two... oh..."

Carrie pulled out of her mum's arms and turned away from her. "I know. It's disgusting and immoral and I deserve everything I get now."

"The men from those photos?" her mum guessed.

She turned back to face her mum. "I tried so hard not to, you have no idea."

"Can't help who you fall in love with."

"Th-that's all you've got to say? You're not going to yell at me, or call me an idiot or tell me how disgusting I am?"

"Darling, I have never been in your shoes, so I can't understand exactly how you feel, but I understand what it means to be in love. I take it they didn't react well when you told them?"

"Well, um..." Carrie looked at a space above her mum's head. "I didn't actually tell them. Not in person anyway. I don't even know if they know yet."

"What do you mean?"

Having to say the words out loud, Carrie knew how ridiculous it sounded. "I wrote a letter telling them, and that we couldn't see each other again, and Bodhi's sister was going to drop it over at some point today. They don't know I've left Sydney, well, they might by now, but I don't know because I turned my phone off when I left Nova's house."

"Christ. I know you wanted a coffee, but I think you deserve something a bit stronger. How about we break into your dad's whisky?"

"As long as we don't have to talk about this again until later... I know I need to deal with it properly and that, at some point, I will need to talk to Bodhi and Dalton, but for the next few hours, can I just pretend everything is fine and that I'm on holiday visiting my parents like a good daughter?"

"You're right. You need to deal with it, but it can wait until tomorrow. Your dad will be home soon, how about we go out for dinner, a late celebration for your birthday."

"Thanks, Mum," Carrie said through her tears.

She hoped her mum thought they were tears of relief or gratitude, the tears of a daughter who was getting the much-needed support she so badly wanted from her parents. In reality, the tears stemmed from the memory of her birthday weekend with Bodhi and Dalton, and the unwanted reality check that had put a dampener on their time away, bringing it to a premature end.

***

Watching her father drive up the driveway when he arrived home from work, Carrie thought he was going to have a heart attack when he realised who was standing with his wife. He ran up to the stoop and hugged Carrie so tightly she wondered if her ribs were going to crack.

It was the best surprise of his life, apparently, and for the first time that day, Carrie felt like she wasn't a complete failure as a human being. Then she thought about the fact that her only reason for being there was because she was escaping the mess she'd made in Sydney, and she was back to feeling like shit.

"What brings you to sunny Brisbane anyway?" her dad, James, asked when they were inside and he'd kicked off his shoes.

She stalled and looked at her mum. "Umm."

"James, why don't you go and have a shower. I thought we could take Carrie out for a belated birthday dinner. Don't want to leave it too late though or it will take forever to get a table."

Carrie had never been so grateful for Lindsay's habit of interrupting and mouthed '*thank you*', earning herself a knowing wink from her mum.

While James showered, Carrie took the opportunity to go into the room she slept in when visiting and got changed into something more suited for a dinner out. She looked at her cell phone sitting beside the bed and, remembering her promise to keep in touch with Nova, she turned her phone on and waited for her screen to flash as she was flooded with messages.

Disappointingly, there were only two messages and they were both from Nova. One telling her she'd delivered the letter, and the second sent an hour earlier, asking where she was and if she was okay.

Aware Nova would be worrying about her, Carrie replied, '*I am okay...ish. Sorry I didn't text you earlier, but I had my phone off because I was in full avoidance mode. I guess Bodhi and Dalton didn't care about the content of the letter because I haven't had as much as a 'go to hell, bitch' text.*'

'*Maybe they're in avoidance mode as well, Carrie. Probably think you don't want to hear from them. Someone is going to have to make the first move because no matter what you said in that letter, the three of you need to talk like adults. Be the one to reach out. You owe them that much.*'.

Nova's reply stung, but everything she'd said had been deserved and Carrie couldn't take offense.

'*Were they upset?*' She had to know.

'*Of course they were. What did you think would happen? They'd get the letter and go 'oh well, that was nice while it lasted?*'

'*You know me too well...*'

'*Just take care of yourself, okay? Call me if you need to... I know I'm Bodhi's sister, but I am also your friend and I care about you.*'

'Probably doesn't seem like it, but it means a lot to me xxx' And it did, but now she was feeling incredibly guilty for putting Nova in what had to be an awkward position, acting as the go-between in a situation involving her own brother.

They left for dinner just after six and driving into the Brisbane CBD, Carrie found herself wondering what Bodhi and Dalton would be doing that moment. Considering Bodhi's concussion, she didn't think he would be doing much and doubted Dalton would have left him by himself. Maybe they'd be watching the fourth Die Hard movie, bundled up on the couch beneath their comforters.

Would they think about the empty space between them on the couch? If they did, would they miss her presence or be angry with her for running away like the coward she was? For all she knew they were talking about what a horrible lay she'd been and laughing about how eager she'd been to please them. They could have been playing her that whole time, or at least that's what she tried to tell herself, but she knew it wasn't the case.

She was the one who'd ended it and did not have the right to be trying to make things easier on herself.

"How long are you staying for, Caz?" James asked.

"Not sure, Dad. A few days, I think. I've taken some much-needed leave and am just playing it by ear."

"In other words," he joked, "you'll leave when we start pissing you off."

Her mum punched his upper arm. "Jim! Lay off her!"

"He was just joking, Mum."

"Yes, Lindsay, listen to your daughter. I was just playing around."

"Where are we going?" Carrie asked, hoping to prevent her parents bickering.

Lindsay turned and smiled at her. "Well since it's a special occasion I thought we'd go to this amazing place called *St. James Crabhouse*, if that sounds good to you?"

"Crabhouse implies seafood so yes, sounds bloody good to me!"

How would it compare to the restaurant Bodhi and Dalton had taken her to? Suddenly the prospect of seafood was as sad as it was exciting. The meal she'd shared with the men the previous week had been one of the best of her life and she didn't know that anything would ever be able to beat it.

She wished it was Bodhi and Dalton in the car exploring Brisbane with her. Maybe they'd travel north and spend some time on the Sunshine Coast or go south and enjoy the sun on the Gold Coast. It was hot enough to swim in Queensland and she could imagine the fun the three of them could have going back and forth between the beach and the water. Things would undoubtedly get a bit naughty, but not to the extent they embarrassed themselves in public; beneath the water hands could wander and body parts could be rubbed and teased.

"You okay, lovey?" James asked, glancing at her in the rear view mirror.

"Yes, Dad. Just been a long day, that's all."

"I was going to suggest we could do a bit of sightseeing after dinner, but if you prefer, we can go home," her mum said, sounding disappointed.

Carrie hadn't exactly been a fan of them moving to Brisbane and had resisted becoming familiar with the city that, in her eyes, had stolen her family from her, and she knew it upset her mum.

"No, Mum. It's a beautiful evening so it would be silly not to make the most of it. I'd love it if you could show me around!"

"Oh, I would love to! You don't mind, do you, Jim?"

"Not at all, not if it means a chance to spend time with my two favourite girls."

Was she going to turn *every* innocent remark into something selfish? Her dad had two favourite girls, but all she could think was that she had two favourite men—who could never be part of her life again.

"How is work going, Dad?" Carrie tried to sound relaxed, but inside felt like she was slowly dying.

"I sometimes miss being in a hospital environment, but I love the normal hours I work at the practice! My weekends are my own and so are my nights; means I can take your mum out on dates or away for weekends. It's been a long time since we could do any of that."

"What about the dress shop, Mum? Last time we spoke, you were interviewing for a new bridal consultant?"

"It is wonderful. I'm so much happier than when I was working for Jude. Was a huge scary leap buying the shop here, but I'm so glad I did. There is nothing quite as special as seeing the look on a bride-to-be's face when she finds *the* dress. We've been getting a lot of women coming in specifically for the plus-size range. I'm so happy you pointed me in the direction of Lisabeth Grace, she is a phenomenal designer."

Carrie could tell how passionate her mum was about the shop by the way she hardly stopped to take a breath. It was a nice change from when her parents had still been living in Sydney and she'd been miserable in her job, mostly because her boss was a complete and utter bitch, who treated her like she was too old to understand anything about fashion. Lindsay had certainly shown her.

"I'm proud of you, Mum."

"Thank you, darling!"

"What about Heartbeat, Caz? How goes the publishing business?" James asked

"Stressful, exciting, challenging, rewarding, everything you could want in a job."

"I bought Liliana Tosca's new book last week," Lindsay said. "She's one of yours, isn't she?"

Carrie laughed, "Yes, Lili is a great writer and an even nicer person. I'll tell her you're a fan, she'll get a kick out of that."

When they were standing outside *St. James Crabhouse* in Kangaroo Point, Carrie promised herself she was going to enjoy the meal and the evening. Thoughts of Bodhi and Dalton could wait until they were back home, and she was in bed, where she would be free to cry and not risk the chance of her parents noticing.

The meal itself was good, but it didn't live up in her mind to the meal she'd had with Bodhi and Dalton in Bondi, and she had a feeling it was more to do with the lack of the two men than the quality of the food. Though her usual order when she went to a seafood restaurant was the mussels, she purposely opted for the prawns that night because, as silly as it sounded, she had no memories of prawns that were associated with Bodhi and Dalton.

Yes, she was now officially letting her memories of Bodhi and Dalton dictate what she ate.

Unable to resist, they ordered dessert and the key lime pie Carrie ordered was so divine it made her eyes roll back in her head. It was the most pleasurable experience she'd had in recent times—outside of a bedroom setting, of course—and she'd been tempted to order another piece to take home with her. She didn't, but it was a fair bet that she'd be back for the dessert before leaving for Sydney. Whenever that may be.

The sun was setting when they left St. James and drove the short distance to South Bank, parking near the impressive Wheel of Brisbane. It was one of the first things her parents had done when moving to Brisbane and her mum hadn't shut up about it, making Carrie promise that when she visited, they would go on it together. They hadn't, and it was all her fault—she'd always had an excuse on hand as to why it 'wouldn't work this time', promising they'd do it next time.

Making excuses not to do something because she was jealous of how happy her parents were in Brisbane was just immature, and she wished she hadn't been such a passive aggressive bitch. Who knew when they would be gone? She could put it off and put it off, but how would she feel if her mum died and she hadn't gone on the gondola wheel with her? Awful was the answer, and she'd probably never forgive herself.

"Lovely view of Brisbane from up the top," Lindsay said.

James nodded and put an arm around his wife's shoulders. "Very romantic."

Aaaaaaand down she crashed, bombarded with images of walking hand in hand with both men along the beach at Coogee, of dancing with Dalton at his cousin's wedding, of being tackled into the water at Avoca and the shower that followed. Then there were vaguer memories of the men picking her up from Jess's and taking care of her in her shockingly drunk state. That night, more than anything, had proved to her how much they'd cared for her, and she'd thrown it all back in their faces.

It was too late to start considering whether or not the letter had been the right option, but she was starting to have her doubts. Who knew what would have happened if she'd spoken up and told them how she felt.

Now she would never know.

Her parents were right, the view from the top of the wheel was spectacular, giving a 360-degree view of the city. The sun had just gone down, casting an eerie light over the city, the lights from the buildings of the CBD creating little exclamation points in the darkening haze.

It was indeed romantic, and her thoughts quickly drifted to Bodhi and Dalton, imagining standing between the two of them, all looking out in awe at the sight of Brisbane by night. For as long as she could remember, the beach had been her happy place, whether it was Avoca, or one of the local beaches, it was where she'd go to feel her heart soar and let the endorphins rush. Nothing had ever given her that same feeling of being completely at ease, until now. Bodhi and Dalton made her feel that way, she realised. They were her happy place, a happy place she'd permanently banned herself from.

In effect, she was banning herself from being happy ever again.

It was what she deserved.

***

"You all settled, Pumpkin?"

Carrie looked at her dad who was leaning against the doorframe, an odd look on his face. "I think so! Thanks for tonight, I had a really good time."

He entered the room and looked as if he was trying to make a decision, finally coming to rest on the end of her bed. "Are you sure?"

"I did, Dad. I'm so glad I had a chance to explore a bit of Brisbane with you and Mum."

"Didn't stop you thinking about the reason you ran away though, did it?" Her dad's voice was soft, his tone non-judgemental, but full of the type of concern only a parent can display.

"That obvious, huh?" What was the point in pretending everything was fine, when it wasn't?

"The way you'd gaze off into the distance, your eyes cloudy with misery? Yeah, it was obvious." He took a deep breath. "What's going on with you, Pumpkin?"

"Do you want me to lie and pretend it's something at work, or do you want the truth, even if it will probably change how you see me?"

"You know the answer to that, darling. I hate seeing you so flat and I'm not an idiot, I know it's something to do with the opposite sex. I might be old and a bit decrepit now, but I remember what it's like to be young and to have your heart sent all a flutter."

There was no point lying, he'd get the truth out of her mum when he went to bed anyway.

"Long story short, the two guys from the photos? I stupidly fell in love with both of them and, earlier today, I told them we can't see each other again, and now here I am, under the guise of clearing my head, but really I've just run away."

"Ah, I see." James gave her a sympathetic look. "Can't say I know how it feels to be in love with two people at the same time, but I can imagine it's incredibly hard and that your brain probably feels like it's exploding about now."

"Can say that again."

"I presume it's not quite as easy as just picking one?"

"That's the thing, I can't. But they have never expected me to choose and until I started freaking out, we were quite happy with the status quo."

"If everyone was happy, why the need to call it off?"

"Because they deserve more than me, Dad. They deserve to find the woman they want to spend the rest of their lives with, they deserve families, they deserve to grow old with their soulmate."

"What if you're that person for both of them?"

"It just wouldn't work! How can a relationship with three people be anything other than a complete mess?"

"Two of my families at the practice are polyamorous," James said. "One is quite a young triad, in fact, I had the pleasure last week of telling them they're pregnant with their first child. The other family are quite a bit older, older than me and your mother, and when I saw one of them last, they told me all about the trip they'd taken to Hawaii to celebrate their fortieth anniversary."

"Forty years? Wow."

"It doesn't have to be a complete mess. I have a feeling that as with any relationship, the success or failure is all down to how the individuals grow and adapt with each other, and how hard you work at making the relationship a happy, healthy one."

"It could ruin their careers though, Dad. Jess turned on me in a huge way, she's blackmailing me actually."

James gasped and looked horrified. "Why would she do that?"

"She recorded conversations between the two of us where I told her certain... details... about my time with Bodhi and Dalton. She is the one who leaked those photos to the press, and on the day they appeared, she came over and told me if I didn't pay her she would leak the voice recordings as well. Those recordings... they would leave absolutely no doubt about what I have done with Bodhi and Dalton, and it would create a scandal big enough to destroy their reputations, at the very least."

"Fuck."

Her dad never swore, so to hear that word coming from his mouth was quite something.

"Exactly."

"What did Bodhi and Dalton say about the blackmail?"

"I didn't tell them. It was stress they didn't need. It was me who couldn't keep my mouth shut, and it was my backstabbing bitch of a best friend who did it, so why should I bother them?"

"I don't know either of them, but I can assure you they'd want to know, and regardless of whether they feel the same way about you or not, they wouldn't want you dealing with it by yourself!"

"It's done now," Carrie shrugged. "They don't need to know."

He held his arms out to her and smiled sadly. "Come here, Pumpkin."

For the first time since she was a child, Carrie spent the next hour crying against her daddy's chest, but unlike when she was a child, the comforting hold of her dad didn't magically make everything better. That responsibility lay solely on her shoulders this time.

CHAPTER TWENTY

Carrie was wrenched from a dream about being at the beach with Bodhi and Dalton, by the creaking of the bedroom door being pushed open.

"Carrie," her mum whispered loudly. "Carrie!" Louder this time.

"What?" she groaned, huffing and pulling the blankets over her head as if to fight off a swarm of invisible bees.

"I'm going to work now. I'll be back around three."

"You could have just left me a note." It was like she was a teenager again. "Sorry, I just didn't sleep well. Ignore me. Have a good day at work. Love you."

"Love you too, darling. Make yourself at home."

The door closed again and under her breath she muttered, "Could have at least brought me a coffee after waking me up."

Curtains opened, and Carrie cringed. Fuck, her mum had heard her sounding like an ungrateful little cow, hadn't she? In hopes her mum would think she'd gone back to sleep, she stayed perfectly still and even made some sighy sleep sounds to help with the impression of being asleep.

Light blinded her as the blankets were pulled back and she covered her face with her hands. "Seriously, Mum? What the fuck are you doing?"

"Rise and shine!" It was Bodhi's voice, she must have still been dreaming.

"Oh, and surprise!" Dalton's voice this time, she frowned, feeling very much awake, but it didn't make sense, she was in Brisbane not Syd—

"After the shitty way you left things yesterday, the least you could do is look at us." Bodhi.

Bodhi and Dalton were... What the hell was going on? How could they—

She moved her hands and blinked, allowing her eyes to adjust to the unwanted light washing the room. "What the fuck?"

Standing before her were Bodhi and Dalton, neither man looking especially happy, their faces clouded with something akin to anger, but not quite as vicious.

Dalton put his hands on his hips and pursed his lips. "You ran away from your problem, so we had no choice but to run to ours." The frown lines creasing his forehead told the story of just how pissed off he was.

"I'm sorry, I just—"

"No, Carrie," Bodhi said shaking his head. "You had your say yesterday, now it is our chance."

"I can ex—"

Bodhi wagged his finger at her. "No. We talk, you listen."

"Why the hell didn't you talk to us, Carrie? When you started to feel it was becoming more than a bit of fun, why didn't you tell us? Wasn't it what we all agreed on back at the start, that we'd be open?" Rather than looking pissed off now, Dalton looked sad. Defeated.

"I'm sorry."

"Do you have any idea how hard it was reading that fucking letter yesterday? In front of my sister, no less?!" Betrayal was written all over Bodhi's face. "As for getting her to do your dirty work for you, why would you do that? Don't you think she has more important things to do with her life?" He took a deep breath and sighed, his face relaxing marginally. "It was devastating. To think you thought so little of us that you didn't think we could deal with what you were feeling."

She hadn't thought of it that way.

"What made you think you had the authority to decide what I wanted, and what Bodhi wanted? Don't you think we should have been allowed to make those decisions for ourselves? You took the choice right out of our hands, like you knew what was best for us."

"I didn't think it would make you angry..." Carrie swallowed back tears made up of equal parts guilt and regret.

Dalton sat on the edge of the bed and finally looked at her, really looked at her. "We aren't angry, Carrie. Upset, confused, disappointed, sure. But not angry."

"Maybe a little bit pissed off," Bodhi said and gave her a lukewarm smile. "But mostly, we just wanted you to hear what we had to say."

"I know it was cowardly to write the letter, and even worse to get Nova to give it to you, but I couldn't bring myself to say the words I needed to say, because it made me cry just thinking them. Saying them would have killed me." Her voice was watery with tears, but she forced herself to continue. "I don't care about me, but I care about both of you immensely and I couldn't handle the thought that I could be the reason your reputations were ruined and that your careers could come to a screaming halt all because of me."

"Who is to say any of that would happen?" Dalton asked.

"Well... it just... would," Carrie said, angry with herself for keeping the Jess saga from them.

But it was too late to go into it now. The money had been paid and with any luck Jess would be living on the other side of the world soon, and it would all be a shitty memory.

"Because that trashy hoe Jess thought it was perfectly okay to blackmail her best friend?" Bodhi's words made Carrie gasp.

"You... you knew?"

"Yesterday, when we were trying to get our heads around your letter Nova let slip that you were being blackmailed by that little bitch. She told us all about it." Dalton sounded angry now. "Why didn't you tell us, Carrie? We could have dealt with it *together*, done what we had to do to make sure she didn't see one cent of the money she, for whatever reason, felt she was owed."

The tears came then, oh how they came.

"Move over," Bodhi said to her, toeing his shoes off and removing his pants, followed by the rest of his clothes, while Dalton did the same.

"You don't h-have t-to."

"No, we don't have to, but we want to," Dalton said, getting in beside her as Bodhi got in on the other side and, finally, she was back where she wanted to be, between the two men who'd turned her life upside down in the very best way.

"Don't you get it?" Bodhi said. "We are both in love with you, Carrie."

"Have been since the night we met." Dalton added.

"You can't love me though," Carrie sobbed. "You deserve more, far more than I can ever offer." It was everything she'd ever wanted, but at the same time it was the last thing she wanted to hear.

"What exactly do you think we deserve?" Bodhi asked, looking bemused.

"Love, marriage, babies, exploring the world, an easy and uncomplicated life."

"And why exactly can't we have those things with you?" Dalton asked pointedly.

"For starters it's illegal to marry more than one person, the babies part, who knows if I can even get pregnant? Exploring the world? Well, I guess we can do that, but you guys will want to go island hopping and get crazy in Bali, and I'm too old for that shit. As for easy and uncomplicated? Fuck, what about a polyamorous relationship will ever be easy and uncomplicated?"

Bodhi responded quickly and passionately. "Marriage between three? Illegal, yes, but that isn't to say there couldn't be a commitment ceremony of sorts. Babies? There is more than one way to have one. Travelling? I don't give a damn about Bali and the next trip I go on, I want to explore somewhere full of history, like Greece. Easy and uncomplicated? Who said life is ever easy or uncomplicated? It's not. There is always something cropping up, but I can be myself with you, and Carrie, there is nothing complicated about how much I love you." The last few words were said with so much passion and conviction she was sure her heart skipped a beat.

A glimmer of hope hung over her, but she was too afraid it would vanish if she allowed herself to think they had a chance.

Now Dalton took his opportunity. "The thing is, we're both absolutely fucking mad about you, and I know I speak for both of us when I say that, if it came down to choosing our careers or choosing you, you would win hands down." He looked at her with those big chocolatey eyes and continued. "Our careers might last another six or seven years if we're lucky, or in a split second one badly executed tackle could end it all in the first game back next season. But you... you'll always be there, what we feel for you will always be there. Loving you isn't something that has an expiry date, Carrie. Whether you like it or not, I love you and the idea of losing you hurts a lot worse than the idea of losing my career."

"Wh-what are you saying?"

"What do you think we're saying?" Bodhi asked. "We spent four hours yesterday travelling to and from Avoca Beach on the off chance you'd gone there, then we had an impromptu meeting with our coach at his house, because we needed to talk to him about what had been happening and what might potentially happen if we made you see sense when we eventually found you."

Dalton smiled. "We have his blessing, by the way."

Bodhi continued. "And then we spent two fucking hours convincing Jess that what she was doing was wrong and that if she didn't delete all copies of the recording and leave you alone, we'd be taking the matter to the police. Then we needed to find out where your parents live, at least Jess came in useful there, because she could tell us their names and after that it was easy enough to find the address online. That just left getting up at a horrendous hour this morning to catch the 6:30 a.m. flight to Brisbane, oh, and the prospect of meeting your parents and whether or not they'd even let us in the house."

Hearing the lengths they'd gone to in order to track her down left Carrie speechless, not to mention wondering how Bodhi had said all of that without passing out from lack of oxygen.

For the first time since they'd arrived in her room, Dalton laughed. "Your mum makes the best buttermilk pancakes, by the way."

Remembering what they'd said about Jess, Carrie rewound the conversation. "Hold up, exactly what happened with Jess?"

"What I said, really. We arrived, she let us in, and I think she thought we were there to tell her we wanted her or something, because she said she'd been expecting this and knew you couldn't keep us satisfied." Dalton snorted. "Don't worry, we set her straight on that. We then told her we knew she was blackmailing you and asked if she knew blackmail was actually illegal. I told her if she didn't delete every single recording she had, back-ups included, that we'd be going straight from her house to the police station and laying a complaint."

"She refused to start with," Bodhi continued the story. "Suggested perhaps we could come to a different arrangement, that she'd give you your money back if we agreed to be at her every sexual beck and call, but funnily enough we refused. Told her if she wasn't going to agree that was fine and our next stop would be the police station."

"But she did agree?"

"Yeah, we watched as she deleted the voice recordings on her phone, and on three USBs. We then recorded a video of her, stating she had received thirty thousand dollars from you because she'd blackmailed you. Finally, we got her to sign a written declaration, which we have locked away at home, just in case."

"You-you did that for me?"

"Don't you get it, you silly woman? We love you and we would do anything for you."

"I-I love you too." Carrie declared. "Both of you. So much that it scares me."

"What are we going to do about it then?" Dalton asked, leaning in and kissing her.

"What do you want, Carrie?" It was Bodhi who kissed her this time.

"I want you. I want both of you. I want *us*."

"Carrie Lucas," Dalton said taking one of her hands, while Bodhi took the other. "You have us. Always have, and always will."

For a few seconds they just smiled at each other, it was Bodhi who eventually broke the spell. "Now that you've got us, will you *please* come here and kiss me?"

There was no way she needed to be asked twice and as his lips pressed to hers, she smiled against his mouth, loving the way it felt to be back in bed, sandwiched between two warm bodies.

His tongue lazily swiped against the tip of hers and Carrie arched back into Dalton who was, as usual, nipping and biting at her neck in a way that made her want to claw the sheets.

The act of pressing her hips back against Dalton brought his cock into contact with her ass and Carrie shuddered, remembering the shower they'd shared at Avoca Beach when she'd confessed to fantasising about anal sex. Judging by the way Dalton had started rocking his hips against her ass, she concluded he was thinking about it as well.

Her thoughts were pulled from that of a cock sliding into her ass by Bodhi's fingers plucking her nipple. Gasping when he plucked harder, Carrie ground against Dalton, all too aware of the hardness of his erection against the crack of her ass, making her hips move in tighter circles against him.

Bodhi swapped his fingers for his mouth and sucked on her nipple, softly to begin with, but quickly harder, sucking more of her in and tormenting her with the friction of his tongue.

With mouth on nipple, Bodhi's hand was free to move elsewhere, which it did at a painfully slow speed, following the curve of her waist, over her hips and inward, until her breath was coming in shorts bursts, waiting for his fingers to finally slip into the part of her anatomy that was screaming for him.

When he gently spread the swollen lips of her pussy, Carrie cried out and fought the compulsion to put pressure on his hand in an attempt to take more of him inside her.

"You feel so good," Bodhi whispered. "God, I've missed you."

"I've missed you too," Carrie whispered in reply, then turned her head in Dalton's direction and although she couldn't see him, added, "And I've missed you."

The moment called for her to say something heartfelt, but the only noise that came from her was a moan of the purest pleasure known to woman, at the feeling of two of Bodhi's fingers pushing inside her.

Before they could get too carried away, she knew she had to impart some bad news. "I don't have any condoms..."

"Luckily, we came prepared," Dalton said and tugged on her earlobe before moving from behind her and getting off the bed. Beside the door were two bags they'd obviously dropped when surprising her earlier, and from one of the bag's he took a box of condoms and a small red bottle. He must have noticed her eyes bulging at the sight of the lube and winked at her. "We came prepared, just in case... I can put this back if you w—"

"Bring it..."

She was sure Dalton's cock doubled in size as she said the words and it only seemed to grow in size as he crossed the room to get back in behind her.

Bodhi added a third finger and Carrie forgot all about the bottle of lube as his fingers curled and he rubbed a spot on the front wall of her pussy that felt so fucking good she thought her head was going to explode.

"Oh fuck!" She gasped loudly, her hips moving in time with Bodhi's fingers as he applied yet more pressure and she really did expect her head to explode.

"Do you want one or both of us?" Dalton whispered, his words making her tremble.

"Both of you. Both. I want—"

She couldn't finish her sentence as an orgasm hit out of nowhere thanks to Bodhi and his magical fingers. It snuck up on her so quickly she hardly made a sound, internalising the pressure as a loud, long grunt, lasting so long it threatened to make her pass out.

Bodhi looked very proud of himself and dropped a kiss in the corner of her mouth. "Just when I think you can't get any sexier..."

She whimpered. "Just when I think you can't make me come any harder!"

"Very nice work," Dalton joked, and Carrie couldn't believe the two men had the audacity to high five each other.

Actually, it was fucking adorable, and she looked forward to many more high fives in the future. But there were more pressing matters to attend to in the present, like the overwhelming need she suddenly felt to be filled up at the same time, by the cocks of the two men she loved so dearly.

"If you two have finished... there's something I'd quite like you both to do to me."

"At the same time?" Bodhi asked, and she knew his question was more about consent than shock.

"Yes."

"Oh god," Dalton hissed and buried his face in the back of her neck. "You're going to be the end of me, woman."

"Good."

Though she'd basically insisted they fuck her at the same time, Dalton still took the time to double check. "You're really sure?"

"Yes," she said again, and this time wiggled her ass against him.

His cock felt enormous and she found herself wondering if it would even fit inside her, *there*.

As if he could read her thoughts, he kissed her neck. "I will be gentle and I will go slow, but the moment it becomes too much for you, you tell me, okay? I love you and I promise I won't hurt you."

Opening the box of condoms, he took two out and passed one over to Bodhi, who had busied himself teasing her nipples with his mouth. The other one he kept, and she shook with what was either anticipation or nerves, she wasn't sure which.

"I'll start with my finger, okay?"

Carrie nodded and held her breath as she heard the click of a bottle opening and the unmistakable sound of a thick liquid being squirted out.

And then she felt it, a finger, slick with lube, against her tightest of holes. It felt... surprisingly good, as he moved his finger in gentle circles around the tight ring of muscle, gradually moving closer to the centre until the pad of his finger was pressing against that hole.

Her breath hitched the moment she felt herself opening and expected him to push gently inside, but Dalton stopped with just the tip inside her.

"Is that okay?"

"Yes. It feels... I want more..."

In front of her Bodhi released the nipple from his mouth and focused his attention on her mouth, kissing her long and slow, helping her relax as Dalton's finger eased inside her, up to the first knuckle. When he pulled it carefully out Carrie waited to see what he was going to do next, and when she heard the lube, she had no idea if he was putting it on his finger, or on his cock. She was quite surprised to find she hoped it was the latter.

It was his finger and it moved inside easier than she'd expected, aided in large part by the lube, but also by the effect of Bodhi's kisses.

Gradually she took in more and more of Dalton's finger until she reached the point she was starting to move against it, the sensation like nothing she'd encountered before, and one she wanted to experience further.

She wanted his cock.

"I-I want..."

"Okay," Dalton said and kissed the crook of her neck. "I promise I will be gentle."

"And if you decide you don't want both of us at the same time," Bodhi said looking into her eyes, "Just say so."

Carrie nodded and smiled. "I want both of you."

As if to prove it she moved her hand down and brushed it over the tender tip of his cock. Bodhi lowered his eyelids and frowned. "Do that too much and there will only be one of us in the right... condition... to be inside you!"

"You're an idiot," Carrie giggled and kissed him, very aware of the sound of a condom being put on behind her, quickly followed by the sound of lube.

"Ready?" Dalton asked.

"Very."

She closed her eyes and focused on her breathing as she felt the head of his cock against her tight hole. It had been one thing to take a finger, but taking *him*?

Very, very slowly she felt herself stretching as Dalton pressed against her. The pressure wasn't painful as such, but it was very intense, and she needed to concentrate on inhaling and exhaling through the sensations until her body became accustomed. He took his time inching inside her and when he eventually came to a stop, Carrie moaned quietly, shocked by how good it felt now he was completely inside her.

It was even more slowly he pulled part of the way out of her, pushing back in with care, but with not quite as much caution. He did this a couple of times and, becoming more curious, Carrie started moving her hips subtly, though soon they were moving with purpose.

"Ready?" Bodhi asked, and she groaned just at the thought of having both holes filled. "I'll take that as a yes," he chuckled, and she felt his hand brush against her pussy, followed by the familiar feeling of his cock pressing against her.

"Oh, fuck!" she groaned as her pussy accommodated his cock, quite literally stretching her to bursting point, given the cock in her ass as well.

Bodhi moved against her, his strokes slow and deep, while Dalton maintained the cautious thrust of his hips against her butt, pulling out halfway before sliding in again, creating friction she could feel everywhere.

With two cocks inside her, no spot was going unmissed and the longer they were both in her the more she came to love the feeling of being at the mercy of two men at the same time.

She appreciated Bodhi and Dalton were taking their time to make it pleasurable for her, but soon she found herself needing more and instinctively started pushing back against Dalton, her hips speeding up every few thrusts, until he was fucking her with more force than she'd imagined she could handle.

At the same time, she was moving harder against Dalton, Bodhi was hitting harder and deeper inside her, with a hand on her hip to create some resistance.

The three quickly found a rhythm and before long both cocks were slamming inside her, turning her into a shrieking, screaming mess of ecstasy. She couldn't believe how good it felt and every forceful thrust of Bodhi's and Dalton's hips pushed her closer to the edge of orgasmic bliss. She didn't want to come yet, she wanted to experience all they had to offer, she wanted the pleasure to course through her for hours on end.

Behind her, Dalton was grunting loudly, his fingers tightly on her hip as he pounded her ass, and she knew he was close.

"Oh fuck!" He growled and a second later pushed inside her one final time, the impact triggering the explosions that resulted in her own orgasm, and seconds later while she was still screaming her release, Bodhi's cock hit the back of her pussy and pressed against her A spot, triggering more waves of her orgasm.

The three of them were each lost in their own orgasmic abyss, pleasure coursing like a live wire, frying her brain and paralysing her.

The relief when she finally came down was so much that she began sobbing, aware in the deepest recesses of her mind there were arms around her, and soft words being spoken.

"I love you both, so much," the choke she let out was part sob, part giggle and she lay in that state for quite some time, much to the amusement of Bodhi and Dalton.

"We've got you," Bodhi whispered. "Forever and always, we've got you."

CHAPTER TWENTY-ONE

At 2 p.m. when her cell phone—which she'd turned back on earlier when she was nice enough to give Bodhi and Dalton a break—rang, Carrie was faced with the sad truth that it may be time for them to tear themselves away from the bedroom.

Caller ID proved her suspicions right, the person so rudely interrupting their reunion was her mother.

"Hi, Mum."

"Hi darling, I was just ringing to ask whether or not I should stop at the butchery on my way home to get two more pieces of steak for dinner tonight..."

She laughed. "Very casual, Mum. I like the way you asked the question without asking the question."

"Would you sooner I straight out asked you if you'd come to your senses and had decided to give those dashing young men a chance?"

"For the record, yes, you should get two more pieces of steak, and yes, I have come to my senses and am giving those dashing young men a chance."

Beside her, Bodhi laughed.

"Never been called dashing before," Dalton said.

"You're not mad at me?" Lindsay asked.

"No, Mum, I'm not mad at you for conspiring with Bodhi and Dalton. A bit disappointed you made them your world-famous buttermilk pancakes though."

"They both looked so flustered and nervous, I had to do something to make them feel at home... I've learnt along the way that men respond well to offerings of food."

... she could think of some other offerings' men responded well to but didn't think her mum would appreciate the input.

"Well, they haven't stopped raving about the pancakes, so you did good."

"Speaking of raving, I saw your dad on my lunch break, and he couldn't stop talking about how impressed he was with those two men of yours. We were both a bit apprehensive when they knocked on the door, but they were so genuine and polite and... well, all the things a parent likes to see in the person, sorry, persons their child is so obviously in love with." Carrie blushed as she looked from Bodhi to Dalton. Yeah, she was pretty in love with them. Had been from the start. "Just so you know," Lindsay continued, "you, Bodhi, and Dalton have our blessing. We know it might be a rocky road for the three of you in the early days, but we're here for you – all of you."

"Thank you, Mum, that means a lot to me... to us."

"Right, I'm going to be home in about ninety minutes so if there is anything you need to... do... before I get home, might be a good idea to set an alarm."

"*Mum!*" Carrie was shocked, her Mum wasn't one to say things like that.

The older woman just laughed. "I may be old, missy, but I remember what it was like to be young and in love."

"Gross! I'm going now!"

Her mum didn't say goodbye, just laughed and hung up.

*****

"Your parents are officially the coolest parents ever," Bodhi said standing with his arm around her waist as they took in the view of Brisbane from their private patio at the Emporium Hotel, their two night stay a gift from her parents.

"They have their moments," Carrie said, smiling over at Dalton who was also admiring the view while talking on the phone to his brother Killian, who, two hours earlier, had welcomed his third child and first daughter into the world.

She was dying to get into the rooftop infinity edge pool situated just metres from their cabana suite, but before they did that, there was one more call they had to make.

Nova.

Other than sending her a text message to say they'd arrived in Brisbane and were at Carrie's parents' house, Bodhi hadn't been in touch with his sister, who they all knew would be going insane, waiting to find out if their mission had been successful or not.

Dalton stood up and put his phone in his pocket, grinning as he took his place beside her. "This has been a pretty fucking fantastic day! A baby, a fancy hotel suite, the hottest woman in the world."

Though she rolled her eyes, she loved the compliment. "You know you don't need to sweet talk me, right?"

"I quite like sweet talking you, thank you very much!"

"Who we may have to sweet talk," Bodhi said, "is my sister."

Carrie laughed. "Shall we put her out of her misery with a video call?"

"Let's do this!" Bodhi took his phone from the table he'd left it on when they'd enjoyed a cocktail upon arrival and tapped at his screen until they heard the familiar sounds of a video call connecting.

Nova's image appeared on the screen and she grinned. "I knew it! I fucking knew it! You didn't get in touch all fucking day because you were too busy getting busy!"

"Surprise!" Carrie laughed.

"Please tell me this means what I think it means."

Carrie put an arm around each man's waist and nodded, not caring about the tears glistening in her eyes. "I love these two crazy men, and for some reason they love me back."

"Calum!" Nova yelled. "Calum!"

They could hear Calum muttering and then he came into shot.

"Hey guys!"

"Look! They're together! *Together together*! Like I told you they would be when they came to visit me and Aurelia at the hospital!"

Calum rolled his eyes. "Yes, darling. You were right, I was wrong." He winked at them via the video. "Congratulations though, I'm happy it all worked out."

In the background the wailing cry of Aurelia could be heard, and Nova smiled. "I have to go and feed my little monkey, let me know when you're coming back, and we'll have a little celebration. Love you guys!"

"Bye Nova!" they chorused, and the video call came to an end.

***

Ten minutes later, Bodhi and Dalton were laughing and wrestling in the pool, so Carrie left them to it taking the opportunity to have a couple of minutes to herself. She swam to the edge of the pool and looked out with a new-found appreciation at the city she knew would forever hold a special place in the hearts of the three of them.

Bodhi and Dalton soon joined her, the three of them gazing into the distance basking in the knowledge that together, they could take on the world.

EPILOGUE

Stepping out of the limo Carrie couldn't believe they were back where it had all begun just a year ago, at the annual children's hospital fundraising gala.

And what a year it had been.

Dalton pecked her on the cheek and smiled. "You look beautiful, baby. Absolutely stunning."

"He's right," Bodhi agreed. "You look like a goddess."

She pouted. "You're just saying that, so I don't cry again because I think I look like a massive blimpy whale."

Not caring who was watching, Dalton dropped to his knees in front of her – probably messing up the knees of his tux – and placed a light kiss on her ever-growing bump.

"If your mummy says anything bad about herself again, please kick her until she shuts up."

Around them flashes were going off and she didn't need to look up to know that photographers had their lenses in their direction and were snapping away.

Bodhi moved closer and put his hand on her belly, smiling at her with the pride and awe that seemed to constantly be showing on his face nowadays. Not so long ago he'd been able to span her bump protectively with his hand, but now he could barely do it with two. "You in no way look like a 'massive blimpy whale'," he said reassuringly. "You look like an incredibly sexy woman who is almost twenty weeks pregnant."

"Not if you listen to Nova, little miss '*look at me, I'm 30 weeks pregnant with my second baby and you're already bigger than me!*'."

Dalton stood back up and he too rested a hand on her bump. "You have a whole extra baby in your uterus, so of course you're going to grow at a different rate to her!"

Not long after arriving back in Sydney, they'd sat down and seriously discussed their plans for a family. To Carrie's surprise, both Bodhi and Dalton had been keen to start trying in the middle of the next year, and though she'd expected them to change their minds, they'd been almost more excited than her when she'd gone off birth control in April. They had planned to start trying in June, so they'd agreed she'd go off the pill a couple of months early, knowing it would probably take a few months for her cycle to get back to normal.

Her doctor had warned her period may take a while to arrive, especially because she didn't get her period when using hormonal birth control, so she hadn't thought anything of it when her period failed to arrive in May or June. By the time July rolled around she was feeling under the weather and had a constant headache – so naturally had convinced herself she had a brain tumour.

Bodhi and Dalton went to the medical centre with her and the doctor agreed the constant headache wasn't a good thing and agreed to do some testing, starting with a simple urinalysis. She'd thought nothing of it when the doctor took some of the urine with a dropper and placed a few drops on a test strip. When the two very pink lines came up she looked at it confused and asked the doctor what the test was for, by which stage Bodhi and Dalton were staring at the doc with their mouths wide open.

"Ms. Lucas, I can assure you it isn't a brain tumour," the doctor had said, giving the men a knowing smile.

"What is—"

"Baby, you're pregnant." It had been Dalton or Bodhi who broke the news to her, or maybe both at the same time, she couldn't quite remember.

Either way, she'd left the clinic crying big fat tears of joy.

The following week at the dating ultrasound the doctor had scheduled, it had again been Bodhi and Dalton whose mouths dropped while looking at the screen.

She'd left the radiography department that day completely in shock, not only was she ten weeks pregnant, she was carrying twins.

Carrie was pulled back into the here and now when one of the babies kicked and not to be outdone the other twin kicked even harder a few seconds later.

"Did either of you feel one of *those* ones?"

Bodhi and Dalton looked at her with tears in their eyes and that told her all she needed to know.

"Shall we do this?" Bodhi asked holding her hand and grinning as they walked toward the red carpet.

Holding her other hand, Dalton nodded his agreement. "Time for Baby A and Baby B to make their red-carpet debut."